THE
OPPOSITE
OF TRUST

RODGER CARLYLE

This is a work of fiction about an intelligence conflict that has been largely ignored. The story has been researched from archives on both sides of the Pacific. The times and dates are fictional, and many of the actual operational procedures have been modified to fit the story. The locations and mission types are all factually represented. The characters, except for a handful of historical figures, are all fictional.

*This novel is dedicated to the intelligence officers and airmen
who fought and died in this hot corner of the Cold War.
They are to be recognized not only for their bravery in facing
each other, but also in facing their own political elite.*

MAJOR CHARACTERS

MAJOR ANTON BIDKOV is a pilot in the Russian Air Force and the husband of a political prisoner, a nuclear scientist sent to the gulags for telling the truth rather than what Soviet Union political leaders wanted to hear.

ELLEN WILSON is a former U.S. State Department operative and the widow of intelligence operator, Walt Wilson, denounced during the McCarthy un-American activities hearings, the same hearings that destroyed her career. Ellen and her dying husband exiled themselves to a remote lake in Alaska seeking solitude after their own country denounced them.

GENERAL CHAD GRITT IV is a general in the strategic air command working for the CIA. He commands a small aviation intelligence unit based in Fairbanks, Alaska. His mission is to use aviation assets to monitor the Russian announcements of a strategic bomber buildup and nuclear war capabilities in the Russian Far East.

COLONEL PATRICK MCGRADY is the senior pilot assigned to the Alaska aviation intelligence unit, flying a specialized Boeing

RB-47 intelligence aircraft. Colonel McGrady is also General Gritt's best friend.

- CAPTAIN RICK FLORES is McGrady's co-pilot and a relative newcomer to aviation intelligence.
- LIEUTENANT BOB WALSH is the photo intelligence officer assigned to McGrady's crew and the first black officer in the unit.

GENERAL ALEXI MOLOVIC is the Russian general tasked with preparing air bases for the buildup of new nuclear-capable bombers and overall commander of air forces in the Russian Far East. He is entrusted with keeping the most critical secret in the Soviet Union from America's prying spy flights. (The Russian's actually have only a handful of modern bombers.)

- GENERAL JOHAN BLOVININ is Molovic's commanding officer and CO of the Soviet Air Force.
- SR. CAPTAIN DIMITRI GAGARIN is General Molovic's personal aide.

COLONEL GRIGORI RASPUTIN is a disgraced political officer exiled to the Far East. His assignment is to insure the political purity and party loyalty of the men under General Molovic's command. He owes his personal loyalty to the Stalinists being replaced by President Nikita Khrushchev. His mission is to somehow get back to Moscow and his privileged party life.

CHAPTER 1

THE SLIM RUSSIAN bomber threaded the needle, a narrow gap in radar coverage just north of Cape Lisburne on Alaska's Bering Sea Coast. Major Bidkov's plane raced over flat tundra, navigating his route over the chalky, featureless terrain by the illumination of the northern lights. Traveling at two hundred meters per second and only one hundred meters above the ground, the plane would be a black hole in the tundra in less than six-tenths of a second if he screwed up.

A stopwatch clamped to the yoke hit zero. Turning south, Bidkov found his next landmark, the frozen Killik River, no more than a slight depression in the snow-covered tundra. To the left and right, naked mountains rose, faint shadows in the dark. Bidkov steadied the plane in the center of a valley. Other than the subtle slopes and shadows, the unicolor terrain offered little contrast. He caressed the controls using only the thumb and forefinger of his left hand. His right hand hovered over the throttles, ready to slam on full power if they needed to climb.

But climbing would expose them to American radar to the south. If that happened, he would turn the Russian bomber west and bleed every ounce of power from the two engines trying to return to Russia before enemy fighter planes could cut off his retreat.

He squeezed through a pass in the Brooks Range, only an hour from his target. His co-pilot sat next to him, straining to pick out landmarks. "You have control, Alexi," ordered Bidkov. "You were trained for this, just follow the terrain."

Bidkov struggled to uncurl his cramped fingers. He took a deep breath. The young man next to him made three perfect turns as the plane exited the mountains.

Bidkov's mind struggled to find that unique place only a warrior understands. That place where he can overcome the exhaustion of intense vigilance and stress without allowing his mind to wander, even for a moment. For a few seconds, he failed, his thoughts filled with a vision of his beautiful dark-haired wife before the Soviet government exiled her to a gulag. Bidkov physically jerked himself from the thought by refocusing on the outside terrain. He sensed only a flash as a huge bird he should have seen flew past the cockpit window, sucked into the intake of the turbojet engine behind his seat. *There should have been no birds that bitter Arctic night.*

The engine damage seemed minimal. The only indication of trouble was a slightly elevated engine temperature reported by the engineer. Bidkov began to breathe again. He licked his dust-dry lips. He studied the instruments in the faint red glow of night vision lighting.

An odd vibration shook the airplane. A loud *BANG* filled his ears, as something tore away outside the plane. The exploding engine sent turbine blades tearing through the side of the fuselage, rupturing the axillary fuel tank fitted into the bomb bay. The reek of gushing kerosene filled the plane, burning the men's eyes. Then it ignited, the stench of burning petroleum blocking all other senses.

In general, flying was mostly tedious, hours of driving the bus without even the challenge of other vehicles around you. Military training, especially combat training, emphasized two exceptions: when you were attacking or being attacked, required different thinking, a different focus; and when something was going wrong, when there was an emergency, it required cool, analytical evaluation and actions. You picked the best possible option to save your life and that of your crew.

Internal fire, only two hundred meters above the ground, hundreds of miles behind enemy borders, too low to bail out, nowhere to land, no options available.

The screams over the intercom wrenched Bidkov's stomach. His co-pilot fought to control their Tupelov Tu-16 bomber, hugging the ground and coming apart.

His men were burning, and he could do nothing. The screams of the radioman and the engineer joined those of the burning tail gunner. Then the intercom failed. The nose gunner and the navigator raced toward the blaze, emptying two fire extinguishers, pushing the fire back for a few seconds. The aircraft commander unbuckled his seat belt, moving to get a better idea of the situation's gravity. The tears in his eyes came from the acrid smoke, maybe.

Bidkov had volunteered for this flight, committing his crew without their knowledge. His life ending was almost a blessing, but the others were all young men, most with families. It didn't matter.

Bidkov could feel the heat on his neck, as he wrenched control of the aircraft from the terrified lieutenant in the seat next to him. "We cannot allow the Americans to capture this airplane."

Bidkov banked the plane toward a flat spot in the snow-covered wilderness. "We will crash it through the ice of that lake." He could smell the man in the seat next to him, the smell of human shit cutting through all other smells.

Through the windscreen, the ground rose to meet them. "Give me ten degrees of flaps. We have to stay airborne." He couldn't see the tiny flap indicator needle in the smoke, but the plane continued to sink.

The two crewmen, their fire extinguishers empty, crowded into the cockpit, the fire only feet behind them. Bidkov looked up at his friend, Pavel. The burns on his face made him unrecognizable. "Thanks," he mouthed.

In the distance, on the far side of the lake, he thought he saw a light. "Shit, shit, shit."

The heavy plane clipped the top of a tree, slicing through a dozen more before slamming onto the ice. First came the sound of tearing metal, a bright flash surrounded the pilot, and then, nothing.

❈

Every night, Ellen would sit on the rickety picnic table next to Wolf Lake, letting the northern lights temporarily fill some empty spot. Some nights she could imagine her body converted to electrons dancing across the sky with the aurora taking her somewhere, anywhere but there.

But there was where she chose to stay. Anywhere but there would be filled with the stares and whispers. Maybe it wouldn't be right away. Maybe it would take time for someone there to recognize her or at least her name. So, there she stayed, hours from the next human, a city girl who chopped wood to heat and hauled water from a hole in the frozen lake. If she could get her book published, she might get her story out, then there might be more comfort.

Ellen had married an older man, her boss for more than a decade, and who introduced her to intelligence work. Somewhere in the cabin there were letters of recognition from the American intelligence community and the State Department, even one from a president. Then one day, her husband's career was ruined followed by hers. The McCarthy hearings, a Communist witch hunt in Washington DC, had twisted their decades of service into something un-American. When the efforts to prove they were spies failed, the accuser's narrative simply labeled them "Communist sympathizers."

The accusations against a man with fifty years of service to his country hit her husband hard, but not nearly as hard as his inability to protect his wife. Now he was gone. She was alone, and not the kind of alone you sought for a moment's peace. Ellen's alone was the kind you only find in total wilderness, an alone so complete that few people remembered she existed.

When they first came to this remote lake, Ellen and her husband had taken a handful of files from their former life, the minimums to eke out a civilized living in that remote spot, and rugged, serviceable clothing, leaving the rest of what they shipped in a storage unit in Fairbanks. At Ellen's insistence they brought hundreds of pounds of books. Initially, she concentrated on the works of the ancient philosophers and political writers Plato, Aristotle and Machiavelli. Recognizing that in some way each wrote about the same things as history repeated itself, she migrated to Dante and Chaucer which eventually led her to seek pure escapism through Melville and Twain. As her mood darkened, she found writers that matched her mood. She wondered whether her current fascination with Conrad said something about her mental health.

Around her the needle-shaped trees sparkled in the northern lights, the rounded snow-covered mountaintops glowing. Above, clear dots of glowing stars and planets filled the sky. Even where the waving glow of the green, yellow and pink northern lights washed from mountaintop to mountaintop the brightest dots glimmered like ornaments.

A blast and blinding flash to her left jarred her from her stupor. The sound of an explosion rumbled through the mountains. The air around her compressed then roared on, flinging her hat into the trees. Her ears screamed in pain from the concussion. A fireball rolled from the far lakeshore onto the ice.

At her feet, Jack rose, barking, as the dog team behind her cabin erupted. Only once before, had she experienced such an explosion. In France, only days before the Normandy invasion, she'd para-chuted into a meadow to hand deliver a map and instructions to the French underground. Like the British, the Americans figured out that women agents were less likely to be arrested by the Nazis. Her orders were to ensure that a dozen critical targets were destroyed before the Allies landed. Ellen watched as partisan saboteurs blew up a Nazi train filled with munitions. This explosion was just as powerful and just as deadly.

The woman launched herself from the lakeside tabletop, throwing off the quilt wrapped around her shoulders. She began to run toward the fire.

A pool of burning fuel surrounded the wreckage of a huge silver plane. Ellen circled trying to get close enough to help anyone trapped inside, but the heat was too intense. There were no screams, only the roar of an inferno so intense that the aluminum itself was burning. After five minutes of trying she retreated, stopping to take several deep breaths to calm her shaking.

A hundred yards from the crash, Jack stood, barking at something dark in the snow.

Ellen ran. On the ground next to Jack, a man lay, unmoving except for the heaving of his chest. With no flashlight she couldn't see how badly the man was injured, but he was alive. She knelt next to the uniformed man. Everywhere she looked there was blood, shiny and black in the dim light.

"Wait here," she said needlessly, "I'll go hook the dogs to the sled."

Ellen spent hours sewing up the man's wounds. She set his broken left arm. Bandages covered much of his body. She somehow heaved the muscular man, now clad only in his white boxer shorts, from the floor, where she had been working, onto the bed. There was a large black knot on the unconscious man's forehead.

❄

Bidkov was awake for some time, sneaking short peeks, trying to get his bearings. He was in a bed, but there were no voices, no sounds or smells that he recognized. A man trained to control; the disorientation shook him. He opened his eyes.

"Do you speak English?"

"Da, yes." He suppressed his pain. Hovering over him was a middle-aged woman, green eyes, auburn hair pulled back and tied with a green ribbon. Her face was smooth, only tiny wrinkles next to her eyes giving away her age. She was dressed in canvas pants and a wool shirt. The woman pulled a clean white sheet closer to his chin.

"Would you care for some water?"

"Yes."

The woman helped him lift his head and held a glass to his lips. He drank. Swallowing was torture; his throat burned. Pain meant he was alive. That disappointed Bidkov.

"Where am I?"

"Your plane crashed onto the lake. You were thrown clear of the wreckage before the plane burned."

The man looked up into the shadows of a kerosene lamp flickering on a rough wooden ceiling. "But…where am I now?"

"You are in my cabin. I was up late watching the northern lights. I put you into the sled and brought you here. I set your arm and sewed up most of the places you were bleeding. I was going to go for help until I took a good look at your uniform. You're Russian, aren't you?"

Bidkov took a deep breath. Even if they could not complete their mission, the Americans were not to get their hands on the Soviet Union's most advanced jet bomber or its secrets. He was sure the woman had a gun somewhere. In a place so remote, she would need one for hunting or protection. He would have to find it and shoot himself. He treasured his reputation as a hard man, but he wasn't the kind of man who believed he could survive torture without breaking.

"Come now, Major, there is nothing to fear. My late husband worked with General Eisenhower. He was one of the liaisons to the Russian Navy. You have the ugliest uniforms ever." She smiled and helped him to another drink.

"Da, yes I am Russian."

"Were you going to bomb my country? Are there a hundred more of you out there? Are we at war? I have a radio, but since the creek froze, no generator, so I don't know."

"Where is the rest of my crew?"

"There are no other survivors. I went back to the wreck the day after you crashed. There were no footprints in the snow."

Bidkov fought through the pain to concentrate. Finally, he answered. "There are no other planes, just us. We were delivering a message to your American Air Force that if they attacked Mother Russia, we could destroy them."

"How very Russian of you. Bluster and swagger in front of your foes until you are strong enough to really do something." Ellen contemplated contacting her old friend, General Chad Gritt. His office was at the remote Air Force Base only a day's travel away. That would take a day's travel by dog sled; impossible right away. "Anyway, you are safe here. I'm not going to report you." Behind Ellen, a huge dog rose turned around twice and then settled again next to the stove.

The Russian major studied the rustic house, the frosted windows reflecting the inside of the cabin. Outside it was dark. "Why would you protect me?"

"I am not protecting anyone. You aren't a threat to anyone. The only one you could threaten is me. You aren't going to do that. Right now, you are just a badly injured man." She walked over to the stove and refilled her coffee cup. "When you are stronger, we will discuss what comes next." She slid a chair next to the bed.

"My late husband and I were both with the U.S. government in Washington DC. We needed a change. We both quit our jobs and moved here. John always wanted to live in the wilderness."

"That is quite a change, from your nation's capital to this remote place."

"John was denounced. It was time to go."

"What do you mean denounced?"

"I don't want to talk about it," said Ellen, her face flushing.

"You said 'late husband'; I don't understand that term."

"John died of cancer." The color in Ellen's face slowly returned to normal. "We knew it before we moved here. He died last fall. I buried him near the lake and decided to stay while I wrote a book about our story. My name is Ellen, Ellen Wilson."

"My name is Bidkov, Anatoly Bidkov, please call me Anton. Would you have something to help with the pain, Ellen?"

"Oh, I am so sorry." She picked up a huge green jar of aspirin from a shelf across the room and shook three into her hand. She dropped them one at a time into his mouth, following each with a sip of water. "We used up all of the stronger pain killers the last month that John was alive."

Anton stared at the ceiling before asking, "How much of my plane survived the crash?"

Ellen smiled. "I wondered when you would ask. Not much."

Anton continued to stare at the ceiling. Ellen waited for him to say more. She refilled the water glass. The Russian airman just stared at the ceiling.

"Anton, your plane crashed two days ago, and I haven't slept since I rescued you. This is the only bed, and the floor is cold. Would you mind if I lie next to you and wrap up in a blanket for a few hours?" It has started to snow, so by tomorrow night the wreck will be covered. When the ice melts, what is left will sink."

"I don't mind." A moment later he added, "thank you."

Ellen turned the knob on the kerosene lamp, lowering the flame then blew out what remained. Wrapping herself in a blanket, she stretched out next to Anton. An hour later he felt her roll over, her arm over his chest and her breath against his neck. That was something he had not felt for more than two years.

CHAPTER 2

GENERAL CHAD GRITT stared at the phone on his desk. He knew that it wouldn't ring, at least not yet; still, he stared. *I once thought that leading men into harm's way was the toughest thing you could do but sending men while you sit in a nice warm office drinking coffee is tougher.*

He used his cane to help lift his body from his chair, and headed toward the door, calling for his aide. "I suspect that someone from either the CIA or the Air Force will start calling in the next couple of hours. They always forget the time change. Don't tell them anything until I get the opportunity to debrief Colonel McGrady myself. While we wait, I'm going flying."

He returned to his desk, picking up the phone and dialing. His wife answered. "I'm going flying for a couple of hours. When I get back, I'll take an hour to debrief one of my crews, then I'll be home. If the kids are hungry, don't hold dinner for me, I can eat later."

He knew that Carmen would hold dinner. She always did.

He pulled his heavy parka over the civilian clothes he preferred. While he was career Air Force, his direct boss headed the Central Intelligence Agency and he leveraged that to run his small unit his way. He headed for the parking lot to take the half hour drive to

Fairbanks Municipal Airport where he owned a small hanger for his Cessna.

"The boss is going flying, isn't he?" asked a sergeant just returning from lunch.

"Yup, he usually does," replied a young lieutenant.

"I don't know how he does it, with that bad leg and all. I flew with him once. He uses that cane like a third leg. The man was damn near killed in the war. People have been shooting at him for fifteen years; I don't know why he still does this," continued the sergeant. "He's from a wealthy family. I'd be retired, fishing somewhere warm."

"Bubba, you know why. Even when those goons with the Un-American Activities hearings tried to tar his reputation by tying him to some old friends they'd denounced, he told them to piss up a rope. He is a red, white and blue legend. He's the kind of reluctant warrior that somehow can lead the attack and at the same time cover your ass. It's why we put up with his temper while we all do whatever we can to stay on his staff."

CHAPTER 3

THE CREW OF the American RB47 aircraft was only thirty miles from the Russian fighter base in the Kurile Islands, north of Japan. The pilot rolled the yoke in front of him to the right; pressing the right rudder peddle with his foot; the plane swung toward the north. They would eventually lock onto the broadcast of a Russian radio station in Anadyr hundreds of miles to the north, flying a straight line up the Kamchatka Peninsula before turning east over the Bering Sea, returning to the small Air Force base near Fairbanks, Alaska.

"Heads up out there," said Lt. Colonel Patrick McGrady, "we will be feet dry in twelve minutes. One at a time, the crew of the intelligence aircraft responded, including the two men in the experimental electronic reconnaissance pod loaded into the bomb bay of the aircraft. Two extra crewmen with no safe way of ejecting from the jet worried him.

The B-47 was Boeing's newest bomber, a six-engine plane with thousands of miles of range. McGrady sat in the front seat of the bubble cockpit that looked like something glued to the top of the sleek fuselage. Behind him, the co-pilot searched for Russian fighter planes. In the nose, the intelligence officer waited for his chance to steal Russia's secrets with his cameras.

Five years before, one of the first B-47s had roamed around

Russian airspace for hours. The Russians didn't have an interceptor that was fast enough to catch it, or even climb to the altitude that they now flew at. *That was five years ago,* thought McGrady.

"Bob, we should be just east of Petropavlovsk in thirty minutes. We need a complete photo sequence of the runway and the parking ramps of the base. The brass wants to know if that Badger is still there."

"You get me near that airbase, and I will get my Kodak out. If it's still there, I will get you a picture. I just hope there aren't a dozen more sitting on the runway. From the poop-sheet on the TU-16, that bomber could be over Anchorage in less than two hours after leaving Petropavlovsk. I know we have fighters ready to shoot them down. But the way our fighter pukes party, they probably couldn't get their boots laced before the Russians leveled the whole city."

"Colonel," called one of the men in the recon pod, "I am still black on the POV radio channels." The place designed by Boeing engineers to carry nuclear bombs in the lethal bomber, carried instead a rectangular aluminum box. Inside, two men sat at consoles that could steal the secrets of Russia's electronic defenses while at the same time allowing the operators to listen to Russian radio communications, even communications from base to base.

"Good to hear, Blackbirds. Hopefully that means no MIGs screwing up the mission."

Colonel McGrady reached above the back of his seat and snapped his fingers, pulling his facemask off to avoid any conversation going out over the intercom. "Rick, I'll do all the flying for the next hour. You concentrate on the skies around us. Four MIGs jumped the guys who got that TU-16 Badger on film last week. They never heard them over the radio. Our guys got lucky, the Russians were late to the party and ran short of fuel before they could close."

"I should have joined up five years earlier," said Flores. "It's more dangerous now."

"They haven't caught one of us yet," replied McGrady, "but they keep getting closer."

Captain Rick Flores acknowledged the order. "On." He flipped a toggle in front of him to warm up the search radar. There was no way he would actually transmit, until forced. You never knew who might be looking for the signal. "I can confirm that all of the radios are in standby. We are giving the bad guys nothing to home in on. I just hope that any fighters on the field run out to take a look at the Navy before we get there."

"Those Navy guys have guts," said McGrady. "They cruise those old propeller planes just offshore in front of us like bait, so we can tell the brass what happens when the Russians see them."

"Low and slow, better them than us."

McGrady tapped the throttles on the six turbojet engines up slightly, increasing their speed to four hundred knots. He checked the altimeter for the third time in ten minutes. It still read 35,000 feet. Their planned course would put them over the Russian peninsula for just over ninety minutes, dodging Russian radar and hiding from Russian fighter planes.

Below the aircraft, the beauty of Kamchatka was blanketed in white. The endless volcanic mountains sent tendrils of steam into a blue sky covering a landscape of forests and lakes. Frozen rivers snaked from the mountains to the blue ocean visible only a few miles to their east. To the west, a massive inlet ran for hundreds of miles along the peninsula. *This place is too beautiful for a battleground,* thought McGrady.

"Captain, I have heavy chatter on the POV channels," called one of the men in the recon pod.

"Eyes open all, it looks like the Navy is about to get a visit. Let's get all of this down."

"I hope that those Navy guys are far enough offshore that the Ruskies leave them alone," offered Flores. "That old propeller job they fly couldn't outrun a ruptured duck, let alone a MIG."

In the distance, the bay leading to the small town of Petropavlovsk Kamchatka was materializing out of the icy haze. Lieutenant Bob Walsh began the process that would capture the entire village and especially the air base on film in such detail you could read the numbers stenciled on the tops of the vehicles. "I hope the Navy attracts all of the attention and the Russian Air Defense Forces miss us entirely," he added to the conversation.

"Damned insensitive of you, Bob. The gold wings have a place on this earth just like we do. The bars in Kodiak would go broke without the Navy."

"What do you have down there, Blackbirds?" asked McGrady.

"I count chatter from four MIGs. That new radar site reports that the Navy is twenty miles offshore at twelve thousand feet, cruising at… let me convert this to knots, two hundred and twenty knots."

"Any chatter about us?"

"Nope, just the Navy. But Russian operations just ordered two more aircraft to ready status."

In the previous two months, the crew had flown over Russian territory three times. Standby aircraft were routine, if anything about covertly flying over a country like Russia was routine. The Soviet Union killed people they didn't like or exiled them to camps where they were either worked or starved to death.

McGrady remembered one of his intelligence briefings about the risks in Russia. The story was, that one of Old Joe Stalin's lieutenants stopped for a shoeshine on a street in Moscow. The shoeshine boy set one of his grimy boots on a picture of Old Joe in the newspaper he was kneeling on and found himself on the way to a gulag the next day. "What would they do to the crew of a plane sent to spy on them?" he mumbled. No one responded.

"One minute to cameras on," came a call from the man who sat in the seat originally planned for a bombardier.

Inside the experimental B-47 Stratojet, reworked for reconnaissance and now designated the RB-47 to indicate its new mission, there was silence. The next three minutes, and two more similar sessions further north, were the primary reasons they were invading Russian air space.

"Hold it absolutely steady," came an unnecessary command from the camera operator. "Cameras on."

The co-pilot dropped the binoculars he was using into a tray next to his seat. "I recommend a clearing turn after the camera run. I can't see anything behind us." *God, how I want to turn on the search radar,* he thought.

"You all have that. When the camera run is over, we will make a 60 degree turn to the left and then a 120 turn to the right. Anything new over the Russian radios?"

"No, Sir," replaced the conversational "nope" from only minutes before.

"Bob, after you shut down the cameras, grab your binoculars and give Rick a hand covering our ass."

McGrady didn't expect an answer. He knew that the intelligence officer in the nose would be busy monitoring the photo run. He knew his co-pilot would have his binoculars glued to the ground around the runway seven miles below them. He would break every few seconds to scan the skies around them.

"It will be interesting to see the film," offered Flores. "I can't see anything that looks like a jet bomber down there. The photos of the Badger make it look like some kind of spaceship. It's hard to believe that a twin-engine airplane like the TU-16 is as fast as we are with six engines."

"Probably can't carry the load we carry or the fuel for range. I like having a stack of engines out there just in case one or two fail. We probably would make it home. I doubt that a Badger crew would be so lucky." McGrady checked the stopwatch clamped to the control yoke in front of him. Just like during World War II, when the bombardier had control of the aircraft during a bombing run, Lieutenant Walsh was in command of the plane during the photo run, but it didn't hurt to have a second set of eyes charting the time.

"Camera's off," came Walsh's call.

"Hold on everybody, we're starting our clearing turns. Rick, you and Bob keep me posted. If I don't hear from you in thirty seconds, I am going to start the turn to the right."

Two minutes later, the plane was back on its original course, glued to the extremely faint signal from the radio station in Anadyr, hundreds of miles away.

"Great work all," offered Walsh. "It looks like we got some really good footage, at least the film advance indicators show the right amount of film through the cameras."

"There was one thing unusual down there," interjected Flores. "There were three Russian naval ships hightailing it out of the harbor, a cruiser and two destroyers."

McGrady thought about the comment for a minute and then deposited it in the mental file he used for useless information. "We can relax in about fifteen minutes. The Union of Soviet Socialist Republics doesn't like their fighter jets to get much more than a hundred miles from their bases. Stay alert. Next stop is Kyluchi to take a look at the new ramps and runway there."

"We appear to have about twenty knots of crosswind right on the left wing," came a call from Walsh. "Your crab angle will be about ten degrees. That cuts our ground speed to about three hundred seventy knots. Kyluchi in fifty minutes."

"Matches my calculations," agreed the co-pilot.

McGrady smiled. "Rick, take the plane for a while." I am going to grab a cup of coffee and then I'll spell you on the binoculars." He unscrewed the cap from his Thermos and filled the porcelain cup he preferred over the Thermos cap.

The coffee was warm, and the cream he preferred gave it a slightly oily feel in his mouth, but it was welcome. Petropavlovsk was the most dangerous target on their mission. There were two different Russian Air Forces at the base; one dedicated to projecting power across the Pacific, and one for defense only. Not far from the airfield was a submarine base. He sipped from his cup. Finding a Baby Ruth bar in his pocket, he tore off the wrapper and devoured half of it before turning back to his coffee.

The Russian air defense radars pointed out to sea. With luck, he and his crew had flown by the bases undetected. If not, the two

Russian Homeland defense fighter bases further north could still make things very interesting.

"Okay guys, grab a cup and whatever you brought for a snack. I am going to take the chance of turning on the search radar when we get within twenty miles of the base outside of Kyluchi. We will operate it for one minute only to make sure there is no welcoming party out there."

Finishing his candy bar and coffee, McGrady spent twenty minutes searching with the binoculars, and then relieved his co-pilot on the controls. Flores opened a Thermos of black coffee and unwrapped two stale muffins, careful about food and drink in the pressurized cabin.

"The next two are on us," quipped Rick. "We will be over the targets more than a half-hour before the Navy comes by."

McGrady just smiled. "Hey Blackbirds, any trouble for the Navy back there?"

"Nope, the MIGs just reported them and did a flyby a few miles inland. They are headed back to base now. I did get some funny stuff on the radar monitor. Looks like it might be a new type of radar, but I don't know. I recorded the signal. I'll see if I can identify it, or maybe the folks back at the base can."

Forty minutes later, the crew began a replay of the camera run over Petropavlovsk, but this time over the small village and base near Kyluchi. They skipped the routine of clearing turns, instead choosing to run a one-minute radar sweep after the camera run. Then it was on to the newer base near what the maps of Kamchatka called Ossora.

The crosswind increased the further north they flew, requiring the pilots to increase the angle of the nose of the aircraft into the wind. Wind drift would deliver them to their next target. To new pilots, the idea of the nose pointing a different direction than the flight destination always seemed odd. To an experienced crew, it just meant that their speed over the ground slowed.

"Yo, Captain," came a call from the recon pod. "I think I just figured out what that odd radar signal was back at Petropavlovsk. I believe it was search radar from one of those ships Captain Flores saw. If it was, they had to see us."

"Anything else odd?" asked McGrady.

"Yup. In the last half-hour, I've been getting a lot of encrypted traffic on the high frequency radio relay stations along the coast."

McGrady began to process the information. He didn't like it.

"One minute until cameras on," called Walsh. "Keep her straight and steady."

In civilian life, the repetition of directives would drive any manager mad, but in the military, it was part of the checklist to make sure that everything needed to complete the mission was accomplished.

"Captain," called a voice from the Blackbird pod. I am monitoring the air defense radio channels. I just picked up an alert. It's nice of the Russians to use the same POV frequencies everywhere. I didn't hear a launch order, but I would bet that we will have a couple of MIGs up here looking for us real soon."

"Camera's on," came a call.

"Blackbird, keep me posted, especially on any air-to-air chatter. We need three minutes. After that, I would like to continue our mission as planned rather than turn east. If something were to happen to us, the only way the forces of good could find us would be to retrace our planned route. They would start looking along the sixty-fifth parallel, then turn south."

Flores was searching the target area with his binoculars. "I thought I caught a glimpse of a large trash hauler climbing out over the ocean."

"It wasn't a fighter, you're sure?" asked the captain.

"No, it was a four-engine prop job. In the distance I can see two more Russian ships running hard."

McGrady concentrated on holding his course. In the distance, he could see the edge of a weather front directly in front of them. "Blackbird, what do you make of all the ship activity?"

"We reset one of the radios for the guard channel the Russian

Navy uses. The chatter is constant. It seems our commie friends have lost something. It's all about specific search grids. We'll stay on it. I am also picking up air-to-air transmissions on the POV channels, no voice just clicks."

McGrady checked his stopwatch. They needed one more minute of steady flight for Walsh's cameras. "You all heard the Blackbirds. I think we have some unwelcome callers on the way up." He thought back to his early career, flying F-86 fighters in Korea. Everyone monitored each other's radios, so when the enemy was around, they used coded clicks to communicate. By the end of the war, the North Korean MIGs, most flown by Chinese or Russian pilots, were doing the same.

He watched in amusement, as the hand clicking off seconds on his stopwatch slowed to a crawl. If he needed to crank up the power and head out over the North Pacific from Ossora, they wouldn't have enough fuel to reach Fairbanks.

"Camera's off," came Walsh's call.

"Rick, crank up the search radar. If there are MIGs up here, it's because they know we are here, so there's not much reason to hide."

"I have them, four of them. Two aircraft are busting ass to catch up to two in front of them. They are heading south, climbing through ten thousand feet. They think we are still on the way, and they are setting up an ambush."

McGrady bumped the throttles up and watched the speed indicator inch toward five hundred knots. He swung the nose of the aircraft directly north, eliminating the adjustment for wind drift. "How far back are they?"

"About twenty miles, but someone just reported our radar. Both flights are turning. They are tracking us, recommend shutting down the radar."

McGrady ran the information through the flight computer in his head. "This will be close." The fighters could only fly about one hundred knots faster than their current speed, and they were twenty miles behind and needed to climb another 25,000 feet. "They may be able to close in enough to make a firing pass before they have to call it off because of fuel. If they do get here, they won't have time to maneuver; they will try to crawl up our tail. Rick, leave the radar on. Keep track of the MIGs, if they get close, sting them."

Flores reached over and armed the twin cannons in the tail of the RB-47. "I'll send a few bursts of fire out in their general direction when they close. Maybe I can convince them to head home. They can discuss how they chased the big bad Americans out of Russia over a vodka or two." Flores was happy no one could see the nervous tick on his left cheek. If they went down, the closest rescue helicopters would run out of fuel before they ever reached them.

At the speed they were flying, you could almost see the fuel gauges wind down. If they forced to stay at 500 knots, they were going to need to divert to the American Navy base at Shemya in the Aleutian Islands for fuel. The good news was that there was a gas station out there. The bad news was that they would have to break the radio silence maintained since their mission launched. Someone was going to get an ass chewing if they did.

"If we are going to get shot at, I want you two Blackbirds to climb out of your nest and get your cold weather gear and parachutes on. I will give as much warning as I can," called McGrady. "Whatever you do to prepare for the loss of the airplane, you had better get started on."

Flores released his seat and rotated it toward the tail. "I have them back there. I'll let them get close enough to see the tracer ammunition before I fire." The MIGs were tiny aircraft, with swept-back wings and like the B-47, and small clear canopies glued to the top. The entire front of the plane was an air intake for its single, engine giving the impression of a fish about to gulp down its prey.

Only Flores could watch the MIGs. The bitter flavor that comes when you are frightened and helpless filled the other's mouths. Only the co-pilot could see death approaching.

Three minutes later, the airframe began to vibrate as the two heavy guns in the tail sent out their stream of lead. Flores fired two short bursts in the direction of the fighters approaching from the left. Both broke off, turning hard toward the east. That was too easy.

He shifted his attention to those on the right, both of which had used the time he was focused on their friends to pour on the power. The lead plane began to spit a stream of fire at the huge American plane. The stream curved from the nose of the MIG slowly downward, passing only a few feet below. "Get the Blackbirds out!" he shouted.

"You heard the man," called McGrady. "Get out of there."

Flores watched as the lead MIG attempted to raise its nose to walk the stream of bullets up toward the RB-47. As it did, the MIG's speed drained away. He sighted his two cannons toward the Russian fighters and unleashed a ten second burst of fire.

His fire passed over the MIGs only a hundred feet above the bubble canopies of the two stubby jets. First the wingman, and a moment later the lead MIG dove away from the shells. In the distance, he could see the two aircraft evading his first burst, now turning and scrambling to catch up.

"They are still on us," he advised.

"Just hold them another two minutes," replied McGrady.

Flores was just about to open fire for the third time when everything around him went gray.

McGrady pulled the power on the six straining engines and pointed the nose of the aircraft down, trading altitude for airspeed, the plane dropping 5,000 feet after entering the cloudbank. "If they come into the soup looking, they will have to do a three-dimensional search," he mumbled.

"Bob, you can tell the two black ops guys, that they can crawl back into their pod. I need them to monitor the Ruskie aviation chatter. Tell them to let me know when the bad guys head for home."

"Captain," came a call, "were still here. We need more than two minutes to secure our gear and prep the self-destruct devices in case we are shot down."

"Don't tell me anymore," barked McGrady. "If there is a next time, you had better move your butts. If you are still in the pod and we lose the aircraft, you are both dead men."

"Captain, we need to get our CO with yours. We need to be on the same page on this. They both need to be talking to General Gritt. It's up to him to sort this out."

"My orders are to jettison the pod if we are going to lose the plane," answered McGrady.

"We understand, Sir, but all of our manuals need to go into a self-destruct box before we can leave the pod. If the pod survives, the manuals must be destroyed. It takes more than a couple of minutes."

Thirty minutes later, McGrady banked the bomber, now cruising at a speed that maximized fuel economy, toward the east and home. He broke out of the clouds just south of St. Lawrence Island in the Bering Sea and set up a long decent toward Fairbanks.

CHAPTER 4

"GENERAL, I HAVE Moscow on the phone. It's the senior aide to our new Defense Minister. He is asking about Major Bidkov's airplane. He wants to know what in the hell a TU-16 is doing in the Far East and who sent it."

General Molovic dropped his cup. He stared at the coffee stain, thinking how difficult it was to get tailored uniforms four thousand miles from Moscow. "Tell him that I am working on an answer. Tell him I suggest he get some sleep since the communications between Khabarovsk and Petropavlovsk are acting up again. I will call tomorrow. And Sergeant, get the bastard's name and phone number."

How in the hell was he, or the other Air Force brass he was working with, supposed to know that Georgie Melenkov would be ousted as Defense Minister? Hell, just months ago Melenkov was the man chosen to replace Premier Stalin. How could they know that Field Marshal Zhukov, Russia's greatest war hero, would agree to take his place? "Sergeant, get me General Blovinin. In person, don't leave any messages. And Sergeant, no one, and I mean no one, is to hear about either call. Think of that order as life and death."

Molovic leaned back in his chair. The fog outside was clearing. Brilliant winter sun shimmered along the hoar frost covering the branches of the trees just outside the windows. Small puffs of wind sent ice crystals flickering. The city was on the downhill side of winter. The ice in the Amur River would breakup soon. The spectacle and sound of the ice blocks crashing in the newly freed river reminded him just how unimportant he really was. He loved both the rebirth and the realization. Molovic just hoped that he would be alive to see it.

His aide, a senior captain, picked up a decanter of Moldovan brandy. He reached under the counter below the windows for two glasses. He set both glasses on Molovic's desk and poured two inches into one glass. "You look like you can use a drink, comrade general."

"Thank you, Dimitri. Please join me. How could we know that a great warrior like Zhukov might object to sending a strong message to the Americans?"

"I will check on the overdue bomber one more time, General."

"God, how I hope that it is down somewhere in the ocean and that the entire crew sank with the damned plane. If he has disappeared, we can blame the whole thing on Major Bidkov. Maybe we can blame the Americans, you know, say that they shot him down for straying too close to Alaska."

Dimitri Gagarin picked up the phone on his boss's desk and gave the operator instructions to reach the Air Defense commander at Petropavlovsk, then hung up, knowing that getting a call through might take ten minutes or more.

"General, neither of us want to spend the rest of our lives in some gulag. Maybe we should tell the Defense Minister who authorized this mission."

"No, Dimitri. If there is anything I have learned in the last twenty years, it's that anyone who shows initiative better be right. If they fail, everyone associated with them sinks in the same boat. Besides, you and I were right there in the meeting when this idea was cooked up. The Air Defense Army doesn't have any aircraft capable of dropping leaflets on an American base a thousand miles from Russian soil. They are really pissed off over the American planes flying over Russia and we were more than happy to help them send a message."

"We." Dimitri slammed the clipboard he carried onto the table, almost launching his boss out of his chair. Hell, neither he, nor the other aides were even allowed into the room when the plan was finalized. Still, would a hero like Zukov, a man who sacrificed an entire armored division in the Great Patriotic War just to lure the Germans into a fight where he could destroy them later, consider his role? "You are right, General, all we can do now is stick together."

"Just smile, Senior Captain Gagarin. It appears that you no longer have to lock up Major Bidkov and his crew until we know whether we make them heroes of the Soviet Union or shoot them for treason."

The phone on Molovic's desk rang. Gagarin picked it up, the conversation brief. "There is no further word on the missing Tupolev 16. They were ordered to adhere to strict radio silence, so from the time the plane climbed out of sight of the airbase, there has been no contact."

"Is that all, Dimitri?" asked his boss, refilling his glass. "That is nothing more than what we knew twenty hours ago."

Dmitri patiently sipped his brandy. He was using the time to figure out how to deliver the rest of the message. He took another sip and painted on a smile. "The Air Defense Force commander has been ducking telegrams from Moscow, asking about the plane. He will have to answer, somehow, by tomorrow. The Navy Commander down in Vladivostok has sent his fleet out to search. He is happy to help. He hasn't reported his action to Moscow yet, but he figures word will slip out. By the time his ships return to port, they will be unable to go to sea again until they are refueled, and the fleet is very short on fuel."

Molovic filled his glass a third time, just as the sergeant tapped on the door. "Yes, have you found General Blovinin?"

"Yes, Sir. He is gathering some other officers together. It's early morning in Moscow, and not everyone he needs in the meeting is in the office yet. He will call back in an hour."

"Fine work, Sergeant. Please let me know as soon as the call comes in." He waved his hand, dismissing the non-commissioned officer.

"Now the question is, will those in the meeting come up with some plan to cover all of our butts, or are they going to throw us under the bus?"

Molovic stood, picking up his drink. He resettled in the overstuffed chair between the bookcases, setting the drink on one of the shelves. The huge room seemed somehow smaller than it did the day before. He picked up an English language book from the same shelf and opened it. He skipped the section on French, English and American generals, choosing the section on Russian generals of the Second World War. He read the two pages on Zhukov, rereading several parts, his English rusty. He'd never known, nor had any Russian who wasn't there, that by the end of the war, Marshal Zhukov and General Eisenhower, now President Eisenhower, were friends. "What do you think, Dimitri, will they throw us under the bus?"

When Molovic and Gagarin finally headed for home that night, they still didn't know the answer to that question. All they knew was that Blovinin, overall commander of the Air Force, would be on a plane headed for Khabarovsk that night. That and Molovic had ordered the communications center in Petropavlovsk shut down.

The Commander of the Air Defense Army objected vociferously, something about an American bomber flying right over their bases that day. Molovic didn't care, or rather he was incapable of caring. Gagarin helped his drunken boss down the stairs and into his staff car, directing the driver to get him home. Then Gagarin called his wife to tell her he would be working late. He started his car and headed over to the apartment of a bar girl he knew who could always cheer him up.

CHAPTER 5

FAIRBANKS, ALASKA

THE AFTER-FLIGHT DEBRIEFING for the crew of the RB-47 was a polite exercise designed to check off that box. McGrady agreed to assemble the crew for a more thorough debrief the next day. The two men from the recon pod would get some sleep and then work with the Electronic Intelligence (ELINT) group to pull all of the information gathered into a report. McGrady didn't know their names or ranks. That was something he didn't need to know. All he knew was that if their work was really valuable; they might become a permanent part of the crew. Until then, he called them what his boss did, Blackbirds. The man who invented that name was a no-show.

Flying for more than a dozen hours, Brady was so wired that he knew there was no chance of sleep. He called his wife.

The Cottage Bar was a favorite with the rich and infamous of Fairbanks. With the expansion of the military role in the small city, it had also become a hangout of many officers and their wives and girlfriends. Like all of the local watering holes, there were two-dozen pegs behind the bar, a gun check for the pistols the local miners still carried.

There was a groan from the Alaskan bartender when McGrady ordered a martini. He carried the drink to an empty booth in the corner facing the door.

A tall muscular man dressed in heavy canvas pants and a red-checkered wool shirt burst through the door. He hung the cane he carried on one of the pegs next to someone's Colt .45 revolver. His blue eyes surveyed the gloomy room in one sweep. He hung his sealskin parka on a coat rack and stuck one finger in the air as he limped toward McGrady's table.

"Thought you would be here," said General Chad Gritt. The two men shook hands. Gritt tugged his heavy sweater over his head and folded it onto the wooden seat. Hard seats were hell on the scarring and unevenly repaired bones in his hip, damage from a friendly fire accident.

The bartender set a shot glass, shaped like a shotgun shell, in front of the man who looked more like a gold miner than an Air Force officer. Gritt tipped the double shot of Jack Daniels, savoring the bourbon around his mouth and tongue before swallowing. He handed the glass back to the bartender. "One more and a large water, Tony."

He smiled. "Did you find it?"

"We'll know after intelligence studies the film, Chad, but we didn't see anything obvious."

McGrady and his boss had developed a private code, a bland language, which allowed them to discuss the highly classified recon missions without really saying anything.

"God, I hope you are wrong. There are some things that we just can't lose," continued Gritt.

"Maybe we need some help analyzing what we already know," replied McGrady. "You know someone outside the party who can give us a second opinion on where to look? I know you have access to other resources looking for the same thing. Maybe someone in the State Department has some intel."

"Not a bad idea, Pat. There must be a few old Russian hands that survived the un-American activities hearings in congress. Even though the boss back in DC gave us the mission, it's a lot better idea than waiting for something to go boom." Gritt drank half of the huge tumbler of ice water that the bartender left in front of him. "We can discuss it tomorrow at the office after we see what the film shows."

A petite brunette slipped through the heavy insulated door, unbuttoning the gray fox coat that shut out the ten-degree night. She unwrapped the gray wool scarf that covered her head and neck. Both men watched Sue McGrady make her way across the half-filled room.

"I didn't know you two were expecting a child," said Gritt.

"Damn, she's only five months along," replied McGrady, "you don't miss a thing."

Both men stood as Sue slipped into the booth next to her husband, who held up the palm of his hand toward the bartender as she slid past him.

"Don't worry, Pat," she started, "I know the drill by now." She tilted her head, kissing her husband's cheek. Sue turned to Gritt and placed her hand on his. "Is Carmen joining us? Pat and I are going out to dinner later."

"No, she'll have dinner on the table when I get home. Both kids had a busy day, and little Chad has a basketball game Saturday night. It's my night to make sure he's caught up on his homework."

The bartender took an order for an Orange Crush from Sue.

"Let me guess," continued Sue, looking at Gritt's clothing, "you spent the day flying that little plane of yours."

"Your wife knows me too well, Pat." He smiled at the woman. "You are right, of course. I usually try to fly whenever one of my teams is…uh, traveling. I guess it helps me feel like I am still part of the real Air Force."

"You don't have to explain the bus man's holiday to me, Mr. Gritt. My dad was a long-distance truck driver. We drove somewhere for every vacation. Besides, all that Pat talks about is about how much fun it was when you brought that little float plane north from the factory last fall."

"It's on skis now. I am still learning to judge the snow conditions in flat light. I started flying with my dad when I was ten, but this is my first airplane on skis. It's really hard to see mounds and holes in the snow from the air. Everything is white."

Gritt turned to the man across the table. "An inspector from the Aeronautics Board approached me while I was refueling in town this morning. First one I've seen in Fairbanks. He saw my uniform coat with the wings on the seat next to me. That coat with the old wings has saved my fanny three or four times. If one of those guys ever asks for my license and medical certificate, I'm busted."

"Why don't you apply for your medical again?" asked Pat.

"After I was wounded, I was grounded. They found other things for me to do. When I applied for a medical after the war, the first question they asked was whether I'd ever lost or been denied a medical, either as a civilian or by the military. I should have lied. Anyway, they have accepted my application and the approval of a flight surgeon four times, but they never process the paperwork."

"So, you fly without the proper paperwork?" interjected Susan, shock on her face.

Gritt smiled, stopping to frame his answer in a way that this strait-laced daughter of an Oklahoma trucker would understand. Before he could answer, McGrady came to his rescue.

"Sue, it's kind of like breathing. For someone who loves to fly, having some faceless clerk tell him he can't, when there is no logical reason, would be like telling him to hold his breath until he dies. The human body just won't allow it."

"Would that same rule apply to a woman who needs to go home next Christmas to introduce her family to her new baby?"

Gritt slipped from the booth. "That is my queue to head for home. Perhaps we can arrange a couple's dinner for the weekend." He turned to leave, then stopped. "I didn't go into the office, Pat. What time are we getting together tomorrow?"

"Two."

"See you then." Gritt made his way across the floor, wrapped his torso in his heavy fur parka, and handed a ten-dollar bill to the bartender. He plucked his cane from the peg behind the bar and headed for the old 1943 military jeep he cherished.

"The general didn't finish his drink," observed Sue.

"He never does. He also paid for ours," offered her husband, picking up the double shot of Jack Daniels and dumping it into his empty martini glass. He then used a spoon to transfer some ice from the water glass that Gritt left, adding a splash of water. "He has been trying to get me interested in bourbon since we first met."

The bartender placed Sue's Orange Crush, wrapped in a napkin, in front of her.

"At least he's not one of those snobs who looks down their nose at anyone who doesn't drink Scotch," answered Sue. She drank half of her soda without coming up for air. It was a habit that she picked up on sweltering afternoons around the municipal pool in Oklahoma.

"Where to, for dinner?" asked Pat.

❦

The briefing the next day started with a young major passing out dozens of eight by ten photos, clipped together in the top left corner. Present were McGrady, Walsh, Flores and two men from Gritt's staff, as well as two men whose job was photo assessment.

"We will spend the next few days giving the photos you men took over the three targets, a second, and then a third examination," started the major. "For today, we have only spent about twelve hours on the film from Petropavlovsk. All we know for sure is the TU-16 that was on the ramp eight days ago was not on the ramp yesterday. We will look at the hangers and two other structures at the airbase that might be big enough to shelter the Badger. We have techniques that we use to give us a rationalized opinion on whether that aircraft is in one of them. We do not have an opinion at this time.

"The first look at the bases at both Kyluchi and Ossora are more interesting. Both bases are exclusively Russian Air Defense bases, not Russian Air Force bases. As such, they have only housed fighter aircraft. At both bases, however, the Soviets are building new hanger facilities that could be used to work on larger aircraft. In both cases, the hangers could be used for TU-16 aircraft or even the bigger turboprop that we know the Russians are working on."

The major took a break to refill his coffee cup. Gritt used his cane to help stand. "Nice work so far, Dan. How long until you can give me a report that you want to sign off?"

"Maybe another three days," answered Major Dan Greiwe. "On the issue of whether that TU-16 is undercover, we will first want to measure the structures to see if you can fit a plane that long into one of them. The Badger has a really long nose and is closer to the ground than most Russian aircraft. In the photos of the one in Petropavlovsk, they built a longer tow bar so that the tractors already at the base could move it. We will look to see if we can find that tow bar. It is about fifteen feet longer than the normal ones used."

In front of him, the eyes of the aircrew began to glaze over.

"None of us needs to know exactly what magic you and your team are working with, only whether the Badger is still there, or on one of the other bases, offered Gritt. Washington is very worried that the Russians are moving one or more of their advanced attack squadrons to the Far East. The Soviet press keeps touting that they now have a thousand modern bombers and at least that many nuclear bombs. Even one Badger with two nuclear weapons could take down most of Alaska's air defenses and open a doorway through central Canada for attacks into the mainland."

"We get it, General. We will keep looking but remember, if we don't see that TU-16, that only tells us where it isn't. To find it, we may have to expand the search and maybe even increase the frequency of flights in hopes of catching it exposed."

There was a groan from the three-man crew of the RB-47. McGrady stood. "Can you tell us anything from the intercepts from the recon pod? The Blackbirds seemed busy for the entire flight."

"I am sorry, Colonel McGrady, but I have nothing from the ELINT gathered. Their mission on this trip was to test the intercept and monitoring technology. Any actual data from this mission is secondary to the technology evaluation. Those guys are all some type of black, off the record operations, at least for now."

Gritt was bothered that Major Greiwe, his second-in-command, wasn't being completely honest with McGrady and his crew. The major's interpretation of the monitoring security orders always erred on the side of revealing nothing. Maybe that was better than revealing too much.

"We think we were picked up by Russian Navy radar on a ship leaving the harbor in Petropavlovsk and they relayed the sighting to the mainland. The Blackbirds seemed to think that a report about us was being sent over their radio relay stations along the coast. When we got to Ossora, they sent up four MIGs to find us. Thank God we got there ten minutes faster than they thought we would. They were behind us but managed to get damned close. I'm sure the armorers reported that we used the guns to fight them off."

"Pat," interjected Gritt, "I can tell you that the Blackbird's primary interest will be monitoring Soviet military telecom. After a request from the director of the CIA, I personally suggested that they use their new toys to look for clues as to where the Soviets might be holding as many as two dozen members of flight crews lost on recon missions, and others missing from the Korean conflict. Having specific goals helped them evaluate their capabilities." Gritt smiled. "Any other help they provided was because they don't really know you and still think you are a good guy. Oh, and they were probably committed to helping save their own asses."

McGrady ignored his boss, turning his gaze back to Major Greiwe. "Are you telling me that we might have to go right back out there to look for that damned Badger?"

"That, Sir, is not my call."

McGrady shifted his gaze to Gritt.

"Pat, that will not even be my call, at least not right now. When Dan's crew is finished, we will ship everything we learn to Elmendorf in Anchorage for a second look. They will send it on to DC In any event, it sounds like it will take Dan's troops the better part of a week to really search through what you already brought home. No new mission for at least three weeks is my guess."

Gritt headed toward the door. "Unless there is something else right now, let's all get back to work." He looked around and found everyone standing, fumbling with coats and briefcases. "Dismissed."

CHAPTER 6

FOR THE FIRST five days, the Russian pilot mostly slept. Ellen had learned little about the man or his mission. She couldn't tell if the tears she watched him discretely wipe away were from pain or sorrow. On the sixth day, Ellen awoke to the man trying to rekindle the fire. She sat up on the edge of the bed, fully dressed.

"You speak really good English. I am surprised."

Anton dropped a match on the moss and kindling and added some split wood. He slipped past the woman onto the bed. Sitting, he pulled a pillow between his back and the rough log wall. Wearing only briefs, he was covered in goose bumps. He pulled a blanket up over his shoulders.

"You once said that your husband was denounced," answered Anton.

"Yes, we have a real problem in this country. One of our senators stirred up the nation. He has the whole country looking for communist spies."

"Do you believe that there are Russian spies in America?" asked Anton. He smiled, not a joyous smile, but one that is used when you know the answer to the question just asked.

Ellen cocked her head, a wry smile on her own face. "You know there are. Anyway, everyone who has ever worked with Russia is under suspicion. John was denounced as a communist sympathizer. My name came up during the hearing. My job at the Department of State involved studying your government. I guess that made me suspect too."

Anton nodded his head. Her story surprised him. "We have similar stories, in a way," offered Anton. "My wife was with the Soviet Nuclear Research Bureau. That is why I speak English; we both took intensive language lessons. Her job was to interpret documents smuggled from America, and I helped her with that." Anton was staring at something invisible on the ceiling. "I guess that is an admission that my country did have spies in America. Anyway, just before Premier Stalin died, she was accused of espionage and sent to one of the labor camps. I haven't heard from her in two years."

"Was she a spy?"

"God no, her only crime was documenting how advanced American technology was."

As the fire heated the cabin, Ellen motioned for Anton to lie down. She reached under the bed for a box of medical supplies purchased when she and John moved to the cabin.

"And John's crime was to try to convince congress that Russia's weak industrial base wouldn't really be a threat for years to come."

"Both sides are paranoid," replied Anton. "They will kill us all."

Anton lay flat, gripping the edge of the bed.

The Russian major winced, as Ellen snipped the gauze used to cover one of the dozen places where his flesh was torn. Where a wound was in an arm or a leg, she'd wrapped gauze around and around the torn flesh, ripping the end and using the two strands to tie it in place. She pulled the gauze away from the six-inch tear in Anton's thigh.

"The skin is healing, and I don't see any new redness in the tissue," she started. "Your cuts were all very clean, probably caused by ripped aluminum or the glass of your windscreen." He grimaced as she pulled gently on a strand of thread that held his torn flesh together. "The only thing available was cotton thread to sew the wounds. It will hurt when I tug out the stitches."

"It hurts when you touch them; every place you bandaged itches terribly."

"That's good, usually that means it is healing." Ellen opened the big bottle of iodine antiseptic next to the bed and soaked the cotton pad in her hand. She swabbed the surface of the wound with the bright orange liquid. She could feel Anton's muscles tighten from the stinging, but he said nothing. It took a few minutes to replace the bandage.

"Would you like to rest a few minutes before I clean the next wound?"

"No, I prefer to get this over with. I just wish you had a bottle of vodka so that when you finish, we could celebrate surviving this torture."

"I told you, John couldn't drink any alcohol with the medications he was taking. Alcohol made him even sicker. When he quit drinking, I just couldn't drink in front of him."

"My dear Ellen, I am trying to make a joke. How could I ask for more? For days you have nursed me, fed me, and even helped me walk out to that outdoor toilet. If I could, I would purchase thirteen roses and present them to you at the best restaurant in the city."

Ellen smiled, sweeping a strand of her dark red hair from in front of her eyes. "It has been nice having the company. I didn't realize how lonely I was." Ellen clipped the next-to-last bandage. "You never talk of your wife. Was she pretty, as well as intelligent?"

"Yes, of course." Anton's eyes misted, but only for a moment. He changed the subject. "She was the daughter of a famous scientist. He was the head of the physics department at a university. When I met her, she was working on her doctorate, and I was a mere soldier from a small farming village sent to the university to study aeronautical engineering. Other men tried to get her attention, but her work was my only competition for Natalya's assiduity. She studied all of the time, and then at the institute she worked all the time."

"You have no children?"

"No, although we were trying to have a child when she was arrested."

"John and I didn't have children either."

Anton rolled over on his side, exposing the last bandage on the back of his left thigh. He clenched his teeth as Ellen pulled the crusted bandage away, and then washed it gently with warm water before soaking it in iodine.

"I am sorry for you and John. But perhaps it was for the best. When the political police arrested Natalya, all of our friends pretended they didn't know me. We both became outcasts. I can't imagine what it would be like to be a child in school facing that. Premier Khrushchev has condemned the political arrests, but they go on."

"In America, our experience was just the opposite. After John was denounced, dozens of our friends and colleagues rushed to our defense. Even his old boss, President Eisenhower, called to offer his support. Were it not for the cancer, we probably would have stood our ground." She bandaged the healing wound. "After the Rosenbergs stole the plans for the atomic bomb and gave them to Russia, a small minority in this country began seeing communist spies behind every tree." Ellen carefully taped a new bandage over the wound in Anton's leg. "Do you know which gulag they sent your wife to?"

"The two letters I received were sent from some place called Amur-3."

Ellen helped Anton to a chair while she changed the sheets. Then she rose and walked over to the counter where she did her dishes. Kneeling, she opened a small door in the floor and began pulling on a rope. A small food box slid from the homemade cooler, set into the ground. She carefully unwrapped a bottle, setting it on the floor, and then lowered the box again, closing the trap door.

She rummaged through the silverware box on a shelf below the kitchen window and then grabbed two glasses from the same shelf. Placing a bottle of cabernet on the table she began struggling with a corkscrew. "I have never mastered these damned things," she finally admitted.

"Here," offered Anton, "let me help. I thought you didn't have any alcohol."

"I saved this one bottle to drink a toast on the anniversary of John's passing. That day is still months away. Anyway, I thought the bottle might be put to better use."

"I don't understand."

"Anton, what I did at the Department of State was study what the communists did in their own country and write reports to project what might happen if they gained power elsewhere. Did you know that only ten percent of those sent to the gulags ever returned?"

Anton jerked the cork from the bottle, handing it back to Ellen, but remained silent. She poured each glass one-third full.

Ellen continued, "the gulags in the Amur region were closed right after Stalin's death and all of those who survived were sent home."

The only noise in the cabin was Ellen's huge dog gnawing on a hind leg bone of a caribou, long before stripped of any flesh or tendons.

"Please share this bottle with me. We can drink to love."

"I will share your wine, Ellen." He held the glass in his right hand, covered in bandages where he had lost a finger in the crash. "We will toast to your John and my Natalya."

Ellen couldn't tell whether the look on his face was of sadness or anger. He was mostly silent the rest of the day and into the evening.

Lying next to the Russian airman, she couldn't stop thinking of what life in the gulags must have been like. She must have lain there for an hour before she felt the man's fingers slowly stroking her hair.

"You should sleep, Ellen," he whispered. "My head has known the truth for some time. Only my heart refused to understand. Now sleep, please sleep and thank you for this day."

The next day, Ellen helped Anton dress in some of John's old clothes and bundled him into a military green down parka. The two of them hobbled across the lake to the snow pile that covered what little was left of the plane.

"Before the last of the wreck sinks, I should come out here and look for the remains of my crew. They deserve a decent burial," said Anton.

"After the wreck cooled, I dug through the scraps of metal and ashes with a shovel," replied Ellen. "I found almost no bones or any sign of other men on your airplane. I don't know how much fuel your plane carried, but the wreck burned for hours after the crash."

"It is for the best. No one must know about our mission."

"You have said that before, Anton. Am I now in danger?"

The tall Russian put his least damaged arm around the woman's shoulder and pulled her against his side. "No, our orders were to make sure the plane didn't fall into American hands and if we crashed, that none of us be captured."

"There is nothing left under the snow that any engineer would find interesting," offered Ellen.

"I can see that."

"And you are the only survivor."

"I meant it is best, because I am never going back. My general convinced me to fly this mission with the promise that he would intervene and get Natalya freed."

The two started a slow walk back toward the cabin, Ellen's huge dog, Jack, bounding through the new snow in front of them.

"John and I bought this old mining claim. It was the most remote place we could find. We needed the quiet. It's hard to figure out why your own country betrays you."

"I understand. I buried myself in my flying, to prove they were wrong."

Ellen slipped her arm through his. "Anton, I am really short on medical supplies and with two of us to feed, I am getting short on food. Sometime soon, I will need to go into Bettles and arrange a flight to Fairbanks for supplies."

"What is Bettles?"

"It is an old mining village about sixty miles from here. There is a huge airstrip that was used during the war as a refueling base for the airplanes we gave Russia, to fight the Germans. I can get a flight to Fairbanks from there, and I can be back in four days."

"Will Jack go with you?"

"I can leave him here. All I need are the sled dogs."

"That would be nice."

CHAPTER 7

THE SLEEK YAK-25 jet taxied to the end of the runway and then turned onto the adjoining taxiway. Normally, the arrival of the commander of the Russian Air Force would require a formal reception, a band and the attendance of all of the local dignitaries, but not on this day.

The small two-person jet slid to a stop on the snow-covered tarmac. A vehicle, fitted with a set of stairs pulled up, and two men climbed out of the cockpit, stopping to stretch cramped legs and backs. They returned the salutes of two privates holding the doors of black staff cars, and then climbed in.

The younger man would be sipping a nightcap in the officer's quarters, across the runway, in minutes. The older, General Johan Blovinin was on his way to the private residence of his old friend Alexi Molovic.

A fur trader made the mistake of supporting the czar, losing everything. He'd built the fifty-year-old palatial house occupied by the Commander of the Russian Air Force–Pacific. From the driveway, Blovinin could look out over the endless plain to the east and the frozen Amur River. His host met him at the door; his informality rooted in thirty years of friendship.

"How is it that we are not blessed with the company of the political commissar?" opened Blovinin, sarcastically.

"I reported trouble with radio broadcasts from Nome, Alaska. I told him that all that tribal music, you know, that crap American kids listen to, was twisting the minds of our young recruits at the eastern bases and suggested that he take a quick trip to figure out what might be done," answered Molovic. "Please come in."

"It is good to see you, my old friend. Remember, Alexi, when we stood on the tarmac at that air base in Fairbanks and I told you that you should stay, that you would make a very good American politician?"

Molovic laughed. "And I told you that it pissed me off to see our country begging for hundreds of American airplanes when we had the best aviation engineers in the world, but no plants to build their designs. We have fixed that haven't we, Johan?"

"We certainly have, although our output is still a fraction of the Americans. Is Sofi home?'

"No, I suggested she go visit our daughter. I really didn't know how all of this would work out. Her train should reach Lake Baikal the day after tomorrow. We have the house to ourselves."

The driver dropped a small duffel bag inside the door. The man confirmed that he was to pick up both men in the morning, and then headed back to the warmth of the running vehicle.

"Come, sit in the parlor while I pour us a couple of vodkas."

Blovinin unbuckled his bag and passed a bottle of bourbon to his host. "I thought it might be hard to get anything but vodka out here in the wilderness." He laughed. "Since our talks will center on the Americans, I thought we might recreate one of the evenings when we sat in one of their bars and drank their whiskey."

Molovic disappeared into the kitchen, returning moments later with a bowl of ice and pitcher of water. He scraped the seal off from the bottle and opened it, pouring two inches of the brown liquor into each of two glasses, adding ice and a splash of water. He walked over to where his old friend stood looking down on the frozen river and handed one of the glasses to Johan. "To a long life and even longer retirement," he offered nervously.

"God, how I hate being old," replied Blovinin. "With refueling stops and one short overnight rest, it took thirty hours to get from Moscow to here. When we were young, sitting in those horrid seats they fit into fighter planes was an adventure. Now it is just agony on my old bones, but we needed to meet quickly."

"Try the stuffed chair on the right. It is my smoking chair, the most comfortable in the house."

"No, I'm tired of sitting, probably for some time. I believe I will stand while we talk. To your health," offered Johan, returning his host's toast.

"Just how bad is this? I mean, just how seriously is the Defense Minister taking the loss of one TU-16?"

"Alexi come now. You know that losing one of our newest bombers is hardly a matter that he would take lightly. But more importantly, no one is telling him what happened. I figure we have about forty-eight hours to have a well-thought-out report on his desk. I doubt that I have to remind you that Zhukov is not above personally shooting anyone he suspects is lying to him."

"It's not just us, Johan. There were ten people in the room when the decision was made."

"That is true, but irrelevant. The final decision came from my desk and the operational plan came from you. We were right, of course. However, the younger officers are more afraid of the secret police and the political commissars than the Americans."

"Then we must tell the truth right up to the border in the Bering Sea. We must admit the plane is missing, with the loss of all hands. We will insinuate that the Americans shot it down over the ocean, in international waters, and we will plead that we needed to test their new radar sites in order to plan a counterstrike."

"As I said, Alex, you are the politician. But let me throw one tiny wrinkle into your strategy. What if the Americans shot it down over land and have the plane and the crew? I know that they haven't made any claim, but if it were me holding one of theirs, I wouldn't make it public until I had wrung every drop of intelligence out of the wreck and the crew."

Molovic finished his drink and refilled his glass. He didn't think to ask his old friend whether he was ready for another. He didn't see the tractor pulling a huge sled out on the ice of the Amur or hear the train whistle in the distance. He was conscious only of the tumblers falling in place in his brain. "We will admit that possibility exists and explain how we have one of their planes and crew as a bargaining chip."

"But, my old friend, we don't."

"Then we will just have to get one."

Blovinin turned from the frosted multi-pane window to stare at his old comrade. "We have tried, have we not? My staff forwarded a report last night, of an attempted intercept of one of the American spy planes just days ago. Our own radars never picked it up. How is it that the Navy can see them, and we can't?"

"All of our installations are fixed and designed to search out over the Bering Sea for a massed bomber attack. The Navy radar is designed to look all the way around the fleet at sea. If those fools in the Duma would ever approve the expenditures for airport radar, we could look everywhere too."

Molovic reached for his friend's empty glass, but Blovinin shook his head. "Even with the radar sighting of the airplane, we could not find it over a peninsula protected by multiple airbases and dozens of fighter planes."

"Johan, we did find it, but by the time we got the messages decoded we were just a minute late. The American plane outran our fighters and disappeared into a storm front."

"Then, just exactly how do you intend to grab one of theirs?"

"I have been discussing the incursions with the commanders of the Air Defense Forces. The Americans always seem to fly the same two tracks. They enter our country just north of the Kurile Islands and fly a straight line almost to Anadyr, and then turn for home. Sometimes, they fly the route in reverse. When they do, they appear to line up with their powerful propaganda radio station on the northern coast of Japan's Hokkaido Island."

"If we know their routes, then why in the hell can't the defense forces stop them?"

"Johan, the defense forces never know when they are coming. They do not seem to have any schedule, and they fly anytime they will have enough light to take their damned pictures. This is not Moscow; we are always short of everything, especially fuel. Our radar can seldom detect them. We watch for their airborne radar or a radio transmission. They never transmit until they are right over one of our bases, so our colleagues over in Air Defense always start behind. Their newest bombers are as fast as our fighters."

"They will lose the speed advantage in the next couple of years, Alexi."

"That will not help today, old friend. But I have an idea. I think the northbound American flights are lining up with our radio station in Anadyr. It is the most powerful in the Soviet Union, because it has to cover an area almost a quarter the size of America. If we had a radar site that could detect the American planes when they first started their run, we could lure them far enough inland to trap them. If we are lucky, we could salvage something from the wreckage and capture the crew."

Blovinin handed his empty glass to his friend. "My doctor would be really pissed off if he knew about more than one drink, but I think it is a tool that will help us fill in this crazy idea of yours." He walked across the room and settled into the overstuffed chair offered earlier.

Molovic refreshed the drinks and settled into the chair across the ornate Chinese table from his friend. "We will actually need three radars, so that we can track the intruder's progress."

"We are not getting funds for radar. But, in the name of protecting Mother Russia, I might be able to talk the commanding admiral of the Pacific Forces in Vladivostok into participating in an exercise to rid the country of the American intruders. The Navy's newest cruisers all have advanced air defense radar."

"It was one of them that sent the message that started the chase this week," replied Molovic. "We have to cover a peninsula that is longer than Finland. We will need to spread them out along the peninsula, and we will have to dispense with the complex reporting code that requires lengthy decoding."

"Let us assume, Alexi, that I can arrange that; how do we lure the American plane inland?"

"We will build a duplicate radio broadcast station on a mountaintop a couple of hundred kilometers west of Anadyr. When it is ready, we will switch the existing station off. If I am right, the Americans will not notice the subtle change in direction until it is too late."

"Alexi, I am suddenly hungry," offered Blovinin with a smile.

"The party has a villa, only about ten miles from here, where we can get dinner. Afterwards, we can spend an hour in the banya and then find some massage girls to help us relax. I'll drive."

"No, my friend. I've only finished two drinks, I will drive."

CHAPTER 8

GRITT, DRESSED IN fatigues, with no insignia of rank, sat in the front of the briefing room, studying the Blackbird report. Most generals in the U.S. military preferred a grand entrance, their aides ordering those seated in the meeting to attention when they entered a room.

Gritt, however, had spent his early career working with a joint Army-Navy special intelligence group. He'd been badly wounded on a mission. That experience beat the excess ego out of the man.

After his new bride nursed him back to health, he'd been "loaned" to the Office of Strategic Services, America's World War II intelligence operation. In 1947, when that group became the CIA, Gritt moved back to the Air Force, rising in rank in the Strategic Air Command. He always chaffed under formal military command structure.

Gritt was pigeonholed as an intelligence officer with most of his postings in air reconnaissance. He'd flown with his aircrews over Korea, Russia and China, as they photographed hostile installations, and later gathering ELINT – electronic intelligence. His expertise landed him back with the CIA by the end of the Korean War. While he no longer commanded any aircraft, anything he or his boss, Allen Dulles wanted, the Strategic Air Command accommodated.

As Gritt marked the critical pieces of the report with the pencil that always stuck out of his shirt pocket, the room slowly filled. Finally, it was Gritt who rose, muttering a totally unnecessary, "at ease, be seated."

In the back of the room, the twelve-man Blackbird team sat uncomfortably knowing that Gritt was about to discuss information that their operational orders considered classified.

"My thanks to the men in the back of the room. Someday soon I hope that I can introduce all of them to you. Until then, I suggest that you assume that they are critical to your mission and if you see any of them downtown, you might buy them a drink." A nervous laugh rose from the back row.

"Before we get to the discussion of next month's missions, let me touch on three highlights from the ELINT report. First, there are no new radar signals other than an occasional signal from the Russian Navy. This is important because the radar towers that you men have photographed at each of the Russian air bases, are so far just wasted steel and cement. This finding confirms what the recent photo recon is showing.

"Secondly, there is Russian chatter about several new installations to collect high frequency radio traffic from our planes and probably also from the Alaskan mainland. This explains the odd construction that you have photographed recently. They appear to be Krug antennas. But they may also have other uses, so it is absolutely critical, that all of you maintain total radio silence. Even in an emergency, you will under no circumstances break radio silence except on close in approach to an American base."

A hand shot up in the front row.

"Yes, Tony."

"In the past, we were allowed one message if we were under attack and one if we were losing the plane, Sir."

"You are right to interpret this as a change in orders. We will give the Russians no help in tracking any flight or finding any downed crew or aircraft."

"Then how in the hell can anyone find us, Sir?"

"We will be experimenting with two parachute canisters. One will be dropped if you are under attack. It will transmit a thirty-second coded burst transmission at noon each day for thirty days. A second canister will be deployed if you are losing the airplane. It will also send a thirty-second burst fifteen minutes after noon each day for thirty days. These will be used to set up a search pattern. You will each carry a short-range emergency radio. You will switch it on at precisely twelve-thirty each day and wait for a coded call. Only after you authenticate the call will you respond."

Gritt looked around the room. All of the men were volunteers, and all understood the policy of no man left behind. He understood that the new procedures did not change that policy, but it might make rescue more difficult. He sensed their unease. "These canisters are experimental. We are tasked with the field-testing. The brass didn't ask us to like this but think about it—we've yet to get any lost crews back from the Russians. If you lose your ride, it's critical that we find you before Ivan does. Any more questions or comments?"

The faces around him were all lost in thought, but there were no hands. He wandered over to the coffee-urn in the corner and refilled the battered porcelain cup he almost never set down.

"Finally," he continued, "the Blackbirds have some intercepts that indicate that the Soviets are preparing an old gulag northwest of Khabarovsk as a military personnel interrogation facility. This may be the breakthrough I have been looking for. None of the intel guys here, or back in DC, can think of any military personnel valuable enough to justify a new base, except perhaps, some of the aircrew still missing from Korea and the Navy and Air Force personnel missing on reconnaissance missions over the last three years. You all know our motto: none left behind." He waited for the murmuring in the room to subside. "Our first priority this month, continues to be to looking for that missing TU-16 in the Russian far-east and any heavy bomber build-up in the region. The guys flying out of Thule, Greenland will be looking for the same thing along the northern border."

Gritt leaned against the heavy oak table in the front of the room. "We will develop a plan to go find this new interrogation facility. If possible, we would like to take our people back."

The rest of the meeting was taken up with the nuts-and-bolts discussions of a crack military unit planning operations. Gritt turned the meeting over to the Colonel who actually commanded these Strategic Air Command crews.

After the meeting broke up, McGrady found Gritt eating a ham and cheese sandwich in his office, a map of eastern Russia spread out on his desk. "We still on for dinner Saturday night, Chad?"

"Yup, Carmen is making some of her moose meat enchiladas. Both kids will be out, so it's just the four of us, Pat."

"Sounds like fun. I'll bring the beer."

Gritt slid his chair back, motioning McGrady toward the chair across the desk. "I don't think we are going to waste a lot more time looking for that one TU-16. Still, everyone back in DC would feel a lot better if we knew it wasn't flying recon missions for a massed bomber strike. It isn't your turn in the barrel, but you and your crew are the best we have here. I would consider it a real favor if you could make a pure photo run up the east side of the Kamchatka Peninsula. They may be hiding it on the other side of the peninsula. See if you can find it."

CHAPTER 9

WOLF PACK LAKE, ALASKA

ANTON USED HIS fingernails to scrape the frost from inside the cabin window. A hundred meters away, smoke rose from the metal chimney of the steam bath. He absent-mindedly rubbed his wet hair with a towel. Only twenty minutes before, he'd lunged from the steaming banya and trotted to the wooden frame out on the frozen lake. The trap door in the ice, normally used to draw water, sat open. He'd dropped the towel he now used to dry his hair, and jumped into the open water, submerging well over his head. The water was exquisite as it washed away the sweat and the heat from the steamy room. He kicked to the surface, gasping.

He'd folded his elbows on the wooden frame. In the distance, he could see the shattered trees from the crash of his plane and behind that, snow covered everything up to the tops of the rounded mountains that were the foothills of the Brooks Range. Above the mountaintops the sky was a soft powder blue, indicating a late winter weather change as the air finally held some moisture.

The water was brutally cold, but also life giving. His wounds healed enough, so that they no longer required bandaging. It was good to be clean, good to be alive. He left the guilt he felt at being the only survivor, betraying the promise he made to himself to end his own life, in the cold lake waters. It might come back, but for now he was free of it.

The cold left an ache in his broken arm and any effort to push with it, shot pain throughout his body. After trying to push out of the water several times with one arm, Ellen called from the cabin. A moment later, she was trotting down the packed snow trail, extending both arms to help him out of the water.

She helped him wrap the towel around himself. "You go dry off and get into the clean robe I set out for you. It's my turn. I will be up in thirty minutes," she said.

As he watched, the door of the steam bath banged open, and Ellen dashed toward the lake, her towel clutched in her left hand. This woman was at least five years older than his wife, but she wore the years well, and work around the cabin sculpted her into a shape you might find in one of those Western European magazines advertising tropical beach vacations.

She had to be watching me, or she wouldn't have known to come help me out of the water, he rationalized. Ellen lifted herself from the water and began vigorously toweling her body. Natalya's hair was coal-black, which she hated. She always wanted soft yellow hair and talked of how lucky Western women were to have inexpensive systems to change their hair color. Those were available only to the party elite in Russia. Ellen was a natural redhead. She seemed to like being a redhead. Steam lifted from her skin.

She wrapped the towel around her long hair and looked up at the cabin. She waved. From somewhere, Jack raced out onto the lake to romp next to her as she started up the trail. Anton turned from the window; his face flushed. He took a seat next to the stove.

By the time Ellen reached the cabin, she had wrapped the towel around herself. "I assume you were watching," she laughed. "From everything I observed, you seem to be all male."

Anton poured a cup of tundra-tea from the pot on the stove. He tipped the cup to his lips, burning his tongue on the scalding liquid. He spit the tea back into the cup.

Ellen laughed. "It's all right, I just wanted to offer you a bit of incentive to stay here with Jack, while I run into Bettles this afternoon. I will be gone three or four days."

Anton rubbed the tip of his tongue with his thumb and forefinger. "I wasn't planning on going anywhere," he mumbled. He thought for a moment. "I liked what I saw."

Ellen laughed again. "I have always been a tease. I like the attention that comes with being reasonably attractive."

"You are more than that," mumbled Anton, his tongue now throbbing.

"We will take it slow," answered Ellen. "We don't want any of your wounds to reopen, and that arm needs more time to heal."

"I am not one of those macho bastards that always has to be on top."

Ellen laughed that laugh that he was growing to love. "Each lover is different. We will have to work out what works for us. Now lie down on the bed so that I can coat your stitches with Iodine to make sure you don't get any infection from your swim. The sting of the iodine should take the fight out of you."

An hour later, Ellen drove the six-dog team out onto the lake, headed toward the outlet stream that was the first part of the trail to the old mining village. She didn't look back. Her head felt like it might explode. She took three or four deep breaths to calm herself. She'd debated right and wrong and the meaning of loyalty for days. One more betrayal might be all it took to push Anton over that final cliff. But staying in America wasn't as simple as walking out of the wilderness and applying for a driver's license. And once upon a time she had taken a loyalty oath. She was good at compartmentalizing, separating the insanity of what the McCarthy hearing did to her family from her love of country.

She stopped near a fallen tree just out of site of the cabin. Brushing away a foot of snow, she tugged a small drawstring bag hidden the day after the crash. She opened the bag and examined the folded flyer that she pulled from a charred pile at the wreck site. The two tags with serial numbers pried from what used to be airplane parts were next, and finally she examined a Russian Military ID, partially melted around the edges. She was sure that Anton would have been furious that Pavel somebody carried the ID onto the plane. The last thing in the bag was a roll of film. The last frames on the roll of twelve pictures were the still smoking remains of Anton's jet.

The team made good time on the frozen creek and then the Koyukuk River on their way to Bettles. She found a plane from Fairbanks just landing on the runway as she pulled into town. She boarded her team with friends at the old trading post, and an hour later, she was winging her way southeast.

❖

Anton sat on the cabin steps, staring out onto the alpenglow of the surrounding mountains. He closed his eyes; the vision of Ellen toweling herself filled his mind. He blinked, as Jack dropped a stick at his feet. He launched it down toward the banya and then closed his eyes again, trying to find his last vision. Instead, the green eyes and raven black hair of Natalya smiled at him. It was almost like she was reading his mind, sending a message.

His dinner of Spam and left-over fry-bread rumbled in his stomach all night.

CHAPTER 10

THE MI-4 HELICOPTER settled into the clearing near the summit of the round top mountain three hundred kilometers east of the town of Anadyr. Three temporary wooden shacks rested on blocks only a hundred meters from the ice-covered helicopter landing pad. Alexi Molovic, general of the Russian Air Force, unstrapped himself from the machine that he considered little more than a death trap, and jumped to the ground, followed by his aide, Captain Gagarin.

The two men were ushered into the relative warmth of the broadcast booth of the radio facility that Molovic dreamed up only weeks before. Blovinin had commandeered the equipment destined for a propaganda radio station targeting Japan. Two engineers, one Air Force and one from the Secretariat of Public Communications, greeted the men. "Are you ready to test the facility?" barked Molovic.

"Not quite yet, comrade General," offered the civilian. "We just raised the last section of the tower this morning and the actual antenna is being installed as we speak. It will take another two hours to finish the connection. While two men work at the top of the tower, the last of the cables will be tightened to keep the tower upright in the wind."

Molovic's glare would have frozen the men in the building if they hadn't been so cold already. The general was ready to pounce, but his attack was interrupted by the starting growl of the diesel generator in the next building. "How can you broadcast with that noise in the background? Won't the noise of the engine drown out the voices in this room?"

The Air Force major, trying to warm his hands over the inadequate heat of the oil pot-burner stove, answered without the courtesy of turning toward his powerful visitor. "Normally, we would have stuffed the empty space between the outside and inside walls with shredded paper to insulate the buildings, but as you can see, the wood for the inside walls never arrived. And, the closest supplies of newspapers are in Anadyr."

Gagarin started to reprimand the insolent major but stopped as he noticed the political corps insignia on the man's collar. His boss bailed him out. "You must have a plan to solve the problem. With any luck, the facility will only have to operate for a month or two."

"I have sent two teams down the mountain and out on the tundra to cut pieces of moss. Now that you are here, we will use the helicopter to lift them to the mountaintop. We plan on packing the moss between the frames. We will cover the inside with the canvas tarps we used to cover the electrical equipment before we finished the buildings."

Molovic reluctantly gave the major credit for problem solving. He stepped over to the wooden counter that served as a broadcast booth. There were two microphones and two turntables for records. On the other side of the counter, three large metal cabinets spewed cables and cords toward the counter and through a hole in the floor. "I assume the power cables run to the generator and the large cable runs to the tower," he offered.

"Your observations are correct," replied the civilian engineer. "We will be able to duplicate everything that the station in Anadyr can do."

The political major turned from the stove. "I hope you are right in your thinking, comrade General. If you are, we might accomplish both of our tasks at the same time. This station should have the power to make our broadcasts more accessible to the people of the north. They will no longer have to listen to the American station on the other side of the Bering Sea. That's why the political corps signed off on re-tasking this equipment. The added power should also make it easier for the arrogant capitalists to aim their planes in this direction."

"When you see Colonel Rasputin, please extend my thanks for the loan of the radio station equipment. It will serve both purposes, and after I catch one of the American reconnaissance aircraft you may move the station if you wish." Molovic smiled, as he looked away. In Russia, once the facility was completed it would never move. Instead, it would just decay into one more rusting edifice to inefficiency and intergovernmental competition.

The political major nodded his head. "It is probably better for us to test the station after dark anyway." He added a "Sir" only as an afterthought. "From what you have told us the Americans only fly in daylight when they can take pictures. It would be bad to have both stations operating at the same time if one of their aircraft was in the air today."

Molovic heard the engine of the helicopter come to life. "That is well thought out, Major. Perhaps you should think about transferring to the operational Air Force where you can actually use that intellect." He didn't wait for an answer. "I would like to watch the helicopter depart for its first load of moss. Perhaps one of you will be good enough to explain what the men on the tower are doing."

The four men pushed through the double canvas tarps that acted as a door to the building. It was nice to be away from the reek of oiled cotton. The political officer glared at the senior officer, determined to come up with some wrongdoing that he could report. It was important to ensure that no one was above the authority of the political corps.

Molovic watched the helicopter lift off in a surging wind, swinging dangerously close to the tower. From the top of the tower, he heard a scream. All four men watched, stunned, as a body fell, bouncing from crossbeam to crossbeam. The plunge lasted so long that a half dozen men were waiting at the bottom to break the man's fall.

"How is he?"

"He is dead," came an answer from a sergeant cradling the man's head.

The major looked over at his civilian partner. "He is one of yours, Vladimir. Do you have another qualified technician to finish his work?"

"He was one of my best technicians. The man has a wife and two small children," replied the civilian now kneeling next to the twisted body.

"That is not what I asked you."

The civilian stood; hands clenched into fists. "No."

"Then you will have to climb the tower yourself and finish. If we do not finish tonight, I will not be able to ride back to civilization with the general. I am not going to freeze another night in a sleeping bag. I suggest you tie yourself onto the tower like my man has."

Molovic and his aide walked to the edge of the clearing, staring at the huge orange sun already low on the horizon. "Dimitri," started the general, "I am a loyal party member, but if I were ever the defense minister, the first thing I would do is ship every member of the political corps to the most remote gulag in the country and then order the location erased from every map."

"I agree, Sir. But we must remember, if it weren't for the politicos, we wouldn't have a radio transmitter."

"Sometimes I envy the Americans, Dimitri. At least they are smart enough to leave their politicians in their capital, thousands of miles away from most of their military. Do you think it is safe to ride in a helicopter at night?"

"You are so old school, comrade General. If it doesn't have a propeller, you don't like it. I am told that a helicopter is safer than a fixed wing aircraft at night. It can fly slowly, and if something happens, the rotor acts like a big parachute."

"Maybe I am too old, Dimitri. Maybe I should be really worried about the Americans and their atomic bombs, but to tell the truth, I am more pissed off that they are flying over here and making the last days of my career difficult. If it weren't for the politicians on both sides, we old soldiers would find somewhere to go fishing together and probably tell lies while we got drunk." He shook his head. "I think I hear the helicopter returning. I want to make sure that we take the body of that boy who fell with us. He deserves a decent funeral where his wife can bring his children."

CHAPTER 11

THERE WERE TWENTY-FOUR empty chairs in the briefing room. The only people present were McGrady and his two-man crew, the general and two briefers.

"Pat, you will be flying the 'A' bird today. I think this will be the last flight looking for the missing Russian bomber. This is a pure camera mission. I have orders to fold the ELINT folks into our actual command. A new bird with expanded electronic capabilities will replace the 'B' bird. It should be ready in the next week."

McGrady scowled. "General, we would all feel better if we had those Blackbirds along. On the last run, they warned us of the MIGs before they ever left the runway."

"Pat, I agree that the Blackbirds offer another layer of safety, but today's mission has only one goal—to see if the missing TU-16 is still in the theater to make sure there isn't a bomber buildup. After today, every mission will have ELINT capability."

McGrady looked over at Rick Flores and Bob Walsh shrugging his shoulders. Both gave him a quick head nod to thank him for trying.

"Colonel," added Gritt, "this mission will follow the new security and radio procedures. Your bird has been fitted with the new emergency radio canisters." Gritt paused for a moment then smiled. "Today would not be a good day to use them."

Dan Greiwe, the general's intel officer, handed a small packet of mimeographed sheets to McGrady's team. "The weather folks are predicting a strong low pressure along the Aleutian Islands. That counterclockwise circulation means you could have eighty mile an hour headwind on your outward leg. You will be launching early this morning so you can stop in Japan. You will refuel at Chitose Air Force Base before going north over Kamchatka."

"The Russian long-range radar pointed at Japan can see any aircraft more than 2,000 feet up," replied McGrady.

The mission briefer uncovered a large wall map in the front of the room. "The Navy recon flights appear to have uncovered a gap in the coverage. If you fly west about a hundred miles and then parallel the Kurile Islands to the north, you should be able to evade any plotted radar."

"What the hell were you before you joined the Air Force?" shot McGrady. "Any plotted radar; sounds like some legal disclaimer."

Gritt erupted in laughter. "You called that one right; Pat. Josh came to us from JAG. He transferred, at his request, to try to make a difference. He is giving you the most accurate assessment we have. He and Dan have worked on this for twenty hours a day for the last three days. It's the best we can give you."

"General, for some reason, I am more nervous about this flight than any since my first. I don't like it. I don't like going back out this soon. The Ruskies have learned that they can see us with their naval radar. If they have figured out how to work together, this could be a hot run."

"Pat, just think of how much trouble we have with inter-service rivalry, then multiply it by ten, that's the Russian military. Why do you think they have two separate Air Forces? Your concerns are why we have to go now. If we give them another week or two, they may work this out."

"So, after this mission, we might as well all go home," quipped McGrady.

"Part of the upgrade on the 'B' bird is advanced radar jamming. When you get back Boeing will start retrofitting the 'A' bird," answered Gritt. "I'll see if I can clear you and your crew to ferry the plane to Seattle for a little R & R."

The second briefer stepped to the front of the room. "Colonel," added the planner, "you will rely on altitude and speed. If you stay at forty thousand feet, the MIG-15's can't reach you. If you keep the pedal to the metal, the MIG-17's will have a very short range. We considered the MIG-17 our designation the type 38, even though we estimate only about a dozen in the entire Russian Far East. You will leave Japan with full fuel tanks. Quick in, quick out, then come home."

McGrady turned to his photo recon officer. "Bob, any problem with the extra altitude or speed?" McGrady knew the answer before he asked. Gritt's staff would have done their homework.

"No Sir, I can fine tune the lenses to within a hundred feet. The speed just means we will take fewer pictures while over the target." Walsh picked up his slide rule and a minute later announced, "If we only have to shoot the airbases, I can cut the camera 'on' time to one minute and fifty-five seconds."

"Anything else?" asked McGrady. "If not, I would like to get this over with."

"Mind if I ride out to the runway with you?" asked Gritt.

"Nope," replied McGrady. "We can use all of the immoral support you can muster, General."

The four men piled out of the International Travelall where half a dozen men buzzed around the Stratojet. Both McGrady and Flores did a complete pre-flight inspection, while Walsh climbed into the bomb-photo compartment and began calculating the routing and navigation information given him. Gritt stood in front of the right wing, his breath making tiny eruptions in the bitter air.

The B-47 Stratojet, built by Boeing, was a totally new design from the firm's famous bombers of World War II. The swept wings with six engines still amazed Gritt, and he took every chance to study the huge plane that looked like a fighter jet on steroids. To a pilot, airplanes were art, and this was the Mona Lisa. Bathed in artificial light in the pre-dawn darkness, the huge plane looked like something from ancient mythology.

McGrady pointed at the open hatch and then at Flores, who climbed into the heavy bomber.

"Don't ask me why this trip gives me the willies," he offered to Gritt, "but it does."

"Maybe the MIGs on your tail last time. Maybe knowing your wife is carrying a baby. Maybe some intuition from somewhere we will never understand. It's not like back in '56 when the Russians couldn't fly as fast or as high as a B-47. But we're still better at this. Just pay attention to your nerves," added Gritt. "Keep everyone on their toes, all the time. Use your radar sparingly when approaching the targets but use it. I'll see you in the bar after you land."

Gritt arrived at the briefing in uniform, a very unusual event. If the reason was to send a message that today's mission, was all business, it was wasted effort. From the time McGrady had slipped out of bed at three that morning, ready to end a restless night, he'd been focused. McGrady snapped a salute to his senior officer who was his own age. He wondered how senior officers felt about sending their troops into harm's way. Then he locked the thought away in his often used "unnecessary question" file.

Gritt remained standing in the same spot for twenty minutes as the crew readied the plane. As McGrady slipped into his seat, Gritt turned to leave, ending up sprawled awkwardly on the pavement.

Inside the plane, Flores tapped McGrady on the shoulder. The sight of the general, born and raised in Alaska, unlacing his shoes, then standing in his stocking feet was just the shot of humor they both needed. They laughed until it hurt, as the general, now on his hands and knees, used a pocketknife to chip away at the ice binding the soles of his shoes to the tarmac.

"Now that's a cheechako move, standing in one place long enough for your warm shoes to melt the ice on the runway and then freeze again."

"Well, that's our fearless leader. But you have to give the guy credit. Most generals would be waiting in the warm car," replied McGrady.

Gritt sat in the open front door of the Travelall, tying his shoes. He stepped from the vehicle to watch the huge silver plane climb into the southwest sky.

A Jeep slid to a stop. From it, a sergeant emerged and approached the general, snapping a salute. "Sorry to interrupt your visual, Sir, but Major Greiwe just called. He says some woman has been trying to reach you since early this morning. He doesn't know why, but she says it is important." The man looked at the pad he carried. "She says you will know the name, Mrs. Captain John Walter Wilson."

Gritt turned and started toward the Jeep. "How about a ride, Sergeant?"

"What about your car, Sir?"

"I am kind of partial to Jeeps."

CHAPTER 12

GRITT ASKED THE young private outside his office door to get Ellen Wilson on the phone. "She says she is staying at the Fairbanks Hotel," he added. Then he turned back to Greiwe, ignoring the pile of work on his desk.

"Did Ellen say what was so important?"

"I didn't talk to her, General. When I got back to the office, she had called four times." He handed Gritt the message slips. "Who is this, Ellen Wilson?"

"She married the Navy Captain that first recruited me into intelligence work, just before the Second World War. I worked with her and her husband later with the OSS before they moved over to the Department of State. She and Walt moved into a remote cabin out by Bettles a couple of years ago, looking for some solitude after tangling with Joe McCarthy's goons."

"What in the hell can be urgent in the middle of nowhere?"

"I don't know, Dan, but I will find out. The woman is never a waste of time. She can put together the pieces of a puzzle like no one I have ever known. Besides, she was the one I was drooling over before my wife walked into a party and threw her lariat around me." Gritt watched his subordinate's reaction. "If you repeat that to my wife, you will find yourself on guard duty at one of the remote radar sites." He laughed.

"Sounds like a job for a bachelor," replied Greiwe.

"This sounds like all business. When she and Walt came through on their way to the old mine site they bought, John confided in me that he was battling cancer. If they need help, I am the guy. I owe them a lot."

Gritt was kind of pissed off that he couldn't go flying while he waited for McGrady's return, but of all of his friends, the Wilsons would be the last to ever ask for help. He started through the pile on his desk, trying to find something that might hold his interest.

Four hours later a private buzzed Gritt on the intercom. "A Mrs. Wilson on the line for you."

"Have you had breakfast yet?" asked Ellen. "If not, I am buying. I know it's noon. You can pick the place. I am in the mood for one of those huge Midwest farmer's breakfasts, but it has to be somewhere we can talk privately."

"Ellen is everything OK?" asked Gritt.

"No, Chad, it is not. And yes, maybe it is really good. I will explain at breakfast. I saw one of your planes roar out of here early this morning, so don't give me the, 'I am needed here' excuses. I know how you work. You won't do anything important until it comes back."

"Be there in an hour," answered Chad. He checked his watch. As he hung up the phone, he wondered how the hell Ellen knew that the morning plane was connected to him.

Ellen apologized. When she couldn't reach Chad early, rather than waste time she'd started her shopping. After they placed their order, Ellen started with the loss of her husband and her decision to stay on the homestead.

"I am so sorry about Walt," responded Chad. "He opened the door for me, and a lot of young men. He left a lucrative oil company career to protect his country, and he did it superbly. He didn't deserve the shit he took at State after his name came up at the un-American Activities hearings."

"There was a lot of garbage flying around," answered Ellen, who had traded her jeans and wool shirt for a business suit that would have fit right in on Madison Avenue. Her suit turned heads in Fairbanks, Alaska. "We would have survived, and probably been right back to where we were before someone let Joe McCarthy out of his cage, but the medical diagnosis changed everything."

Chad motioned for the waitress and pointed at his empty coffee cup.

"I married a man more than twenty years older than me. My life was all business, and

after his wife died, it just seemed right. It kept the vultures away while I put my degrees in international affairs and European history to work." Ellen sipped her coffee. "When Walt got sick, I realized that we'd been lovers and partners, but I had never been much of a wife. Honestly, I hadn't thought through how tough it would be to watch the man I spent almost half of my life with die before my eyes. But I would never have changed a minute."

Chad watched over Ellen's shoulder as the waitress emerged from the kitchen. "Is that why you called, to tell me about Walt?"

"No," replied Ellen. "Let's eat breakfast first; you can update me on what you are doing, and Carmen and the kids. Then I am going to ask you for a hard promise before I can get to why I left the homestead to find you."

"If I can, I will," answered Chad. "There isn't much I can tell you about what I am doing though."

Ellen laughed. "Tell me about the family. Then I will tell you what I think you are doing."

Gritt didn't realize how hungry he was, as he devoured his meal, using the moments between bites to brag about his family to an old friend.

"This is what I think you are doing up here," started Ellen. "I think you are coordinating recon over-flights of the Russian Far East. I think you are trying to keep track of the bomber threat to the West Coast. I also think you are monitoring what new aircraft are being staged in eastern Russia."

Chad wasn't really surprised by Ellen's analysis but having spent most of two years in the bush, it was startlingly on the money. "I can't comment."

"Okay, that's what I thought," replied Ellen. "Now for the commitment. I made a promise to someone who has been giving me information. It is someone who I think could be the love of my life, someone with very similar experiences to my own. I don't know that he feels the same, but I want to find out. I promised him that I would not betray his confidences." She stared at her coffee. "There's more than one reason to betray my commitment to him or I wouldn't be here. Still, you can make this a lot easier."

Chad reached across the table and put his hand on hers.

Ellen wiped away a tear. "You can't disclose anything I tell you or show you without his permission and mine. If you agree, I think we might be able to help you with your job."

"Ellen, this mysterious person can only be one place, back at your mining claim. I could send a platoon of army scouts out there this afternoon to arrest him as a possible enemy asset."

"You could, but you won't. First, the paint that Joe McCarty sprayed all over Walt and me would probably get me arrested too. McCarthy is gone, but there are still people in high places who believe in what he was doing. The FBI intercepted Walt and me on our way through Seattle the year before he died. Second, the minute I left, I am sure this person searched the cabin for my rifle, and he has little to live for if I betray him."

Chad thought through the conversation. Ellen was one of the few people in Alaska that truly understood security disclosure obligations. He loved his job and in only four more years he could retire, although he had no intention of doing so. But, if this source really could help define the Russian threat, there was an obligation to follow the lead. Besides, Ellen's description of the risk to her was spot on."

"OK, I'll bite. On one condition, I want to meet your new friend myself."

"I will arrange it."

Ellen retrieved the sack she hidden after the crash from the small pack at her feet. She dumped the contents on the table.

Chad picked up the serial number plates and then the leaflet, and finally the ID tag. He pointed at the exposed roll of film. "What exactly am I looking at?" he asked, a haunting fear in the back of his head."

"A Russian bomber crashed on my lake about four weeks ago. Only the pilot survived. His mission was to drop a load of these leaflets on your base to send a message that America should stop flying over Russian territory and to let us know that we are just as 'at risk' for a secret attack, as they are."

Chad sat stunned. "What is left of the bomber? It could be an intelligence treasure trove."

"Nothing, there is nothing but melted blobs of aluminum. The wreck burned for hours. Much of it sank through the melted ice. You have a photo of the burning wreck on that roll of film."

"Ellen, there must be something."

"Nothing recognizable."

"That leaves the pilot. He's the one you are protecting."

"That I am. He deserves better than being paraded through Washington. He agreed to the flight in hopes of getting his wife released from a gulag. She was imprisoned for telling that prick, Stalin that American technology was years ahead of theirs. She was a nuclear engineer."

"So, this man not only knows about the Russian TU-16 bomber but has information about their nuclear program," stammered Chad.

"I didn't say that the plane that crashed was a TU-16."

"We have been looking for that plane since we got a picture of it six weeks ago. Shit, shit, shit." Chad stood. "Ellen, can we get together for dinner?" He never thought to apologize for the language.

"Sure, you know where I am staying. What's wrong?"

"Now my turn to ask for a promise. No disclosure, period. Promise?"

"I promise."

"The plane that went out of here this morning is looking for that TU-16."

Chad threw a ten on the table and headed out the door, tugging gloves over his now sweaty hands.

He jumped into his battered old Jeep and slammed his foot down on the starter. The engine whispered to life, all that a flathead four-cylinder engine could muster. He shifted into first and floored it, shifting into second at fifteen miles an hour. For the first time, he wished he were driving something with power.

The guard shack at the base waved him through; still, it took a half-hour to get to his office. "Get me operations at Chitose, Japan."

The call came through quickly, which was a shock. What wasn't, was the operations chief's stonewalling on what was classified as a top-secret flight. Somehow, both officers worked out a conversation that gave Gritt the information needed.

A half-hour later, he sank into the overstuffed reading chair under the window. McGrady's RB-47 had finished refueling at Chitose only an hour before his call and was now flying its mission, observing total radio silence.

Back at the hotel, Ellen changed into something more appropriate for shopping in the tiny Alaskan city on a zero-degree morning. Repacking her suit in a small trunk, she picked up Anton's bloody jacket. Before leaving the cabin, she'd removed all insignia from the coat. She held it next to her cheek as she called the front desk, inquiring about any laundry in town that might be able to clean the jacket by tomorrow. "God, I hope that I am doing the right thing," she mumbled as she hung up.

CHAPTER 13

"FEET DRY," ADVISED Bob Walsh. "We just passed over the lighthouse, but I can't see it."

The stress levels always rocketed as the crew left the ocean behind for its run over the long Russian peninsula. Below, a heavy cloud cover blanketed everything on the lower Kamchatka Peninsula. The complete absence of any Russian aircraft, as they penetrated the air space over mainland Russia, was a good omen.

"Shut down the radar," ordered McGrady.

Flores switched the radar to standby. "I don't have anything like the Blackbirds have to work with, but I think we were being painted by some form of radar. It may have just been a ghost or false signal," he added a minute later, "whatever it was, disappeared after a few seconds."

McGrady settled into his seat, thankful that a refueling snafu in Japan offered the crew an opportunity for a meal. The airspeed indicator was as close to the red line as the B-47 could muster in level flight without burning all their fuel. The altitude was locked on 40,000 feet. "At the speed we are traveling, we will finish our photo run in just over eighty minutes," he offered over the intercom.

"We should be able to pick up Anadyr radio in about twenty-five minutes. We will fly a straight line to pick up all four targets."

Walsh liked straight lines; it made it easier to calculate time between camera shoots. "We have only about ten knots of wind up here, right on the tail."

"How long until our first camera pass?" asked McGrady.

"Twenty-two minutes," answered Walsh.

The three-man crew settled in for an hour over enemy territory.

In the seat behind McGrady, Captain Flores sat studying the instruments in front of him. Since his first report of possible radar, he'd remained silent.

"You're not your nervous talkative self this afternoon," said McGrady.

"That radar may or may not have painted us again. It is very weak and only lasts about fifteen seconds. I see something about every ten minutes." A muscle below Flores' left eye began to twitch.

"The skinny from the Navy appears to be right," replied McGrady. "You saw no indication of detection all the way from Chitose."

"True," replied Flores. "It's just that I have never seen any radar at the bottom of the peninsula before."

"Keep monitoring whatever it is, Rick." McGrady hadn't lost any of his discomfort from that morning. "I want a radar sweep for a full minute, before we reach each target."

The crew tried to relax for the quarter-hour before their mission really started.

✸

"Camera's off," announced Walsh. "There was a little surface fog around the airport, but I think I got the runway and all of the parking areas."

Flores dropped his binoculars into the tray next to his seat. "It's hard to tell from almost eight miles up, but I didn't see anything unusual down there."

McGrady reached up and dialed in the radio station at Anadyr.

"The forces of evil must have upgraded their transmitter. Usually, it is all the system can do to align the needle from this far away, but today it came up in seconds."

"Thirteen minutes to the next target," added Walsh.

"Rick, run a quick radar scan, no more than two revolutions. Let's see if anyone is coming up to see what just went by," ordered McGrady.

Flores switched the radar to active. "Nothing, not even a seagull in the air."

Ten minutes later, Walsh dropped his binoculars. "Captain," he called, "I need a fifteen-degree turn to the east. We are straying out over the water instead of holding right on the coast."

McGrady banked the heavy jet slightly and prepared for cameras on. While he waited, he checked the direction finder locked onto the Anadyr radio station. The target was just to the left of the planned track. The joy of using a radio station to navigate was that it never moves. You can set a needle on the NDB instrument and fly directly to that target. "Fire up the radar," he ordered.

"No airborne targets," reported Flores.

With cameras off, McGrady took a moment to think through the tracking problem. "Bob, when you get a chance see if you can figure out whether we have picked up some wind out of the east."

Walsh took a few minutes to finish logging the camera run, and then a few more to run a stopwatch as the plane passed two points where he could accurately measure the distance. "I don't see much, Sir."

"The track from Anadyr looks a little off," replied McGrady.

"It won't matter much between now and the next target. We just need to stay right on the shoreline. When we get a little further north, the weather forecasters thought we might find a couple of hundred miles of low clouds before our last target." Walsh opened his Thermos of coffee and poured a cup. "The Anadyr line has always worked. Nine minutes to the next target."

"I just saw another radar sweep, or whatever this thing is I have been seeing," interjected Flores. "It was really weak."

"Go ahead, activate the radar and take a look. Make sure nothing is out there tracking us," ordered McGrady. His insides felt like they did when he drank way too much coffee.

"Still, not so much as a bird. If I didn't know the Soviets were short on fuel, all this quiet would be worrying me."

It was worrying the plane commander, but he kept his thoughts to himself.

The third target came and went. Again, McGrady was forced to bank the plane to the east as the Anadyr track had slipped them offshore several miles. In front of the plane, a thick blanket of clouds covered the ground for as far as he could see. McGrady wished that he'd skipped the meal in Japan, his stomach rumbling.

"Nineteen minutes to our last target," offered Walsh, studying the line on the map next to his seat. "If the weather guys are right, this cloud cover should be gone before the target. If not, well, we tried."

The men finally began to relax. The final target was a relatively new base with only a handful of interceptors. They were a half-hour from the turn for home.

The clouds below them ended only minutes from the target. "Shit, oh dear," snapped Walsh. We are way off course, out over the Sea of Okhotsk. The target must be thirty miles to our east. I can barely see the shoreline."

The rock in McGrady's stomach became a boulder. "Rick, let's see if anyone is flying out there."

Rick flipped a switch and sat glued to the radar screen in front of him. "Oh my God."

McGrady waited for more. His mouth filled with the taste of stale candy and coffee.

"I have four targets to the east of us and four more to the north. They have to be MIG-17's. All of them are closing on our altitude."

"What about behind us?" asked McGrady.

The question was answered by the *thud* of a string of hits on the bottom of the hull. Two MIG's banked away from below the jet before turning for another firing run.

"They must have been right below us when we passed the cloud-bank," said Flores.

McGrady turned the jet the only direction that didn't have instant death.

"You are turning directly toward the Russian mainland and a major airbase," gasped Walsh.

"We have a lot of fuel. I am going to try to circle back to the south and then cross the peninsula." McGrady knew that the only chance was to run the MIGs out of fuel.

"That radar thing is back in spades," added Flores. "This time, it is constant. We just flew into a trap."

"No shit," replied Walsh. "Those guys were so close I could see their eyes."

"See if you can get the MIGs off our tail," ordered McGrady.

Flores activated the twin cannons in the tail, just as the plane shook again, bullets ripping into the right wing. One of the engines began to shut down.

"Walsh, drop the first emergency radio canister. Flores, shut down number five."

The plane jerked again as more rounds tore into the tail area.

Flores swung the cannons toward the oncoming planes and depressed the trigger. The MIGs sweeping from right to left made them hard to track. He depressed the trigger, nothing happened. "The cannons are down," said Flores. His left eye blinked open and shut with each spasm of the muscle in his cheek.

He looked at the radar in front of him. "There is no way we are going south. There are six planes moving to cut us off."

"Then we go west and hope to loop back to the north. Any fighters west of us?"

"No, Sir, they've left the door open into the Russian mainland," said Flores.

With the nose pointed toward the water below, the plane began to distance itself from the swarm of MIGs trying to bring it down. The radar painted a picture of persistence, but after twenty minutes, the planes behind them began to turn away.

"They are running short on fuel," observed Flores, massaging his cheek that now ached.

"I am going to try turning to the north and then back toward home," said McGrady. He looked at the altimeter, which was just winding down below thirty thousand feet.

"The ass end of this bird must look like Swiss cheese," mumbled McGrady. "But except for one engine shot to shit, every gauge in front of me looks Okay. The controls feel fine, just a little spongy in turns."

Both Flores and Walsh confirmed McGrady's observation. "I was too damned busy to get scared," said Flores. His fingers pushed harder at the cramp in his face.

"Not me," replied Walsh. "You two have my black butt in your hands. Don't screw this up."

"Now there's a visual I could have done without," replied McGrady, trying to shake off his nerves. "Flores, keep that radar up, they certainly know we're here."

"It looks like the entire Russian Air Defense Force has gone home for lunch."

That lasted fifteen minutes, until the outside edge of the radar screen flickered with dots. In minutes, the dots turned into a dozen MIGs blocking their way.

"Every damned advanced fighter in the Far East must have been positioned up here," snarled McGrady, as he turned west again. They were low enough now that they were vulnerable even to the almost obsolete MIG 15s.

In the distance, Flores could now see the flash of Soviet fighters strung out in the sunlight. They looked like geese flying south, in the late November South Dakota sky.

"Only these geese shoot back," he mumbled.

"What?" asked McGrady.

"I was trying to wish myself home," answered Flores. "Never mind."

McGrady started to climb again. "Let's hope that there are only MIG 15s this far north."

"I see nothing in front of us, but I am blind below," barked Flores.

The plane screamed over land at the eastern edge of the Sea of Okhotsk. A sting of bullets ripped into the already damaged right wing, tearing into the two inside engines. Parts of the cowlings ripped away, followed by parts of the engines. They began to lose altitude.

"They came up right under us," shouted Flores.

The plane rolled up onto the damaged right wing, then tried to roll onto it's back. Inside the cockpit, everything not screwed down went airborne. McGrady pulled power on the straining engines on the opposite wing and countered with rudder and aileron deflection. The aircraft began to stabilize.

"I can see them now. The MIGs that just hit us are turning for home," advised Flores. "Those guys were close enough to reach out and touch us."

McGrady rolled the ailerons hard left and countered the unwanted turn with heavy rudder pressure. "We aren't finished yet," he snarled into the intercom, wondering why the MIGs concentrated their fire on the wing. He slowly added power to the undamaged engines.

The wounded plane continued west over the mainland before turning northeast again. Their airspeed was down to under three hundred knots, and they were low enough to pick out snow-covered trees on the barren coast in the distance. Fuel streamed from the wing, forming a mist. He checked again. The fuel supplies to the engines on that wing were in the off position.

There was a flash from under the right wing, as an exploding engine threw white-hot fragments into the stream of fuel from a broken fuel line, igniting it into a blowtorch. It took only seconds for the fire to race into the wing itself. McGrady pointed the nose down, trying to increase the airspeed. With enough speed, the wind might extinguish the flames. The airframe groaned, some of it trying to turn west even as McGrady pointed the nose north. Asymmetrical stress was slowly ripping it apart.

The computer in McGrady's head slowed as the viable options disappeared. "Thank God the fuel tanks aren't in the wings. Take a quick radar sweep," he ordered. Below were the mountains of the Russian mainland.

"Nothing out there that I can see."

The mental calculator in McGrady's head stopped. He fought the controls. "Gentlemen, we are not going home today. Drop the second radio canister. It's time to get out of this wounded goose and pray the folks in the Department of State and General Gritt get us home before we die of old age."

McGrady couldn't see Walsh in the nose, but he was proud of Flores, who remained all business.

The aircraft commander turned the plane back toward the Sea of Okhotsk fighting to bring the wounded aircraft into level flight. He pulled the throttles to idle. "From this altitude, the plane will crash into the ocean. I want all of us out of the airplane before it starts to nosedive, eject, eject, eject; and good luck." McGrady wiped tears of anger from his eyes, then closed them, focusing on an image of Susan, and then followed Flores' ejection seat out of the doomed aircraft.

The ejection at hundreds of miles an hour slammed and twisted the men in the air like toys. McGrady's unstrapped helmet ripped from his face, taking his oxygen mask with it. He shut his eyes tightly to keep them from freezing. The stocking cap he always wore under his helmet barely protected him from the cold, as he fought to stay conscious in the thin air. He had no idea where his crew was. All he knew was that the indicator lights showing that both had ejected illuminated before he punched out.

His eyelashes frozen shut, he gripped the risers of his parachute trying to stabilize what felt like the swinging of a pendulum. With no visual frame of reference, it was impossible.

He was semiconscious when his body slammed onto the crusted snow. McGrady lay, gasping for breath, unable to move. The cold weather flight suit he wore kept him from freezing but did nothing to cushion the fall.

Grady wondered how long he laid in the snow before two hands lifted his head. "Colonel, it's me, Rick Flores."

McGrady tugged off a glove, rubbing ice from his eyelids, then opened his eyes. "I don't know if I can move."

"You have to, Sir. You are lying right on the edge of a cliff. If the wind picks up, your chute will pull you over."

"Have you seen Bob?"

"He is coming this way, dragging his chute."

"Thank God, we all got down safely," mumbled McGrady.

"I haven't seen any Russian search planes, but we should get under some cover, Sir."

McGrady rolled onto his side, the pain in his back bringing gasps. He looked around as he fought his way to his knees. "Not a tree in sight, what do you have in mind for cover?"

"We landed right on top of a big round hill. I saw some trees along the valley below on the way down, probably a couple of miles from here. Can you walk?"

McGrady struggled to his feet with the help of the younger man. He put one foot in front of the other. He used up his willpower on the second step. "I can feel some grating in my spine."

"Stay right where you are then. Let me clear your parachute and fold it into a sled."

McGrady felt four hands lower him onto the thin fabric. His eyes clamped, trying to shut out the pain; the contraction of muscles in his face so intense it cut off his hearing.

Flores and Walsh started down the hill pulling their commander behind. The crusted snow generally held their weight except for the moments when a foot would break through, disappearing to mid-thigh. The two men took turns pulling the other from collapsing snow. The men pulled their burden to a small shelf near the valley bottom.

"Wait here," said Walsh, "I'll check the snow under the trees."

Flores watched his crewmate descend a couple of hundred feet before he broke through the crust, buried to his waist. Walsh laid his upper body flat on the snow and used his survival knife in one hand and his pistol in the other to punch into the crust as he pulled himself free. The wind had blown snow from the ridges, filling the valley. What looked like small trees were really the tops of large ones.

The men found a place behind a stand of trees. The small camp they started to build came directly from their winter survival training.

The next thing McGrady saw was the inside of an emergency snow shelter made of blocks carved from windblown snow. Next to him were his two crewmates, all wrapped in a parachute for warmth.

"They will start looking for us in the morning," whispered McGrady.

"The Russians are looking now," replied Walsh. Every half-hour or so, we can hear a search plane come over, and a few minutes ago I heard a helicopter."

"If they don't find us tonight, we have a chance," managed McGrady. "General Gritt will have planes in the air tomorrow to listen for the emergency radios. Try to get some sleep."

CHAPTER 14

FAIRBANKS, ALASKA

THE COTTAGE BAR was almost empty, the afternoon drunks already on their way home to sleep it off, and the evening crowd just getting off work. Over the phone, Ellen Wilson recommended that she and Chad continue their conversation there rather than wait for a late dinner.

She walked past the old Jeep parked in front, stopping to appreciate the soft alpenglow on the wispy clouds to the west. It pleased her that Gritt's men would be coming home in clear air.

She found her old friend sipping a root beer at the table furthest from the door. He pointed to an ice bucket with a bottle of Mumm's Champagne and two champagne glasses. "I thought we could start with a toast to Walt," he offered. "Mumm's is the best champagne you will find in Fairbanks." Ellen tossed her long down parka onto the seat of the adjoining booth.

"I appreciate the gesture, but I have had exactly two glasses of wine since I buried Walt. I'm out of practice and I need a clear head." Ellen leaned back in the booth. "Besides, I know you, and until your crew gets back you would just humor me with a sip or two."

"The guy who runs this place makes a mean spiced cider. He

normally adds a shot of rum or brandy for those who can't handle it straight up."

"That sounds wonderful."

Gritt waived at the bartender who folded the newspaper he was reading under his arm as he approached. "Change of plans, Manny," said Gritt, "if you wouldn't mind, leave the champagne on ice. Patrick will be coming in later; we will open it then. Bring the lady a mug of your spiced cider, hold the winter spirits."

Ellen smiled at the bartender as he turned to leave. She then leaned close to Chad, "I need to finish my shopping tomorrow and head back. I told Anton, that's the Russian pilot, that I would be back in four days. What I need from you, my old friend, is some form of legal status for Anton and a commitment that the crash of his plane is kept secret."

"Keeping the crash a secret is a good idea. The Soviets are all over the board on how they deal with their citizens in our country, especially those seeking asylum. Some they will jump through hoops to get home, some they ignore, and others go out for coffee one morning and die after their first cup."

Ellen sat quietly, the steaming cup of cider in front of her. "I was thinking that political asylum was a real possibility here. In my old job, I helped a number of people who were feeding us information get asylum."

"Ellen, I work directly for Allen Dulles. If this Anton has anything really valuable to trade, getting him legalized will be easy. Tell me, is he willing to disclose what he knows? Or is he one of those zealot patriots, committed to political ideals and his homeland?"

"You mean like you?"

"I had that coming, I guess," said Chad, stifling a laugh. "But bad information is worse than none, so I am just trying to figure out how much I trust this man." He checked his watch for the third time since Ellen's arrival.

"When is your plane due back?" she asked.

"Anytime now."

"You will have to meet Anton. I believe that he feels betrayed by his government and especially the men who sent him on his mission. He will never put Russia at risk, but if he believes that what he knows can really protect Russia and maybe even change it for the better, I think he will cooperate."

"Does he want to go back?"

"He told me he is never going back."

"What if we wanted him to go back, to keep feeding us information?"

Ellen put her hand on Chad's wrist. "This man is no spy, just angry." Ellen smiled.

"He's the man you started out to be before you met Walt. He just loves to fly airplanes."

"He's more than that, or you wouldn't be interested," smiled Chad.

"You're right, he has the intellect that I need. But Chad, being at the cabin gave me a lot of time to think about my life. It's time for me to find a life that is worth living for me and not just my country. Maybe learn what is going on in the world from an issue of National Geographic or LIFE, not some briefing ginned up by smart young kids who want to be head of station someday or a deputy ambassador to Mali."

"When are you going home?" asked Chad.

"I need to get back early enough tomorrow to pick up my dog team. From Bettles, it's about five hours to the lake."

"Why don't I just fly you to the lake? I picked up a sweet Cessna 180 and put it on skis."

"My dogs are in Bettles. Besides, I need to work my way through how I'm going to introduce you to Anton."

Chad checked his watch. "Ellen, I have to get out to the runway."

Ellen took both of Chad's hands in hers. "Just how short on fuel would your plane be by now?"

"If they could do an economy cruise for the whole trip, they might still have an hour left."

"Maybe you can give me, and the supplies I bought, a ride to Bettles tomorrow?"

"You're on. Since the debrief will be short tomorrow, I should be available by ten. That, of course, assumes that my guys get here safely."

"Maybe it will be even more important if they don't. You will send out whatever assets you have to find them and then just stew in your office until you hear something. As I recall, when you are all stressed out, you almost always go find something to fly."

Chad rose to leave, distracted, he barely heard her.

Ellen reached for his hand. "There is one more favor, if you don't mind. I have a radio that will reach Fairbanks, but the only generator I have is water-powered and doesn't work when the creek is frozen. Could you find us a small portable generator and some fuel and arrange for it to be delivered to the lake? It's the only way we will be able to communicate."

"I can't get a generator in the Cessna," replied Chad.

"I don't need it tomorrow. I am sure you know someone with a larger transport on skis, or something."

Chad wiped his nervous face with a white handkerchief. "I'll let you know what I can do tomorrow. I'll call you at the hotel by eight."

❋

Ellen opened one of the new books stacked on the nightstand. She propped her back against the wall and slipped the extra pillow under her knees. Next to her was a tray of cheese and crackers, a treat not experienced in a year. There was also an open bottle of French Cabernet. In the duffle at the end of the bed were three bottles of vodka. The radio in the room halted a music program, with an announcement: "All Air Force search and rescue flight crews are asked to check in with their commanding officers. This is not a drill."

Ellen took a deep breath. Her trip to Bettles would be a very quiet one.

CHAPTER 15

KHREBET KOLYMSKIY, RUSSIA

THE SNOW SHELTER trapped their body heat, warming the air to above freezing. The parachute underneath kept them dry and the layers of parachute over their cold weather flight suits kept them warm, the steam from three men's breathing creating a haze in their snow shelter.

Flores clicked on his survival flashlight and fished two aspirin from the bottle in his survival kit. He helped McGrady sit up enough to get them down with the last of the water from one of their three canteens. "We will need water today," mumbled McGrady.

Flores packed some snow beneath the parachute under the Colonel's head. It was enough to allow McGrady to watch as Bob Walsh pulled a collapsible metal pot from his survival kit. "It's not government issue, but every survival course I've ever taken says hydration is more important than food," offered Walsh. "When all the water is frozen, I thought it might come in handy to melt snow.

"Good idea, Bob," managed McGrady. "Probably better to build a small fire now before the Russians start searching again. We can drink some and refill the empty canteen."

"It's just starting to get light," replied Walsh. "I'll get started."

Walsh pushed aside the parachute cloth door of their igloo shaped shelter. He started out through the low entrance. He froze.

Sitting in front of the door was a man in a quilted white jacket and pants, with a heavy fur hat pulled down almost to his blue eyes. To either side of him were other men dressed exactly the same. Each cradled a rifle in their arms.

"Welcome to Russia, darkie," the man said in a slightly British accent. How badly injured is the man you dragged down the mountain?"

"He injured his back. He can't walk," replied a shocked Walsh.

"You will, to please, throw out your pistols, and then I can have my medic take a look at your man. Now that you are awake, we will brew some tea while we wait for the helicopter."

While Walsh blocked the door, Flores used his pistol to smash the emergency radio he held and then pushed it into the snow under McGrady's head. Then he handed three pistols to Walsh, one at a time.

❃

Four hours later, Walsh and Flores sat next to the hospital bed at a Russian Air Base. McGrady's eyes flickered and opened. "God, I was hoping that the Russians were just a bad dream."

"Nope. Sorry, Colonel," replied Flores. "Their medic thought you might have fractured a vertebra or two, so he gave you a shot that knocked you out while they transported us here."

"Where is here?"

"We are at the airbase at Magadan. They wanted to transport us down to Khabarovsk right away, but it's all socked in by a big storm. The doctor here says you tore some muscles and cracked a couple of ribs, but he doesn't think you have any broken vertebrae.

McGrady looked at the barren cement walls of the room. Someone in Moscow had decided that the room would be painted a pale puke green. Above, a weak florescent light barely lit the room. "Are we alone, I mean, where are the guards?"

"The special forces captain that captured us was here until an hour ago. He left to get himself and his troops some chow. There are Air

Force policemen at the entrances to the building, but other than that, they aren't guarding us. Like the captain says, where are we going to go?"

"We are going to be airlifted to Khabarovsk soon," added Walsh. "There is a general down there really anxious to get his hands on us. Other than that, we have been treated like guests, not prisoners. Are you hungry?"

"I am. Did you two eat?"

"Lunch was reindeer liver and onions and tea. Let me see if I can get you a plate," offered Bob. "They seem really surprised to find a Negro American officer. I'm kind of a celebrity."

"I'm not much on liver," replied McGrady. "Maybe they have something else."

"Dorothy, you are not in Kansas anymore," laughed Walsh. "Everyone on the base eats the same thing. That special forces captain can't wait to get back to his home base where the food is better."

"Come to think of it, I have been trying to cultivate a taste for liver," answered McGrady.

Walsh wandered down the hall toward the smell of stale cooking oil.

"Rick, why all the good treatment? Do you know what's going on?"

"No, Colonel, I don't. I asked that captain what to expect, and he said he wasn't sure. He mumbled something about debriefing us and then trading us for some of theirs, but he didn't know anything, except that his unit was sent up here five days ago and briefed for a search mission for downed American airmen."

"So, the whole thing was a trap," uttered McGrady.

"That's about the size of it. They appear to have spent months of their fuel supply to nail us. I suspect we will know why in the next few days. In the interim, I appreciate the kind treatment. I doubt that it will continue."

Walsh wandered back into the room with a blonde nurse in tow. The young woman set a small metal bowl on the table next to McGrady's bed and smiled.

"Spaciba, Marina," offered Walsh as the woman turned into the hallway.

"Do you speak Russian?" asked a surprised McGrady.

"I have been studying it since we flew our first mission. I don't speak it enough to really communicate, but you can thank me for the tomato and cucumber salad in the bowl. The vegetables are straight out of the base greenhouse."

The next afternoon, a heavy four-wheel drive truck delivered the three Americans to the side of a large turbo-prop plane. McGrady's stretcher was strapped to rings in the center of the floor. The ambulatory men were handcuffed to a frame seat with a cushion about the thickness of a napkin. Any thought of complaint went away when the special forces captain and his men took seats along the other side of the fuselage. Their seats didn't have napkins.

The whine of the turbines starting was almost drowned out by the sound of thousands of metal parts vibrating. Every metal piece of the plane seemed to be fighting the one next to it.

The heavy tires thumped heavily along the rough cement runway as the plane began its takeoff roll. Any thought that the noise inside the aircraft would improve was dashed as the plane climbed for its trip south. The men stared at each other, all wondering the same thing. *Will this contraption shake itself apart before it lands?*

CHAPTER 16

THE EMERGENCY RADIO transmitters were designed to transmit their signal in a burst and then turn off to conserve battery. One would transmit at noon and the second, minutes later.

Offshore of the Kamchatka Peninsula, two Navy search planes based out of Kodiak, Alaska flew at high altitude, three hundred miles apart. Two Air Force planes based in Japan were strung out, one in between the Navy planes and another orbiting close to the Russian mainland west of St. Lawrence Island. All were on station an hour before the radio bursts were expected, hoping for some indication of where the missing plane might be.

Search and rescue aircraft from Fairbanks flew the path between the Bering Sea and Ladd Field. Two more aircraft from Anchorage were combing the Bering Sea itself, looking for survivors. A dozen civilian planes were combing the Alaska beaches. The search was mobilized within hours of the final minute that the aircraft could still be airborne. With the only other recon aircraft still in Seattle, Gritt and his staff were powerless to do more.

Chad's call to Ellen that morning was short as expected. She'd been surprised when Carmen Gritt arrived to transport her and her small mountain of supplies to the Fairbanks airport where Chad kept his plane.

The two women had never been close, their lives intersecting but never long enough to become friends. They worked for twenty minutes to strip away the packaging of the supplies so that they would fit into the cramped Cessna. As Carmen closed up the back of the Ford station wagon, Ellen slipped into the front seat.

"I don't know exactly what my husband's team does," started Carmen as she headed towards the airport. "I know that Colonel McGrady's plane is missing, and that Chad would be flying something, somewhere, while he waited for news. I am glad that for at least the next couple of hours, he will have some company."

Ellen smiled at the woman driving. Carmen's statement was perfect. The rules in the game were that no one, not even family is to know what your mission is. But Ellen and Walt always knew most of what the other was doing. Ellen had felt the same stress that Carmen was feeling when one of Walt's agents or recon teams went missing. The only thing worse was when one of her own 'assets' disappeared.

"I spent too many years in the game and watched men like Chad get ulcers worrying. At least your husband has a release. I think we both knew that the plane was missing when we set up the flight to Bettles last night." Ellen took a moment to appreciate the woman driving her to a ski-equipped plane, where she would pick up her dog team and then head to her log cabin in the middle of nowhere. Carmen wore a long wool skirt and heavy cable knit sweater under a fox coat. She'd taken time to put on makeup.

"I don't know how you live out there. I love the outdoors. The kids and I love it when Chad has the time to fly us out fishing or berry picking. The Gritt family owns a homestead, a private lodge in the Bristol Bay region. But I don't know if I could live without running water and electricity year around. And now you live alone."

Ellen was pleased that Chad hadn't even mentioned Anton to his wife. "It seems like I spent my life in a pressure cooker with the flame turned up high. Now, all I do is write and read, and reconnect with ideas and beliefs that used to be important."

"They made my husband a general in his first twenty years. He has been a remarkable husband and a great father, but it seems we go through one of these intense phases at least every year. Maybe after he gets in his twenty, he will find something less stressful." Carmen pondered her own statement. "But probably not. Every time this country is threatened, he wants to climb back into the cockpit and go vanquish the enemy."

"Hasn't he figured out that war is for young men, men who think they are still bulletproof?"

Carmen laughed. "The thing is, a lot of the men he has commanded have been older than Chad." She turned onto the main road to the airport. "I'm really happy that the military sent us back to Alaska. At least here, my husband has a life that balances out his career. He really loves this place. The kids have grandparents and cousins down in Anchorage."

"Then, even if he leaves again, he will be back. After a couple of years in this country, I finally understand. This is a way of life, not a place. You are lucky to be raising your children here."

Carmen turned onto the road that circled the end of the runway. In the distance, wood smoke billowed from the chimney of the squat wooden structure. The tail of the plane stretched out between two doors pushed almost closed to allow heat to build up inside the hanger. "Do you ever wish that you and Walt had children?"

"No, we were close to Walt's grown children, and as of the time we came to Alaska, they were avoiding having grandchildren. Besides, it probably isn't too late for me yet."

Carmen turned, a puzzled look on her face, but she didn't ask the obvious question. Instead, she pulled up next to the small hanger. "Here we are."

Twenty minutes later, with the back of the warm Cessna stuffed to the roof, Chad taxied toward the runway, monitoring the radio for any incoming air traffic. He carefully studied the runway and the air beyond both ends, before he lined up on the snow-covered path next to runway.

"I can't use the cleared runway with skis," he explained. "You ready?"

"You know, in all the years we have known each other, this will be the first time I have flown with you. I'm ready."

Chad searched the skies at both ends of the runway again. More than half of the planes that used the airport didn't have radios.

The heavy plane staggered into the air. Behind them, Carmen slipped into the seat of the idling station wagon. In front of them, Bettles was almost exactly two hours away.

Chad checked his watch. The earliest he might hear something from the search planes would be in just over three hours, but more likely after they landed, still five hours away.

"I found you a small surplus generator. The base commander didn't know it was surplus until we talked. There is a flight service on the other side of the Fairbanks runway that has a Beaver on skis. I think we can get the generator and a drum of fuel into his plane. I will see if he has an opening in the next few days."

"Thanks for the help. I will start my conversations with Anton when I get in tonight. I found some decent vodka. That should loosen him up a bit."

Ellen waited for a response and got none.

"See if the air charter company will take my check. I have an account here in Fairbanks," requested Ellen.

"With Walt gone, you must be a little short. I'll take care of the charter."

"Chad, Walt left a ton of stock and a government pension. I am from a wealthy family, kind of a trust fund girl. I'm pretty set. Spend your money on your family."

The two spent the next half-hour discussing radio communications and developing a simple code. Chad would have one of his people monitor the radio frequency each morning and again at five in the evening beginning the day after the generator was delivered. The rest of the flight was silent.

❋

Across the Bering Sea, both the northernmost Navy plane and the Air Force plane picked up the radio transmission from the first emergency transmitter at noon Fairbank's time. The transmission was very weak, making it difficult to get a good direction fix. The second transmission was even weaker, but it appeared to come from a site that was almost due west of the first. The search crews were surprised. Both transmissions appeared to be well to the west of the line they were searching. Until each plane landed and filed their reports, it would be impossible to triangulate their findings and get approximate locations.

The good news was that the transmitters were working. The bad news was that they appeared to be well inland and north of the airbase at Magadan. Each crew discussed possible rescue strategies all the way home. No one offered any good ideas.

CHAPTER 17

THE RUNWAY IN Khabarovsk felt like the one in Magadan, surfaced in boulders. The wheels touching down felt like the plane would shake itself to pieces. Like in the era of piston engine airplanes where the engines were built loosely to dissipate the stresses. The Americans guessed that Russian aircraft were built that way from nose to tail. Thousands of parts vibrating with each other, wearing on each other. The three men felt relief when the pilot shut down the engines.

The commander of the small special-forces unit leaped to the ground before the stairs were rolled into place. He was the first one up the stairs a moment later.

"I am sorry," he said to the Americans, as he issued orders to his men.

The Americans' arms were pulled behind their backs and handcuffed; ankle chains were clamped on their legs. McGrady's stretcher was carried to a waiting truck while the other two men were hustled into a staff car. In the front seat, Senior Captain Dimitri Gagarin bit his lip, as Colonel Grigori Rasputin, the base political commander, climbed into the rear-facing seat opposite the Americans. He slammed the door. His interpreter walked to the other side of the black sedan and took a seat as far away from the colonel as he could.

Dimitri's orders were to take all three to the building next to General Molovic's office. He'd personally overseen turning it into an interrogation center. That would have to wait until the Politico finished what Dmitri hoped was a one act play. That play began with the political officer slapping both Americans across from him in the face with a short leather belt he wrapped around his fist.

Rasputin's interpreter listened to the political colonel and then translated. "You are both going to be shot as spies. Your comrade will be strapped to a board so that he can die next to you."

The political colonel hadn't been on the need-to-know list for the arrival of the prisoners, which troubled Gagarin. In the conversation between Molovic and his boss, General Blovonin, it had been agreed to interrogate the prisoners. But the primary goals of capturing an American aircrew was to embarrass the Americans into halting flights over Russia and to use them as a bargaining chip for the missing TU-16 flight crew.

The driver looked apprehensively at Gagarin, as the Politico directed him to drive to the small political prison in the center of town. In the distance, Gagarin could see someone standing in the window of Molovic's office watching. "Colonel," he blurted, "the general is waiting for these men."

"Drive downtown," repeated Rasputin. "The general devised a brilliant plan to capture these spies, but he is not in charge of the prison system. Now that they are here, they will follow the path of the other American spies we hold."

"They may be more valuable for other purposes," offered Gagarin. Just having the colonel in the general's car brought the hair up on the back of his neck, but he was powerless to countermand the orders of this officer.

The car picked up speed, passing between two buildings, turning onto the road to the main gate. The truck carrying McGrady followed. As they approached a guard post, sirens began to blare, and red lights began flashing on the tops of the buildings. Behind them, four jet fighters roared into the sky, turning east. Two guards dropped a heavy bar across the road.

A young lieutenant ran from the guardhouse toward the car. "You will have to take cover, Sirs," he ordered as the driver rolled down the window. "We have a report of American aircraft inbound toward the base. Access in or out of the base is closed. All personnel not assigned to base defense are to follow emergency shelter protocols."

"Take us to General Molovic's office. The prisoners will be taken to the bunkers next to his office," directed Gagarin, stifling a smile.

Behind him, Rasputin's face looked like his great-great uncle's the day he was brutally stabbed, strangled, poisoned and then shot by friends of the Czar, committed to breaking Rasputin's psychological hold on the Czarina. His anger boiled over as the car came to a rest in front of Molovic's office. He lashed out at both men across from him with his belt.

Molovic himself opened the rear door, grabbing the colonel, pinning the smaller man's arm to the doorframe. "Come now Grigori, is that behavior becoming of an officer?"

"You engineered this phony base lock-down, Alexi," screamed Rasputin.

"Don't you mean General Molovic?" Molovic twisted the colonel's wrist until sure he was hurting him. "I was not aware that the insignia of the political corps relieved you of the responsibility of respecting military authority."

The general looked at the two Americans, both bleeding from the nose, with welts and cuts, and unable to wipe away the blood, their hands still cuffed. He turned back to Rasputin, dragging him from the back of the car by his arm, intentionally twisting it until he was sure that the pain was excruciating. "Look what you have done, Colonel. We will probably have to parade these men before the press and diplomatic corps to get what we want. Now, we will have to wait for their wounds to heal. It will be counterproductive to have the world believe we are barbarians."

"These men should be tortured until we know everything we can learn from them and then shot," stammered Rasputin. "At least they should go to one of the re-education camps. If they renounce their capitalist rulers and admit their crimes, we might let them live. They will exist like caged animals in a zoo. Russian patriots will pay to stand in front of their cages and show this swine their bare ass."

"You Politico's need a new procedures manual," said Molovic, his laughter further infuriating Rasputin. "Our new leaders have all repudiated Comrade Stalin's methods. I am surprised that the political corps hasn't sent word to the men they exiled to the Far East."

Molovic turned to the sergeant next to him. "Unshackle these men and take them to the facility we prepared. Find a medic to dress their wounds." He turned to Rasputin's interpreter. "You will translate every word I say. Do you understand?"

The shaken man nodded his head.

"Good. Tell these men that they are my prisoners. Tell them their crime was entering The Soviet Union without proper paperwork, which by our laws can be interpreted as spying. They will be interrogated, and the methods used will be influenced by how they answer the questions."

Molovic waited while the interpreter translated. "Now, the first question. How many of the Russian flight crew from our plane that disappeared in Alaska survived?"

Flores and Walsh stood wiping blood from their faces with the sleeves of their jackets. They looked at one another. Finally, Flores answered. "General, we know nothing about any Russian plane crashing in Alaska."

"This could be a bit harder than planned," muttered Molovic to his aide. "Please get these men to their cells. I am going to check on their injured colonel." Molovic turned to Rasputin. "You were a party to the discussions where we agreed to trade these men for our missing crew. I don't even want to hear your excuse for intervening in the plan." Molovic released his grip on Rasputin's arm. "I need your interpreter until I can find one of my own. You are dismissed until I call for you." Molovic was everything but gentle, as he pushed the political colonel back into the staff car. "Take the colonel to his quarters."

As the car pulled away, Molovic turned to Gagarin. "I want a log of every call that the colonel makes. It is important that we know if he has decided that he is a big deal or if he is working under the direction of someone in Moscow."

As Flores and Walsh were led away, Gagarin started to the communications center to instruct the long-distance operators. Molovic grabbed the interpreter by the arm and turned toward the hospital, a quarter mile away. "You do this work, as I order, and I will see if I can get you a billet in Intelligence and a promotion. Let's go visit the American colonel."

The packed snow beneath their feet squeaked like a rocking chair on a wooden floor, one with loose boards. The young corporal seemed lost. "May I speak honestly, Sir?'

The general smiled at the young man. "I know that honesty isn't high on the list of priorities in the political corps, Corporal, but in combat units it is the difference between succeeding in our missions and dying for the cause."

"Sir, I am afraid of Colonel Rasputin. When he was transferred to the Far East, he brought me with him. He seems to have only one agenda, to somehow get back to Moscow."

Molovic smiled. He would have to find out what Rasputin did, who he pissed off to get exiled. "I need you for a few days. What is your name?"

"Yuri Burin, Sir."

"Yuri, do a good job and you will never have to work with Colonel Rasputin again."

The two men passed through the double glass doors into the hospital. Ignoring the front desk, they turned into the wing where testing was done. The general stopped the first orderly he found. "There was an American colonel brought in here for X-rays of his back. Where is he?"

The orderly led the way to a small room, virtually identical to the one in Magadan, right down to the paint color and the weak light. The general pulled a chair close to McGrady's bed and seated himself.

"Yuri, ask the American colonel his name."

Patrick's answer was short.

"Ask Colonel McGrady if he is being well-treated, and if he is in pain."

Again, McGrady answered the question honestly.

"Tell the Colonel that he flew right into a trap that I personally set for him."

"The colonel knows he flew into a trap. He says that his crew counted more than forty fighters in the air around his plane."

"Ask him if he would like to know why I would work so hard to bring his plane down."

McGrady nodded, requiring no interpretation.

"The Soviet Union has lost a plane on a mission over Alaska. We believe that the Americans are holding the crew. We will interrogate the colonel and his two men about their plane and mission, then we will be happy to trade them for our missing crew."

Again, McGrady nodded. If the Russians wanted to trade him, and his two men, for some of theirs, that would explain the good treatment so far.

"Ask the colonel how many of our crew survived the loss of our plane in Alaska."

McGrady thought through his options. It might be better if this general believed that there might be Russian airmen in American hands.

"The colonel says," stated Yuri, "the Americans have been looking for a missing TU-16. But he doesn't know anything about finding it or any survivors."

Molovic couldn't stifle a huge smile. A young doctor tapped on the door, two X-ray films clutched in his hand. Molovic motioned for him to join them.

"Tell us Doctor, what do your X-rays tell us about the colonel's injuries?"

The doctor walked over to the window and held one of the films up against the pane. "This one tells us nothing. I apologize for wasting the film." He held up the second. "This one tells us that the colonel cracked three ribs right along his spine. He probably did some serious muscle damage at the same time. Other than wrap him in a cast from his waist to his arms, there is nothing we can do. It will just take time to heal. We should get him into a cast before he does any more damage. But I can definitely see that he has no actual fractures in his spine."

Molovic nodded to Yuri, who translated for McGrady.

"Thank the doctor for me," uttered McGrady, both pain and relief on his face. "Is there any possibility of some pain medication? The back hurts like hell."

Yuri translated, guessing at the meaning of the American slang.

"Tell Colonel McGrady that he will be taken into an operating room where they will put his torso into a cast. How much pain medication he gets will depend on how he answers the questions we will have for him, starting tomorrow. Until then, we need for him to have a clear head."

Molovic rose as Yuri translated. Then he headed for the door.

McGrady's survival and interrogation training assured that got the message. He began to steel himself for what he knew was coming.

"Ask the colonel if he has any further questions before I let the doctor take him away."

"Just one. Will you be notifying the American embassy of our capture so that they can get word to our families?"

"When the Americans come clean about our missing aircraft and crew, we will cross that bridge," offered Molovic without Yuri's help.

McGrady sat stunned, as did the interpreter.

Molovic smiled at each of them. "I spent almost two years in Fairbanks early in the war, helping to move aircraft to Russia. I didn't think my English would come back, and we, Colonel, are lucky to have Yuri here to help us avoid misunderstandings. You will meet my aide, Senior Captain Dimitri Gagarin tomorrow. He speaks no English. Yuri will translate. You will feel better if you talk to him."

Molovic sauntered into his office, a man who'd bet everything and won. He had the sergeant in the outer office arrange quarters for Yuri away from Rasputin before retreating behind the double doors of his office. He poured himself a tall brandy and then picked up one of the three phones on his desk, ordering a call to his friend, General Blovinin in Moscow. It was time to get the diplomatic part of the plan in motion and to find out what was driving Rasputin.

CHAPTER 18

ELLEN ROLLED FROM the bed, quickly wrapping herself in a robe that years before found its way into her trunk during a visit to the Waldorf in New York. She wadded up one sheet from the four newspapers carried from Fairbanks and stirred it into the ashes in the bottom of the barrel stove. She carefully stacked some moss-covered twigs from spruce trees on the paper and then three sticks of split spruce kindling.

Taking a match from a holder on the wall, she struck it on the front of the barrel, then held the burning match to one edge of the paper, rewarded instantly with a small flame. As the kindling caught, Ellen added pieces of split spruce, stacking them across one another like a tic-tac toe game and closed the cast iron door. She smiled, remembering the hours and cursing it took her late husband to cut the opening in the end of the barrel with a chisel. She adjusted the slide in the door's air grate to allow more air into the young fire.

She set the coffee pot prepared the night before on the heavy iron plate bolted to the top of the barrel. Throwing off her robe, she slipped her nude body back under the sheets and curled up around Anton. Everything but her head felt incredible. She rolled over to look at the aspirin bottle sitting next to the vodka bottle on the table. Both were three-quarters empty. She decided against aspirin.

Anton rolled onto his back, his hand resting on Ellen's thigh. "Good morning BB."

"Just who is this BB? There is no one here with those initials."

"Don't you remember my greeting when you pulled up in front of the cabin yesterday evening?"

"You said, welcome back beautiful bird."

"And you said that you weren't a bird. But I think you are a beautiful arctic bird. One that hides itself under layers to ward off the chill, hiding its beauty underneath."

"Well, Major Anton Bidkov, I am not hiding anything now."

"BB, I have the eyes of a pilot, and you have the attention of every nerve in my body. Beautiful bird fits you perfectly. I think we were both dreaming of last night while you were gone." Anton fought off the vision of Natalya that flooded his mind.

"Anton, I have never had a nickname, and I am not sure I like beautiful bird."

"BB fits you. It will be my secret name for you for as long as we are together. You don't have to like it; it should be enough that I do."

She smiled. For years, Ellen got almost anything she wanted from John Walter Wilson, one of the most powerful men she'd ever met. This upstart Russian was already challenging her. She liked it. "It will take a half-hour to warm the cabin. We should find a fun way to pass the time." Ellen slid her hand onto Anton's thigh, and then up.

Their breaths billowed into the ten-degree air as Ellen and Anton sat on the steps of the cabin, watching the trees across the lake turn from grey to gold as the sun rose. Each held a mug of black coffee. Jack sat in front of them absorbing ear scratching from both humans. Behind the cabin the sled dogs still slept, exhausted from the pace Ellen set getting home.

"You must think I am a tramp," started Ellen.

"If that means that you sleep with many men, I do not think that."

"I normally don't sleep with a man that I have known less than a month," answered Ellen.

"You slept with me the third night," joked Anton.

"I don't mean sleep-sleep."

"I like you Ellen Wilson," answered Anton. "We were both lonely, but, more importantly, some greater power went through a lot to bring us together."

Ellen pulled Anton's hand away from the dog and kissed his fingertips. "Anton, I have a generator and fuel coming in the next couple of days. We need it to communicate with an old friend. He has agreed to help you stay."

"I don't intend to go anywhere, BB."

"It's not that easy. You are a Russian officer who flew his plane into American airspace and crashed. While we both know you weren't attacking this country, most rational people would categorize what you did as hostile."

"I don't know that word."

"Anton, flying a bomber with the intent to drop anything on an American airbase could be construed as an act of war."

"What if we dropped ten thousand roses?"

Ellen looked up. Anton's face was bathed in a mischievous smile, like the one her younger cousin used to get when he dropped a worm down her blouse or talked her into opening a shoe box full of leaping frogs. Maybe that was the attraction. This man still knew how to play.

"Anton, I am serious. It is only a matter of time until we have to explain how you got here and why that is not dangerous for my country."

"Who is this friend?"

"He is the man who you were trying to send a message to, when you flew from Russia. His name is Chad Gritt, the something or other. He comes from a long line of Chad Gritts. I have known him since before the Great War. We worked together several times. He was a pilot, or rather is a pilot like you. He is a general in our Air Force, but he isn't really military."

She watched Anton's body stiffen. "If he is a general but not really military, then just what is he?"

"He studies potential adversaries and keeps track of risks to this country. Remember, both my husband and I did the same thing until we retired. He just uses airplanes to fulfill his mission."

Anton sipped his coffee quietly for a full five minutes. "Is this the general who sends his planes over eastern Russia and takes pictures?"

"That's him, although there are men like him in Europe and Greenland doing the same thing. Every speech that your new Premier makes talks of hundreds of bombers loaded with thousands of nuclear bombs ready to strike Europe and North America. My husband was one of those who stood up and said that it was all posturing, that the Soviet Union couldn't ramp up their manufacturing fast enough to have those capabilities. That's what got him denounced."

"Lying officers like your friend are what got me here," said Anton.

"Then I guess I owe them a big thank you."

Anton reached over and squeezed Ellen's hand. "I don't trust generals, especially political generals."

"More coffee?" asked Ellen, rising.

"Yes, thank you. I am not going to some American gulag," he added.

Ellen reached down and kissed the top of Anton's head. "Anton, America has no gulags. We have prisons for actual criminals, but we have no political prisons. You being here will end in one of two ways. You will either stay, or somehow, someday, you will go back to Russia. Oh, there will be a bunch of bantering between the two governments if you are going back, but America isn't going to keep you here against your will. The last foreign spies shot were during the Great War, Germans caught in civilian clothes, sent here to sabotage American industry." Ellen paused as she tossed her now cold coffee out onto the snow. "I will swear that you were in uniform when I found you." She handed the empty cup to Anton.

"You know that I don't want to go back."

"Then Chad is the guy we need to talk to. He has friends in places that can make it easy for you to stay and stay in a way that your former country doesn't send an assassin to make sure you don't betray them."

"They wouldn't do that."

"Anton, that is exactly what I used to study. Russia is a country that locked up a young woman for telling the truth about something she was asked to study. Do you think they would bat an eye about killing someone who might embarrass them?" Ellen opened the door to the cabin and headed toward the coffee pot, leaving Anton and Jack to stare at each other.

When she returned, she carried a map of Russia and the coffee pot. "I kept some of my old working files. Grab the cups and follow me."

Without waiting for Anton, Ellen headed toward the lake and her wooden picnic table. She used her sleeve to wipe the frost from the table, and then refilled both cups. She unfolded the map.

"Each of the red marks on this map represents a gulag that America has been able to pinpoint. There are hundreds, all built to detain people who the leaders of your country feel threatened by. I believe there are even gulags with American aircrews, some captured in the Great War while America was supplying hundreds of airplanes to defeat the Germans. The Soviets secretly smuggled out dozens of men, who landed their damaged planes in Russia after bombing missions over Japan, most handed over to American government officers in Iran. The Russians had a non-aggression pact with Japan, so they didn't want the Japanese to know that they were repatriating the Americans. But those repatriated men observed other air crews in Russian custody…crews that never made it home."

"Can you show me the camp where they held my wife?"

Ellen traced the Amur River from where it emptied into the ocean north of the city of Khabarovsk. "It would be one of these, upriver from this city. There are several. I don't know them by name."

Anton touched four dots, one at a time. There were tears in his eyes. "Are there really American pilots being held?"

"There are. Some from the Korean conflict, some from the

previous war. We believe that there are air crews were captured while trying to photograph Russian bases to accurately calculate the bomber threat to America."

"Your country is probably holding Russian aircrews."

"Anton, I would know. There isn't a single Russian airman being held by this country." She took a chance. "Does Russia send recon planes over the United States?"

"No, and your country shouldn't be flying over Russia," replied Anton.

"Neither country trusts the other very much. You are right, we probably shouldn't be flying over Soviet airspace; both countries are obsessed over the threat of the other. But don't you think it's better to have American planes with cameras over Russia than planes with atomic weapons?"

Ellen watched Anton walked down to the edge of the snow-covered lake. The professional in her realized that this was the moment to use the dissidence in the man to tip him toward a commitment. Deep inside, she knew how he was feeling. She waited and watched silently.

Finally, Anton turned, throwing the contents of his cold cup onto the snow. "I believe you. The documents that Natalya was studying were all taken from America. The people who stole them were obsessed with the threat. The men who sent me are obsessed with planes carrying nothing more dangerous than cameras. Both sides are crazy."

"Anton, men are dying because no one can stop this madness. One of Chad's aircrews is missing right now. They were trying to keep track of your one Tupolev bomber."

"Is this Chad man someone who would help stop the madness?"

"In a couple of days, a plane is going to land on the lake. It is bringing a generator so that we can use my radio. It will take a couple of days to get it all set up. We can ask Chad to fly out here. You can talk to him yourself."

"I don't want an American Air Force plane landing here. Your friend might bring military police to arrest me. Hell, they might arrest you too."

Ellen laughed. "He will come alone in his own personal plane."

"Your friend actually owns an airplane?"

❋

That afternoon, Ellen put Anton in her sled and took him on the loop around the lake as she checked her rabbit snares. They arrived back at the cabin just before dark. Anton had the six rabbits they collected cleaned before she could unhitch the dogs.

"That was quick," commented Ellen, as she started to feed the team.

"I grew up on a farm. If it took more than a minute to skin a rabbit or five to pluck a chicken, I would go to bed without supper. My father was mean and a drunk. I volunteered to fight the Germans when I was fifteen just to get away from him. After the war, the army taught me to fly."

"How old are you now?" asked Ellen.

"I am thirty-five." Anton looked back at Ellen. "How old are you, BB?"

"I am thirty-nine. It is a perfect age. I am old enough to know better and not old enough to care."

"Care about what?" asked a puzzled Anton.

"Everything, especially what people think about me. All, except you."

"I liked last night a lot," replied Anton. "Perhaps I shouldn't admit this, but I woke up feeling a little bit guilty."

"Wouldn't Natalya want you to find a new love?" asked Ellen.

"She came to me as an angel while you were gone. She said exactly that. But when I closed my eyes a moment later, I could see her alive and scowling."

CHAPTER 19

KHABAROVSK, RUSSIA

MCGRADY SAT ON the narrow bench, his torso encased in plaster from his hips to his armpits. Across from him, Flores and Walsh picked at thin pancakes smothered in some kind of black goo. "You two look like you went a couple of rounds with Rocky Marciano."

"There is a war going on between the regular Air Force guys who engineered the trap and some guy who the Air Force calls a politico. The scrapes you see are from the politico trying to intimidate us before some general, damn near broke his arm to stop him."

"That would be General Molovic. I met him yesterday. He is the head honcho in the regular Air Force out here. What I remember from the briefings is that every unit has a political officer whose job is to ensure the purity of thought in the unit. They enforce commie doctrine. I doubt that the field commanders like their meddling, but I don't know of any reports of real conflict."

"There is between these guys," replied Walsh. "I didn't understand much of what they were saying, but words weren't necessary. The general damned near ripped the political colonel's shoulder apart trying to stop him from hitting Rick and me with a leather belt that he keeps wound around his hand."

"Anything else happen before they locked me in my room last night?"

"That's about it," Flores said. "They fed us about seven. That general says we can expect to be interrogated by one of his men today."

McGrady pointed at his ears and then at the light overhead and the radiator under the window. "Here's what I know from my conversation with Molovic. The Russians really believe that one of their surveillance aircraft crashed in Alaska. They believe we are holding the crew. I told them our side was looking for a TU-16, but we knew nothing about any crash or Russian aircrew." He motioned for his two men to lean closer. "Assume they are listening," he whispered. In a loud voice he added, "neither the general nor our side seems to know where that TU-16 is. Hell, Alaska is huge; it could be anywhere."

"I am surprised that they are allowing us time together before they interrogate us," whispered Flores, as he washed down some of his chewy pancake with weak coffee.

McGrady shook his head and rolled his eyes. "That's probably why the Politico is involved – he realizes the regular military isn't very good at this." He leaned forward. "Let's not give them any help," he whispered.

Flores picked up the conversation. "We don't know anything about their missing plane, so why wouldn't they keep us together? We're just an aircrew tasked with keeping an eye on their air buildup. We don't know shit."

Walsh smiled and nodded his head. "They know we aren't going to tell them anything they don't already know, any more than one of their flight crews would tell American interrogators."

McGrady swallowed what was in his mouth and then whispered, "I think our plane made it to the ocean, so at least for now they don't have it. They must have gun camera film from the attacks. Here is what we tell them – six engines, 4,000-mile range, three cameras with directional arc, 500 knots max speed. We will hold out, but feel free to tell them what they already know."

Flores leaned back. "We are just dumb flyboys who know nothin'. Why so much effort to bring down a plane taking pictures?"

"They want to trade us for their missing crew," answered McGrady.

"That may be why the general seemed to be genuinely angry with the political officer for roughing us up," said Walsh, his hunger finally overcoming his reluctance to eat the tasteless food.

✳

In a control room, only thirty feet from where the men ate, the interpreter Yuri sat compiling notes while across from him Dimitri Gagarin waited for breaks in the conversation for updates. Dimitri checked his watch. The schedule gave the Americans another ten minutes to finish breakfast before they were led back to their individual cells. He'd never done an interrogation, but the Americans seemed talkative. Besides, the list of what the general wanted was short and the most important question had already been answered – the Americans knew about the missing TU-16. If they hadn't found it, they were looking for it.

On the other side of the base, Grigori Rasputin hung up the phone. His call had awakened his father who learned that his calls could come at almost any time. Grigori smiled; his father was going to track down an old duck-hunting buddy. Grigori suspected his calls were being tracked, so when the new Minister of Internal Affairs, MVD, was ready to talk, his father would place the call to avoid suspicion. He'd briefed his father the same day he was been told of the plan to capture an American plane. If Molovic's plan succeeded, Rasputin could count on another five years in purgatory, but the plan failed. That was his opening.

For now, the Russian government couldn't parade the Americans before the world's cameras. He'd seen to that. He'd expected Molovic to negotiate for the release of the three Americans once he had them under lock and key at a political prison. Now all he could do was play out the hand and hope that his father could help. His simple plan to get back to Moscow was creating a major political crisis.

Rasputin hoped that exposing the plot to fly one of Russia's most advanced bombers over America and losing the airplane would erase the shadow over himself and his family. That bitch daughter of the former deputy minister of the MVD accused him of rape. They'd both been drunk, and Grigori knew she wanted him as much as he wanted her. But now the deputy minister's opinions meant nothing. The hardliners were poised to take down the reformers in the Air Force. Grigori Rasputin was the key witness and informer.

For all he knew, the entire TU-16 flight had really been treason. Handing the Americans one of the most advanced weapons in the Soviet arsenal, especially by senior officers was unthinkable. Their story to drop leaflets on an American base was hard to swallow. His help bringing those responsible to justice surely trumped any lies that little tramp told her father. He, Grigori Rasputin, would be a hero when the hard liners again ruled Russia.

Mid-morning tea was being served in Moscow when four men presented themselves to the pretty redhead who screened General Blovinin's callers. Two of the men took seats next to the hallway door while the other two handed their credentials to the young woman. "We need to see your boss. It is urgent, a matter of national security," said the older of the two men. He removed his hat, disclosing a head with little hair. He unbuckled the belt of his long black leather coat and allowed it to fall open, revealing a shabby brown suit that hung loosely from a thin frame. The man's face scared the young woman. It was the face of someone comfortable with death.

The woman pressed a button on the intercom in front of her. "General, there is a colonel from the Ministry of Internal Affairs and a general from the KGB. They need to speak to you."

Before Blovinin could respond, the KGB man in the shabby suit was opening the outer door to the general's office. As was his custom, Blovinin hadn't closed the inner door.

CHAPTER 20

KHABAROVSK, RUSSIA

GAGARIN'S INTERROGATIONS DELIVERED a minor trove of information about the American bomber and the strategies used to photograph Russian air bases. His report to Molovic confirmed almost everything they surmised. The captured crew flew only the intelligence model of the aircraft. They claimed to know nothing of the tactics that might be used by the Americans in an actual nuclear strike. The crew didn't know how many bombers the Americans had ready to launch, which didn't bother Gagarin or his boss, since that information was available, compiled by agents in America's Northwest through simple observation of Boeing's manufacturing facility.

The trap had been a success. The Negro officer let it slip, that their flight strayed off course. The ruse with the radio station worked. The similarities between the MIG 15 and the newer MIG 17 worked just as planned. The Americans believed they were above the ceiling of the MIG 15's. They couldn't tell the difference between the two MIG fighters from a distance. By stripping every possible kilogram from a dozen MIG 15's, Molovic's team increased the number of fighters capable of intercepting the American plane by a factor of four. It was unfortunate that two of those modified MIG15 fighters, the ones that first damaged the American plane, crashed when they ran out of fuel; minimum fuel was part of the plan. In the end, it was four of the MIG-17 advanced fighters that closed on the American plane and shot it down. The film from their gun cameras confirmed that the pilots followed orders. They'd aimed for the wing and the engines rather than the fuselage. It was simply bad luck that the Americans had just enough altitude to allow the damaged plane to glide to the ocean.

Molovic ordered Gagarin to complete his report then get a copy off to Moscow as soon as possible.

The only puzzling thing was that after three days, no one called to confirm that they wanted the Americans sent to Moscow. Blovinin was going to personally parade them before the diplomatic corps and the press. The Americans needed to acknowledge they held the Russian air crew. Every day his men were in American hands, the risk increased that one of them would give up the critical secret. Russia didn't have enough TU-16s or other advanced bombers to mount a major strike into America.

As Gagarin left, Molovic put in a call to his old friend and boss, Blovinin. He wanted an update before he left for dinner and drinks at the Party Dacha. Strangely, he had to demand that Bolvinin's lap cutie transfer the call to his old friend.

"Now is not a good time to talk, Alexi," answered his friend. "I have visitors from both the MVD and the KGB in my office."

CHAPTER 21

KHABAROVSK, RUSSIA

MOLOVIC WAS DRUNK when they came to arrest him. He knew that there was little that Blovinin could do to stop the nonsense when he'd hung up the phone, two days earlier. Blovinin would throw him under the bus in order to keep the plan moving. The only thing he didn't know was how far under the bus he was. Maybe the truth would be recognized. Their plan to protect The Soviet Union from constant American spying really was a good idea. Maybe, Blovinin, by surviving, could help resurrect him some day. But his career in the Air Force was over.

He called his wife as soon as he learned that a special MY-4 bomber was in route from Moscow. Like the TU-16, only a handful of MY-4 long-range bombers existed. Stripped of most of the crew of eight, there were plenty of seats for whoever was coming to make his life miserable.

He could hear the fear in his wife's voice, as he told her that she might have to suffer through some reports in the Party papers, claiming that he was an American spy. He genuinely felt sorry for the shame that his family was going to have to endure. They, beyond all others, knew that there was no way he would betray his country.

Dimitri Gagarin called him early that morning with the news of the Moscow plane. Molovic suggested that his aide meet the plane and guide whoever was arriving to his home. "The more you cooperate, the greater the odds that all of this will not taint you," suggested Molovic. "I am going to tell them that this was almost all my idea and that I used my authority to send the mission to America and to capture an American plane. The others need to be protected long enough to finish the plan. We need to know how much the Americans have found out about the TU-16 and what is going on with the crew."

Perhaps it was logical that McGrady's crew were not informed that their colleagues had found the missing plane. "Just do me one final favor, Dimitri; if Major Bidkov didn't destroy the plane, if he let it fall into American hands, then when he is repatriated, shoot the bastard."

The agents sent to arrest him allowed him to pack a small bag before hustling him into the back of his own staff car where Gagarin sat staring out the windshield. Two hours later, he found himself in handcuffs, in the military waiting room of the train station. Across from him sat the three Americans, their faces freshly bruised. The two men sent to arrest him sat at a table in the corner, pouring through files with Rasputin.

"Colonel Rasputin, you will regret your betrayal," spat Molovic.

Rasputin asked the KGB men for a few minutes alone with the general.

"Perhaps. But being a general does not give you the right to betray your country, Alexi," replied Rasputin. "I have been called back to Moscow to testify against you. I will be leaving in the next few weeks. Until then, I will be helping these men build their case. You should be getting used to your new quarters by the time I sleep in my own bed, in my Moscow apartment."

"Am I not going to Moscow to face these charges?"

"No, Alexi, there are obviously some in Moscow who do not want to hear your lies. You are going to the same interrogation center as your American comrades here. The KGB men and I have been tasked with getting the truth out of all four of you."

"You can't send a general officer to a prison camp," snarled Molovic. "Even in Russia, a man who has served his country for forty years deserves a trial."

"Not a prison camp. You are headed to Amur-3, one of the old gulags east of Khabarovsk. It is being remodeled to accommodate the American airmen we hold. It is a perfect place to check your phony stories against what they tell us."

"What about trading these men," started Molovic, pointing at McGrady and his crew, "for the missing Russian aircrew?"

"You personally chose the officer for your alleged mission to stop American over-flights. The man you chose is the husband of a spy, who did terrible damage to Russia's nuclear armament efforts. She is dead, and you gave her bitter husband one of our most advanced airplanes and sent this obvious spy to deliver it to the Americans."

"You know that is all a lie. Besides, you approved of the choice. You provided the information about Major Bidkov's wife that convinced him to accept the mission."

Rasputin walked over to where Molovic was chained. He leaned down and whispered in his ear. "Only three men know of my screening of Major Bidkov, you, me and him. Personally, I think he and his crew are dead, crashed in the Bering Sea. But there are a lot of facts in my statement, are there not, Alexi? Enough facts to convict you and you know it. It is fortunate for you, that some in Moscow do not want a trial."

Rasputin rose, gathering up his notes. He stepped from the drab military waiting room into the ornate lounge for civilian travelers, stopping to sneer at Molovic before closing the door.

The penal car was as barren as the inside of a shipping container. There were no windows in the heavy steel walls, riveted to the steel ceiling and floor. The Americans sat on metal benches; their hands shackled to loops above their heads. Flores and Walsh could see just enough of their boss to see the pain twisting his face, tears dripping onto his plaster cast.

Molovic sat across from them, careful to avoid any communications with the Americans. The handcuffs he wore were clamped into a ring between his knees, making it impossible to move. In less than an hour, the pain in his aging back mirrored that of McGrady. At either end of the car, uniformed KGB officers now sat, machine pistols in their laps.

Hours later they felt the car being added to the rear of a west bound train. There were two types of trains on the Trans-Siberian Railroad. Express trains rushed between major cities along the five-thousand-mile route, going from Khabarovsk to Moscow in about five days. This would not be an express.

Molovic tried to place Amur-3 on the map in his head. Another hour passed before the train lurched into motion. The blazing lights overhead made it difficult for the men to sleep. The pain from being frozen into one position, as the metal seats beat their spines from below, made it impossible.

Even the milk run should reach the siding that serviced the old gulag in a day, thought Molovic. Perhaps he would know one of the men who ran the camp. If he did, he might be able to negotiate some tiny margin of comfort. No one who had ever served with him would believe the ridiculous charges against him. Maybe he could explain the strategy of trading these three Americans for his missing crew and shield them from physical abuse that would taint Russia's bargaining position.

The train stopped a dozen times before the men in the penal car sensed a change. Behind the car, they could hear voices and clanking, as train crew disconnected the caboose. Then the train pulled ahead, turning onto a siding. Their car was disconnected, plunging it into total darkness. The two uniformed guards switched on flashlights and played them on the inside of the steel door. Off to the side, the men could hear the train backing down the main tracks and the sound of the caboose being reattached. Then the train pulled away, leaving almost complete silence.

An hour later, the unmistakable voice of Rasputin could be heard calling outside. "It's fucking cold out here. I don't know what the holdup is, but the trucks from the camp won't be here for another hour."

Whether it was an hour or three, was impossible to tell, but when the door finally slid open daylight flooded the car. The Americans could barely move, taking minutes to relax their arms from above their heads. Flores and Walsh helped McGrady from his seat onto the floor. While their flight suits buffered the cold, McGrady's hospital pajamas left him shaking uncontrollably. They slid him across the floor to the door, prodded all the way by the guards.

One at a time, the men were manhandled into the back of an open truck. The driver, a middle-aged woman, grabbed a basket from the cab and wrapped each of them in a couple of wool blankets. She helped Flores pull a worn pair of wool socks over McGrady's feet. There was no effort to secure their shackles to the truck. "Why would they?" muttered Flores. "We can barely move."

The two guards climbed into the warm cab. As the truck began to pull away, Molovic was shoved into the back seat of a small van. Rasputin and the two KGB interrogators climbed in behind him and the van followed. Two other trucks stopped next to a boxcar, now disconnected along with the penal car. Some men began unloading freight.

Once their truck started to move, both Flores and Walsh added one of their blankets to those covering their colonel.

The narrow track twisted through a forest of mostly birch trees, stripped free of leaves by winter winds. The packed snow made it difficult for the driver to keep the truck moving without sliding. Behind them, the van seemed to bounce from one side of the dirt road to the other. "I could walk faster than this," offered Walsh, startling his companions with his voice.

"I doubt that," replied McGrady. "I doubt that any of us could walk a hundred yards right now. Besides, wherever we are going has to be warmer than where we are."

They followed the rough track for an hour before they broke out of the forest. Both Flores and Walsh watched as the road wrapped itself around a lake to their left. The high hills on either side were covered in spruce and birch trees. The lake itself was covered by clear ice; the snow that fell on it blown against the far bank forming huge drifts. The prevailing wind was obviously from the direction they were heading.

As they reached the end of the lake, the road twisted along the banks of a mostly frozen small river that flowed toward the lake. It was probably another quarter-hour before the truck pulled up in front of some two-story concrete buildings. Two of the buildings were situated next to the river and the third directly in front of where the truck parked.

There were no fences, no gate. The only obvious security was a tower next to the road where two guards, outfitted from head to toe in fur, waived them through. The KGB guards, from the train, climbed from the cab, and trotted toward the front building. The driver lowered the tailgate and motioned for the men to climb down. As they started to move, she followed the guards, leaving them standing.

A few minutes later the van slid to a stop. The driver followed those in the earlier truck, as Rasputin and the two interrogators pulled a badly bruised Molovic from the van. They pushed him toward where the three Americans leaned against the back of the truck. Then Rasputin and the two KGB men turned towards the closest building, leaving Molovic and the Americans standing in a bitter wind.

"Just what did you do to deserve this?" asked McGrady, struggling to stay on his feet. He could barely see the Russian, his eyelashes frozen together allowing only a squint, his arms so sore he couldn't raise them to pinch away the ice.

Molovic turned his back to the buildings. "It is a long story, Colonel. I sent the TU-16 your country is searching for. It was unarmed except for a ton of leaflets warning America to stop flights over my country. As you know, the plane disappeared. I don't know that I believe that you don't know anything about the missing plane, but I assure you that the men who accompanied that prick politico, don't."

Molovic reached into his coat and tugged at a pack of cigarettes. He tapped one out and pulled it from the pack with his lips. He handed the pack to McGrady who managed to get a cigarette to his lips before handing the pack to Flores. Molovic stood, struggling with his lighter before Walsh took it from his hands and helped the three smokers light up.

"I will be questioned about the others who helped plan the American mission, but I just can't remember who they were. I must be getting old." Molovic looked at each of the Americans. "This camp doesn't really exist. You will meet men here who have been captive since the 1940s. I am told that there are flyers captured in the Korean conflict, and even one from just a year ago. These are the men who have refused to renounce your country since their capture. Why my country still holds them, I don't know. There is little they could tell us that our spies don't already know. I am really sorry that you are here. You were to be traded for my crew, not added to this group of men who are of no value.

I would guess that we don't know what to do with them. We can't tell the world about them; we have claimed for years that they don't exist. Even the thugs who did Comrade Stalin's dirty work don't want to murder them in cold blood. It is a new day in Russia." Malovic's laugh on his smoker's throat doubled him over in pain.

"Are you telling me that we are no longer going to be traded for your missing crew?" asked McGrady.

Molovic turned to McGrady. "I can't imagine them letting you know this camp exists, that these men exist, and ever setting you free. I predict that you will live a longer life in Russia than I will."

"Just how did our two countries fuck all this up?" asked Walsh. My dad was in the engineering corps that helped build the Alaska Highway during World War II. It was used to move supplies that helped our Russian allies beat the Germans."

"I don't know," replied Molovic. "I told my aide, just a couple of weeks ago, that if the politicos would get out of our way, the warriors would go get drunk, sort all this out, and then go fishing, at least the old ones like me. God, how I wish you and your military had never started flying over my country."

"It might still work out, General," interjected Flores. "You might still get to go fishing. I even know a couple of American generals who would love to take you."

"Spoken like a true American. That same attitude is why the men in this camp are still here. You Americans still believe in good. You believe anything is possible. Don't stop believing. Those who give in are sent to work camps where they disappear. That is the only advice I have for you."

"Why would they leave us alone out here?" asked Walsh.

"It is part of the psychological preparation for interrogation. They know you can run, but also know you have nowhere to go. They want you cold and dejected."

"Why are you telling us this?" asked McGrady.

"Some of us have been trying to change my country since the end of the Great War. Many of them are now dead. Maybe someone will come to power in twenty years and decide you should be set free. Maybe you will remember this conversation."

A bell rang on one of the buildings. From behind the building a line of barefoot, tattered men formed a line, each carrying two buckets. The one man without buckets led the others toward the river in the brutal cold, crossing through an old graveyard. They waded into the water, filling their buckets and carrying them toward the buildings. The men watched as the prisoners stole glances at the newcomers, shaking their heads.

"I counted seventeen men including the leader," offered Walsh. "If there are the same number in the other building, there might be more than thirty prisoners being held here."

"Why do you torture yourself by counting?" asked Molovic.

"There have to be more prisoners than guards. They should just break out of this place."

"Captain that is the beauty of the system that has haunted Russia since the 1930s. Whoever set up the gulags put them in in places like this. Do you have any idea of where you are? If you run from here, where will you go?"

"But you aren't one of us, General. Why are you here?" asked Walsh.

"I will be here until they can verify my story or piece together a lie that others will believe, and until they feel you have told them everything about your missions and our missing plane. If one of my old friends can convince the Defense Minister that I should be allowed to retire, then maybe I will leave someday. If not, they will just quit feeding me. I will be just one more mound in that grave-yard, and no one will ever know where I went."

The four were still standing next to the truck when the sun disappeared. When it came up the next morning, all four were hud-dled together in the van. At one point in the night, Flores started the vehicle, turning the heat on high, but the truck ran out of gas only an hour later. No one in the building even come out to check on them.

One at a time the Americans were led into the front building. Each man's leg chains were clamped to a ring in the floor of a bare cell with one weak overhead light and two chairs. Molovic was the last out of the van. Unlike the others, he was left standing outside in the cold.

McGrady stared at the walls painted the same puke green as the hospital. Only the cast on his back kept him upright, the pain now so acute that his brain wandered in and out of consciousness. He felt the warmth of the room, a clanking radiator under the window working full time to keep out the cold. The heat added to the tor-ment in his body as it wormed its way into his frostbitten skin. The place stunk of mold.

He was only vaguely aware of the door opening and a man plopping his huge mass into the chair in front of him. "Lieutenant Colonel Patrick McGrady, you may call me John. Like the disciple,

John, I will be the one who can share your story with the world." The man looked at a file in his lap. "I will be the one who can advise the American authorities that you are alive, so that your wife Susan knows that she is not a widow. I can do these things, but only if you tell me the truth so that my boss lets me tell the story. Do you understand, Colonel?"

McGrady managed to nod.

"Good. Before we start, is there anything you want to say?"

"My back is so painful that I can barely keep track of what you say, John."

"Pain medication is very hard to come by in Russia. It is very valuable and only available to men who need it to do what the motherland needs done. Ordinary citizens must bear the pain until their bodies heal. Spies like you are so low on the priority list that only a high political or military officer could arrange it."

"Are you a high-ranking officer?"

"No, I am a lowly foot soldier. But I report to a man who could authorize the help you need. He is in Moscow, but we have a radio-telephone communications link here."

"How about some water then, I haven't had anything to drink since you dragged us out of the cells in Khabarovsk."

"Perhaps I can find you a glass of water after we talk. Now, let's begin. I have six topics for you, and then I will ask you to sign a simple letter acknowledging that you and your crew were spying on the Soviet Union and making it clear that you know such behavior is illegal."

McGrady fought through the pain, trying to keep track of what he was being told. He said nothing.

"Oh, Colonel, I don't expect you to sign this letter today. It will probably take a few days before you are ready to balance your life, and that of your family, with your silly old-fashioned loyalty. Now let's begin. Where did the Russian TU-16 crash and how many survivors were there?"

CHAPTER 22

FAIRBANKS, ALASKA

GREIWE AND GRITT sat hunched over a map of the Russian Far East. Someone had drawn two blue lines from a position just offshore of the northern end of the Kamchatka Peninsula and two red lines from offshore of the mouth of the Anadyr River. One red line and one blue line intersected over the northern end of the Sea of Okhotsk along the western shore of Shelivkova Bay. The second set of lines intersected a couple of hundred miles northwest of there. Both were over land, and both were hundreds of miles west of the planned flight path for McGrady's mission.

"Our offshore flights are well out of range of the small portable radio that Colonel McGrady's crew carried. It's been four days since they went down, do you really think they could survive out in the open that long?" asked Greiwe. "The temperatures there have to be near zero."

"Those guys can last a month, if they made it out," replied Gritt. "The real question is, did the Russians already find them?"

"Meaning no disrespect, Sir, but the other two questions are: how do we get inland far enough to check on them; and even if they are found, how do we get a rescue helicopter that far into Russia to get them out?"

"We take the questions, one at a time. SAC promises that the modified RB-47 will be here tomorrow. The SAC commander demands that we shake the plane out completely before we begin flying it on intelligence missions. I know you are assigned to SAC, just like I am under the org charts, but the head of the CIA wants his men back, and he wants to know what they found."

"Why do I feel my career in the Air Force slipping away?" asked Greiwe.

"You know how to handle this, Dan. You will write me a note, disagreeing with my interpretation that using the plane for a search and rescue mission is just the ticket for a shakeout flight. The planes flying along the Kamchatka Peninsula are all reporting almost no Soviet air activity."

"If you were to find the missing TU-16 at the same time, everyone will be happy," replied Greiwe.

"That is no longer our priority, Dan." Gritt wished he could disclose Ellen's story. "We have three missing Air Force officers. If we can find them, we will figure out how to get them out. Maybe they can get to the ocean, and the Navy can get a sub in there to take them off the beach. I hear specialized subs have even penetrated Russian harbors. Based on where the second radio is broadcasting, they are only a few miles inland of that inland bay."

"So, you are going to order the B crew to fly a pass over the two radio beacons?"

"I don't have to, they volunteered, as did the Blackbird crew. If we can't raise them on their emergency radio, we will scoot on down toward Japan and see if we can pick up any information from Russian communications."

"You keep saying *we*, Sir."

"The new electronic recon bay is designed for four Blackbird operators. Until the newly trained crew gets here, we have only two operators and a couple of empty seats. It makes sense for me to monitor the operations on the shake down flight."

"Did Director Dulles agree to that too?"

"I think we have reached that old permission versus forgiveness debate, how about you?"

"You know that the new recon bird had the guns and the ejection seats removed, Sir?"

"There is no way to put ejection seats in for the Blackbird crews, so it makes sense to remove them for everybody. The guns have always seemed a bit ridiculous. Any good fighter jock could figure out how to climb up under a B-47 and avoid them."

"We will fly a direct line to the area where we are hearing the emergency transmitters and from there down the peninsula. We will refuel at Chitose. When the new plane gets in, have the ground crew figure out how to mount extra oxygen. One of the things we want to find out, is how high can we fly if we need to, it may take more oxygen."

"All right, General, I am on it. Do you want to set up the briefing for tomorrow night?"

"No, Dan, it will wait until the next morning. We don't have to be over Shelivkova until noon Fairbanks time."

❋

The two men in the cockpit of the RB-47 rolled the airplane into a raceway orbit to the west of the first expected signal from the emergency transmitters. In the new electronic intelligence compartment, the two blackbirds remained silent, focusing on the new equipment in front of them. Both had manuals open in their laps. Gritt sat trying to read from the briefing file, looking for anything he or the team overlooked.

Their routing took the big jet north over Barrow and out over the polar ice pack, turning south over Russia. "Still nothing?" asked Gritt, fighting off claustrophobia in the windowless compartment.

"No, Sir, nothing. We have seen no radar signals at all on this routing, and no radio traffic on any of the Russian Air Force frequencies. Even the commercial radio station at Anadyr seems to be off the air."

"Could it be a malfunction in your equipment?" asked Gritt.

"I guess it's possible, Sir," offered the second operator. "But we tested everything leaving Alaska. We even picked up a radio transmission from a civilian Beaver flying just outside of Bettles, heading to some remote lake with a load of freight. He was asking if he could get fuel in Bettles. We logged all three radar sites on the American side. Everything was working then."

"We ran a radar sweep about five minutes ago, General," came a call from the cockpit. There is nothing in the air around us."

Gritt looked at his watch. It was five minutes before noon, Fairbanks time. Unless the emergency beacons had malfunctioned or run out of battery, they would hear the first transmission in minutes. Gritt looked at the consoles with their red and white lights and glowing dials and instruments. He looked at the overhead, and the floor that cramped the space. *If this is what it's like to protect the country in a submarine, those guys are way underpaid*, he thought. He looked at the two men with him and made a mental note to check into their pay.

"We have the first locator beacon," said the man next to him.

"We have it on the direction finder up here," came the cockpit call. We will be over it in less than one minute."

Gritt wanted to blurt out the heading from that first beacon to the location of the second, but he bit his tongue. This crew was competent, and they all knew the plan, now clipped onto the kneeboards strapped to their legs.

He could feel the aircraft commander throttle back the engines, so that they would arrive over the second beacon at the time it was expected. Somehow, he had missed the communication from the navigator.

The second beacon went off almost directly under the plane. The pilot began to circle. At the furthest console from Gritt, the lead Blackbird operator waited five minutes and then keyed a microphone in front of him, calling out a phony call sign and a preplanned message that McGrady's crew would interpret as permission to transmit back. He waited for a response before making a second call, then a third.

Ten minutes later, the Blackbird operator called the cockpit, asking the co-pilot to try a call on the same emergency frequency using the radio in the cockpit. The Blackbirds switched off their intercom so that they would only hear the transmission if the call went out over the radio. Their radio picked up the transmission loud and clear. There was still no response. The search plane tried again and again to reach anyone on the ground, with no luck. To Gritt, it felt like the pressurized aircraft had developed an air leak, the flow of optimism from the entire crew, almost physical.

"All right, gentlemen, let's assume that the missing crew has a radio failure. Let's do a quick sweep over the land going north from here and then a second a little further inland going back south. Let's get it all on film," ordered Gritt.

The pilot swung the heavy plane onto a northern heading. "Camera's on," came a call over the intercom. I am going to shoot fifteen miles."

With a camera's off call, the pilot rolled the plane into a turn to the left and set up a southbound track inland of the first."

"Camera's on," came the call and only two minutes later, camera's off."

"We won't know if the guys down there left a visible marker until we can analyze the film," said Gritt. "There is no way we can see a message in the snow from 40,000 feet. Let's move on to phase two. Time to see what we can learn from Russian radio chatter on the way to Chitose."

Gritt could feel the aircraft slow even more as the pilot slipped into the second part of the plan. Unless they were challenged, they would spend almost three hours monitoring Russian communications. Their flight plan included dinner and an overnight in Japan before a straight flight back to Fairbanks.

Normally, a night out on the town in Japan would be something to look forward to, but Gritt knew that everyone on board was only thinking of three missing friends in a country known for missing men.

CHAPTER 23

MOLOVIC'S FACE SHOWED welts from Rasputin's belt. He smiled at the asshole sitting across from him, which he knew drove Rasputin crazy. The problem was that Molovic was telling the truth, all except for his claim that he alone ordered the flight to Alaska. His statement of the strategy to capture the Americans was the plain truth, as Rasputin knew, being included in the plan from the beginning. Rasputin's clumsy attempts to trip him up were easily deflected.

"You know, General, that those in the Navy and in the Air Defense forces who helped you bring down the plane still don't know anything about the American captives."

"Colonel, that was part of the plan. Until the conversations with the American State Department get to an agreement on the two flight crews, we don't want any publicity."

"The Americans are completely silent about your missing plane."

"What do you expect? They will stall for time to study the wreckage and to interrogate any survivors unless we make it clear that it is in their best interest to acknowledge the loss of our plane and theirs. They will trade any survivors of our crew for theirs; they always do."

"Not if Major Bidkov gave them the plane. I think it's time to leak the story of our capture of the Americans and their interrogation. With the story public, those who helped you will be ready to talk, even if you aren't."

"Colonel, you do not have the authority to do that. You need to discuss it with your bosses and with General Blovinin before you fuck this up. The offer to trade flight crews is the best opportunity we have to find out what happened to our plane."

"General Blovinin is under investigation. I think he helped you plan the mission to America."

"There are a lot of men far superior to you and your father who don't give a shit what you think. Do you believe that a former MGB general, one pushed out when Comrade Stalin died, has more muscle than the Air Force commander? Men like your father brutalized the Russian people, all in the name of protecting their privileged lives. He should have been denounced. You, and they, cannot accept that Russia must change."

"We will see, General. For now, the political corps is assisting the MVD and the KGB investigation of your treason. My job is to smoke out all of the rats. If I can get the other officers who helped you with these plans, to open up we will get this done quickly. They need to know where the American spies they helped capture ended up. It's time to let them know where the whole affair landed you."

CHAPTER 24

THE OPEN DOOR of the cache banged against the side of the elevated storage shed. Resting on four tall logs, the tiny building's design kept raiding bears and wolverines out of stored food.

"You are quiet again this evening," observed Ellen.

Anton stretched his good arm up toward where Ellen held a large canvas bag full of dried salmon. He grasped the bag. Ellen pushed a handful of hair from in front of her eyes, then swung the door against the biting wind and latched it.

"Not a word, not even a question," continued Ellen, making her way down the frosted wooden ladder.

Anton dropped the bag and reached up to steady Ellen's decent.

"I know that the fish are for the dogs," replied Anton. "I am happy that you now let me help with them. I was feeling pretty useless."

Ellen smiled.

"I have been watching you every day," said Anton. "Chop up half a fish for each dog and boil the fish in that stinking can over the outdoor fire. Pour a ladle of fish and water into each dog bowl and get the hell out of the way to avoid being part of dinner. Repeat the same process in the morning."

Ellen started to pick up the heavy bag.

"Allow me," said Anton. He effortlessly lifted the heavy bag with one hand and carried it to a chopping block next to a steaming five-gallon gas can turned bucket.

"I wasn't talking about feeding the dogs," continued Ellen.

Anton said nothing. He pulled a dried chum salmon from the bag.

Ellen normally took fifteen minutes to chop up four fish, a task that Anton completed in a third that time. They both picked up the chunks from the snow and dropped them into the boiling can. When they finished, Anton effortlessly flipped the bag and remaining fish up onto the edge of the cabin roof to keep it from the weasels that lived beneath the floor.

"BB, I apologize for ignoring you," said Anton. "I want to do just the opposite. I want to be your partner, maybe more than a lover."

Ellen worked to get her windblown hair back under her stocking cap. "I think I would like that, but only if you quit calling me BB." Both people watched until the steaming can of water finally began to boil again.

Ellen used a huge ladle to fill six bowls for the dog team, finishing with a ladle and a half for Jack. Anton placed each bowl as far from the dogs as their chains would reach and jerked his hand away as gnashing teeth lunged.

That ritual complete, Ellen gently took Anton's hand and started toward the lake. She took a seat on top of the old table and motioned for Anton to join her.

"I think I understand your silence," said Ellen. "I can sit here with Walt and ask him for advice, even permission when needed. He was always my treasured advisor."

"You said you buried your husband near the lake," said Anton.

"Under the table. I put the table over his grave to keep the scavengers from digging. He is six-feet down, but until I moved the table, they still tried."

Anton jumped from his seat, zipping his jacket to shut out a sudden chill. He stared under the table. "Maybe that is it. You know for sure."

"Anton, I am sorry your men died. I am sorry Americans are in Russian Gulags. But I am not sorry that you are here. That is selfish of me, but it's how I feel."

"You are sorry, I am angry. I am angry at your country for sending planes over mine. I am angry with my government for their lies and betrayal. I am angry about this crazy conflict that is killing people on both sides. But it wasn't that conflict that got Natalya arrested, it was power-mad men. I am through with all of it."

She patted the tabletop. "The last thing Walt said to me was, now go find the love of your life."

Anton sat. "When I forget my anger, I think I hear Natalya say the same." He gripped Ellen's knee and squeezed. She jumped. A huge smile crept over Anton's face. "I just don't know if her voice is coming from my heart and head or some other part of my body." He watched Ellen's face turn red, but she was smiling.

Ellen finished the dinner dishes, watching the Russian man throwing sticks for Jack outside the frosted window. Behind him, on a stump, he'd placed a bottle of vodka allowing the temperatures now hovering around zero to chill it. The after-dinner drink was becoming a daily ritual.

Ellen hung the dishtowel over the wood stove and lifted her heavy coat from a peg behind the door. She tugged a stocking cap over the hair piled on top of her head and pulled on a pair of mittens. Grabbing two glasses she stepped out onto the porch, watching the man and dog play.

Jack figured out that if he refused to drop the stick after Anton threw it, the man would chase him. When Anton turned around, ignoring the huge dog, Jack would drop the stick and bark until the man started another round of the game. Jack finally tired, dropping under a spruce to reduce that day's stick to wood chips.

Anton picked up the vodka bottle and partially filled the glasses that Ellen extended. She handed one to him. "We need to find a way to help stop this nonsense between our two countries," she said.

"I agree, but we aren't going to start tonight," he replied. "Come, you can see a full moon just rising from down by the lake." She slipped her arm through Anton's as they walked. She pressed her cheek against the bitter cold of the sleeve of his coat. Somehow the gesture warmed her.

CHAPTER 25

KAMCHATKA PENINSULA, RUSSIA

ONE OF THE men locked in the RB-47's airborne communications capsule pumped his fist, bouncing in his seat. One technician punched the other Blackbird in the shoulder and pointed to a frequency dialed in on the equipment in front of him. The second man rushed to dial in the same frequency, and then both began taking notes. Furious writing continued for more than fifteen minutes.

One of the Blackbird operators reached up and flipped a switch, temporarily disconnecting his headset from the radio. "General, I am going to translate this on the fly for you. Some colonel by the name of Rasputin – I am not kidding, that's his name – sent a message to a bunch of senior officers up and down the coast, thanking them for their efforts in capturing an American plane crew. He indicated that the Americans were being held for questioning and trial."

The second operator continued to monitor the radio but slipped one side of his headphones off from his ear to listen to his partner and the general.

Chad didn't know whether to cheer because the men were alive or scream because he knew what they were up against. "What else? Did he say where they were being held?"

"No Sir, but there is more to the message. He evidently told the officers that a General Molovic has been arrested for mishandling state secrets, losing them to the enemy. He was being transported to the same interrogation center as the three Americans."

"Arresting this Molovic guy is stirring up a hornet's nest," said the second operator. "The phone lines are alive with calls from all over the Far East. I need to get back to the radio."

The plane was just crossing the 55th parallel when both operators again began scribbling frantically. One of the men pulled off his headset. "Have the pilot circle. We are monitoring an interesting call." He then pulled the headset back over his ears and continued writing.

Gritt keyed his intercom, ordering a five-mile racetrack course.

Finally, both men quit writing. "Let's go home," said one of the Blackbirds.

Gritt looked at the man, a strange expression on his face. He wasn't used to technical sergeants giving him orders.

"General, we were listening to a conversation between the commander of the Pacific Fleet in Vladivostok and a Senior Captain who was the aide to this General Molovic. The admiral's ships were evidently a key part of the plan to track Colonel McGrady's flight. Their radar isn't dedicated to watching out to sea like the Air Defense radar."

"So, the Russian Navy tracked the plane for the Air Force," offered the co-pilot. "From all of our briefings, the Russian services don't even like each other."

"There is something else," offered the radio operator. "Evidently the admiral and this Molovic guy are old friends, and the admiral is furious over his arrest. He asked this Captain Gagarin where the general was being held, and he is threatening to send in the marines to free him."

Gritt sat absorbing the information. Finally, he asked, "Did this Captain Gagarin tell the admiral where they were?"

Both Blackbirds began searching through their notes, answering at the same time. "He believes the general was being taken to someplace called Amur-3."

"I hate to rain on everyone's parade," came a call from the cockpit, "but I just got a radar warning up here."

"Check it out, Ernie," ordered the Blackbird master sergeant. "I want to continue listening for any other calls until we are out of range of the radio links."

The second operator began searching the radar scanner. "It's the same signature that Colonel McGrady and I saw a month ago. This must be a Navy radar because it is sweeping us with a rotating signal."

"We're at 40,000 feet," called the pilot. "We're above the operating altitude of the MIGs."

Gritt gave the information a minute to sink in. "The flight plan for the missing B-47 was all at forty thousand feet. Somehow they climbed up high enough to shoot him down."

"Maybe they just had a mechanical problem," answered the pilot.

"They dropped two emergency beacons, 200 miles apart. They were under attack. Intelligence reports that the new MIG -17 can reach 40,000 feet. Intel thinks that's their ceiling."

"Let's hope that there are no 17s down here," offered the Blackbird monitoring the radar sweep on a screen in front of him. "I just picked up radio chatter on the Russian Air Defense frequency. They have us and are scrambling MIGs from Petropavlovsk."

"How far are we from the airfield?" asked the pilot.

"The navigator was already plotting the distance. "It's fifty-four miles southeast of our current position," he answered. "It is directly on our route to Japan."

"All right everybody, we are turning southwest. I'll make their run as long as I can," advised the pilot.

Everyone focused on the four incoming jets. "This must be how a condemned man must feel after everyone else leaves the gas chamber," commented one of the Blackbirds. "You just lie there strapped to a table waiting for the sound of pellets dropping into liquid."

"Or maybe it's the hiss of gas filling the room," offered his partner.

"You two are really morbid," said Chad. "Knock it off; focus on getting us out of here."

In the cockpit, the co-pilot tracked the Russian planes on the radar. "Thirty miles out and closing," said the co-pilot.

"The lead MIG just reported passing through thirty-five thousand feet," added one of the blackbirds.

"Shit, oh dear," came from the co-pilot. "MIG-15's can't operate that high. They are on a string for us. They will be here in ten minutes. Thank God they are climbing, it is keeping their speed down."

"We just crossed the coast, were south of the Peninsula," added the pilot.

"Let's crank up the power and see if we can coax another 10,000 feet out of the new girl," replied Gritt.

The pilot pushed their speed from the 300-knot cruise to more than 400 knots. He firewalled the throttles and trimmed the plane for climb. He watched as the rate of climb indicator began to register an anemic 400 feet per minute. No one aboard had ever been beyond 40,000 feet. Engine flame out in the thin air was possible. A stall was possible. For all they knew, God could get pissed off about them invading his space and smite them. All they knew for sure was that below them four Soviet fighters were determined to shoot them down. At this altitude and speed there would be no bailing out.

"What's our current altitude?" asked Gritt.

"We are passing 42,000 and still climbing."

"Take her up at least another 3,000 feet. Let's hope the MIG drivers really can't climb past forty thousand, or that their top-down Russian training has convinced them that they can't," ordered Gritt.

"They appear to have leveled off at 40,000," offered the co-pilot. They are still closing behind us, but below us. If they can get under us, they might be able to get shells from their thirty-millimeter cannons to reach us."

"We just edged past 44,000," called the pilot. "We are still climbing but barely."

"Try leveling us out and run the engines right to the red line," ordered Gritt. "We are not going to lose another plane over here."

"They are holding steady 4,000 feet below us, but they are still closing," reported an excited co-pilot.

Gritt watched the two Blackbirds. The color in their faces was now pale, their shirts wet with perspiration. They no longer reported the constant chatter from the MIGs.

Gritt sometimes struggled with trusting his training early in his own career; coming close to death numerous times, sometimes having to dish out death to others in order to survive. "Listen up, all of you. There are six American brains riding in the most advanced bomber American engineers can build. Let's start using those brains to get this crate home."

"They will run short on fuel pretty soon," suggested the navigator.

"They have a base down in the Kurile Islands that they can land at," replied Gritt. "We may have to hold this altitude and speed all the way to Japanese air space. If those MIGs close another mile, they can make a firing pass."

"That is going to leave us really short on fuel at the rate these six engines are guzzling," replied the pilot. "We are going to have to reduce power in the next few minutes to reach Japan."

"Let me try something," offered the Blackbird sergeant. He flipped a switch on the radio in front of him, and keyed the microphone button, transmitting in Russian."

For two minutes there was silence throughout the plane, interrupted only by the sergeant's voice carrying on a conversation in Russian.

"Whatever you did, worked," called the co-pilot. "The MIGs are losing altitude and turning."

Gritt looked at the Blackbird sergeant with a puzzled expression.

"I told them that if they wanted, we would climb on up to 50,000 feet. They were free to tag along below us, but that we just called ahead, and a full squadron of American fighters was taking off to meet us halfway."

"If this was wartime, I would put you in for a medal, Sergeant," offered Gritt.

"You take Ernie and me to the best Kobe steakhouse in town and buy and were all even, General."

"Might as well make that a table for six," offered the pilot.

CHAPTER 26

FOR THE THREE newbies, there was no food and little water for three days. The guards confiscated their flight suits and boots. They were questioned every two hours leaving them exhausted. The three men now dressed in blue striped cotton pajamas and barefoot were ushered into the office of the camp commander. McGrady's pajama top was open, the garment too small to button over his cast. All rubbed at patches of blackened, frost-bitten skin with fingers that felt full of fire.

On a chair across from the commander sat a tall graying man. His hair was buzz-cut, his skin drawn, his blue eyes deep in his sunken face. The man rose unsteadily as McGrady and his crew were led into the room. "Gentlemen," he started in English, "let me introduce you to the camp commander, Pavel Nasidna. I am Army Colonel, Robert Davis. Welcome to Amur-3."

"Sit," ordered the camp commander, pointing to three stools along the wall under the windows.

"Colonel Davis is the commander of the prisoners held here. He and the eighteen other Americans were brought here to help put this old gulag back into shape. This camp has only one purpose, to help the men who live here recognize the truth. You three may be here for some time," offered the commander with a phony laugh. "It all depends on how quickly you admit the truth." The man painted on a smile, his yellowed smoker's teeth showing through tight lips.

The commander opened a file, spreading three sheets of paper across his desk. "So far, you have all refused to acknowledge that you were spying on my country and that your aggressive and criminal country is using its air power in an illegal war against the Soviet Union."

The commander turned back to Davis, "Bob, how long have you been in custody since you illegally landed your B-25 at a Russian air base?"

"That was December 17, 1944," answered Davis.

"The Colonel has faulty vision," laughed the commander. "After a dozen years, he still can't see that his country's actions have kept him from his family. He doesn't realize that same country has abandoned him. I have known Bob for more than five years now; this is our second camp together. He is a competent officer and a kind man. It is terrible that he will probably spend the rest of his life at Amur-3."

"Bob, you may take the new men to the cafeteria. I am sorry that somehow their files got lost and they have been accidentally deprived of food. After lunch you can show them to their assigned rooms. You are all dismissed."

Davis walked slowly next to Flores and Walsh, who were each supporting one of McGrady's arms. "We can talk in the halls," he said, "or outside. Everywhere else may be bugged."

"What do they want, Colonel?" asked Flores.

"They want you to denounce your country. There are four of us here from World War II, twelve from Korea and a U.S. Navy officer brought in right after we moved here."

"Sir," started Flores, "after a dozen years, no one would blame you if you signed that damned statement. Even the brass would understand that you signed under duress. Wouldn't it be worth it to go home? You are a hero."

Davis stopped, confronting Flores. "Captain, I have known

more than a dozen men who signed that letter. Have you ever heard of one of them being repatriated? Even if our government wanted to bring them home silently, some smart reporter somewhere, would be running with their homecoming story."

McGrady steadied himself. "Why did they allow us to meet you before they turned up the screws on our interrogations?"

"It's all a game. We are all here, because with Stalin dead, no one wants to shoot us. Our guys have been painting and fixing broken windows and rewiring this decrepit old complex for six months. They control the schedules, but we are pretty much free to take care of ourselves. We all know that we are never going home."

"Does that mean we won't be tortured?" asked Walsh.

"No, you are newbies. You have information on current weapons systems and tactics. You don't even realize what you know, information they would like to learn. You will be brutalized for whatever time it takes for your interrogators to realize that you aren't going to give them anything more."

"The only kindness we have seen, was when a woman truck driver gave us some blankets for the ride to this place," said Flores.

"That is the woman we call Aunt Star, for the red star she always wears around her neck. She is the camp medic and the most sadistic person here. She loves to watch, as we are tortured. Sometimes she helps. Be especially careful if she tries to seduce you. She will scream 'rape' and smile as the other guards hold you down while she cuts off your balls."

The three newcomers looked at each other, struggling to believe that the pretty middle-aged woman who had helped them could be so evil.

"Just tell her that you are faithful to your wives or fiancés, and somehow that gets her to back off. But she will forget the conversation in a couple of weeks and try again. Now, we need to get moving if you are going to get any food. They will come looking for you soon."

"Do the interrogations stop after a while?" asked Walsh, walking again.

Davis opened a door to a barren room with four wooden tables and benches. He walked through to a kitchen, where two men in tattered pajamas stood at a stove. The colonel introduced the men, who filled bowls of weak fish soup and helped the new men carry them to one of the tables. One carried a huge pitcher of water and three glasses to the men who emptied the pitcher. The cooks went for more.

Davis looked at Walsh and shook his head. "I have heard we now have Negro officers, Lieutenant, it's nice to finally meet one. And, in answer to your question about the interrogations ending, the answer is no. Every one of us still goes through it every week. If the interrogators are having a good day they smile and let us know that they are just going through the motions, so that they can check a box on some form. If they are having a bad day, it can be brutally painful. These guys know ways to hurt you that you can't even imagine."

"But why, why would they continue?" asked Flores.

"None of them want to be here either. If we were all gone, maybe their exile would end too. Everyone here is a prisoner."

McGrady looked at a fish head in his spoon, and dropped the small head back into the broth, choosing a shred of cabbage and piece of carrot instead.

"I would eat that, Colonel," offered Davis. "Except for the fish we catch or the occasional rabbit or squirrel we trap, we only get protein twice a week. You need to keep your strength up."

Behind them, a door banged open. Aunt Star stood in the doorway, the top three buttons on her blouse undone. She pointed down the hall.

"Eat quickly," suggested Davis. "It is time to go."

Three days later the newbies again saw the cafeteria. Pushed through the door; two could barely walk, the soles of their feet beaten bloody. They'd gone without food, surviving on two cups of water each day. Only Walsh seemed to be healthy.

The cafeteria was full of worn men, all devouring rice and fish broth from chipped bowls. As Aunt Star slammed the door behind the newbies, other prisoners struggled to their feet to help them. Davis was the first there. "Pretty rough. The reason they moved you into the barracks was so that we would have to listen, as they tortured you."

The helpers cleared room at one table for McGrady, Flores and Walsh. Bowls of rice and three pitchers of water were placed on the table. Davis turned to Walsh. "How was it, to listen to that scum torture your crewmates? I assume that you were questioned and threatened, but they never hurt you."

Walsh looked over at Flores and McGrady who'd aged in the three days since they had last been together. "It was the hardest thing I have ever done."

"They didn't torture you?" asked Flores, his eyes twisted into tiny slots.

"Captain," started Davis, "when we first got to this camp, they did the same with Lieutenants Deerwater and Alvarez; both men have dark skin. Let me guess, the message was, 'You don't have to suffer here, your people have suffered enough at the hands of your white capitalist rulers.' It didn't work on a Cherokee or a Mexican any better than it worked on you."

Walsh and Flores ate and drank like animals. McGrady, however, couldn't stop shaking enough to get a glass, let alone a spoon to his mouth. A small man with black curly hair, broad nose and dark brown eyes, slipped the spoon from McGrady's fingers and began feeding him, pausing only to lift the glass of water to his lips. "Do you remember me, Colonel? We went to the academy together back in 1945."

McGrady tried to focus. He rubbed the crust from the corner of his eyes. "Is that you Manny?"

"It is. You were three years ahead of me. We both played base-ball. It is nice to see you again, Sir. I just wish it wasn't here."

The familiar face helped McGrady focus. He smiled at the man. "Thank you for your kindness, Manny. How long have you been a captive?"

"I was shot down in June of 1952, flying close air support in Korea."

McGrady turned to Flores and Walsh, "Guys, this is Manny Alvarez, the best shortstop I have ever seen."

"It will be a few days before they start in again on you," offered Davis. "You can't tell them anything if you are dead. I will assign men to help you."

"Is there any place that I can take a sponge bath?" asked McGrady. "The itch under this cast is terrible, but if I could keep the sweat and grime from trickling in, it might help."

"I can take you down to the river," offered Manny. "We kept the towels of the two men who died after we got here. I can tear one in half for a washcloth."

"Get as much sleep as you can," suggested Davis. "I noticed that political officer who arrived with the KGB interrogators is still around, so they aren't finished with you."

A lean prisoner, one time probably been a real lady's man, sat at the table. Davis introduced him as Navy Lieutenant Calvin Carter, the camp intelligence officer. Flores stared at the new man. He wondered if anyone else noticed that he was actually a little fat in the middle while the other men in the room resembled scarecrows.

Carter caught his stare, a worried scowl sweeping over his face before he spoke. "What is the story with the Russian general who arrived with you? He is the only man here who is guarded all the time, yet he seems to have some grease with the camp commander. I saw him wandering around the cemetery this morning. He stood by one grave until the political officer came out waving a pistol and ordered him back inside. He is being held alone in this building, which isn't normally used for housing."

Flores finished his rice, running his fingers around the bowl. He licked his fingers. "That's the guy who set the trap, where we were shot down. Evidently, he sent a Russian bomber over Alaska on some type of secret mission, and it crashed. We were looking for…" McGrady kicked Flores under the table and shook his head. Flores sipped his water. "He is accused of authorizing an illegal mission and the loss of the plane and crew. These guys even hate each other."

CHAPTER 27

CHITOSE AIR FORCE BASE, JAPAN

THE CREW OF the RB-47 slept in the following morning, all except for Gritt, who sat in a small conference room with three other officers. "We need confirmation that the missing crew is in this Amur-3 place, and we need current information and manning estimates on the facility," he said. Gritt checked his watch. It was twenty minutes before eight.

Across from him sat another one star and four other men. "General Gritt, the Air Force doesn't keep photo recon planes here at Chitose," replied the other general, a smug smile on his face.

Gritt smiled back, the smile that he saved for people who were bullshitting him. He had fought this battle before. It really grated on some officers, to work with someone of the same rank who was fifteen years younger. "Karl, there are two RB-45 Tornado's in Japan. Most of the Tornados left after the Korean War wound down, but two still operate clandestinely here, to keep an eye on the North Koreans and the Chinese. I am sure that if you check with operations, they fly out of Chitose from time to time."

"Those two aircraft are not under my command."

"No, they are still under the command of SAC, operating for the CIA." Gritt unfolded a telegram he found waiting for him after dropping $200 buying dinner the night before. He handed the telegram to General Karl McNamara. "One of those Tornados will be here from Honshu this morning. The aircraft and crew have been temporarily assigned to me."

Gritt switched from his hammer approach to the kid-glove approach that he was more comfortable with. "We will need your team's help with mission planning, fueling, and most importantly, developing the film from the Tornado's cameras as quickly as possible. There are three American lives on the line."

McNamara read the short note "requesting his support," recognizing that a telegram from 'Engine Charlie Wilson,' the Secretary of Defense, was more than a request. "My entire staff is at your disposal," he answered.

"Thanks, Karl. Can you get someone to see what it will take to ramp up the photo lab to handle the film? We won't know how much film until the RB-45 gets back. I also need whatever maps you have on the Amur area, especially any that identify the old gulags west of Khabarovsk."

Gritt opened the weathered accordion briefcase on the chair next to him, unfolding a map on the table. "This is a Navy map, showing the radar coverage plotted along the Russian coastline. We will need any information that you have compiled, to update it. This needs to be a quick in and out mission with few footprints."

McNamara rose, stuffing a well-chewed cigar butt into the corner of his mouth. He turned to the four men next to him, still scowling. "Fuel and ground handling," he snapped, pointing at the major at the end of the line; intelligence updates," he added, pointing at a lieutenant colonel next to the major. "Mission planning," said McNamara, pointing at the colonel next to him. "The Colonel here will grease the skids with Photo Intel." The last man in line was a young captain, with silver wings on his chest, clearly the general's aide. "Cory here will keep me informed and take care of whatever else is needed."

McNamara made a show of walking out the door without a salute, telegraphing who the highest-ranking officer was.

When he was gone, the others took the time to refill coffee cups, giving their general time to get out of the building. The Colonel spoke for all of them. "General McNamara has never liked people stirring his soup. He's a short timer now, almost finished with his thirty years."

Gritt smiled at the men around him. "Smoke 'em if you have them. I hate it when someone stirs up one of my units. But we are all professionals, and this is important."

"Are we looking for the crew of that missing B-47?" asked the captain.

"I can't tell you who we are looking for," answered Gritt. "Personally, I hope to learn something about three friends," he added after a pause, bringing smiles to the other men's faces.

The colonel nodded to the others in the room, dismissing them to their projects. "If you will follow me, Sir, planning will be easier down in operations." He pointed at the Lt. Colonel. "Max will join us with our latest radar and surveillance charts."

"Oh, and Max, bring along that old map from when we were plotting Russian military bases. It has dozens of locations in the Far East, where we looked at facilities that turned out to be abandoned gulags and industrial sites. It's the best map we have to identify where this Amur-3 might be."

The general's aide led them into the hall. "I will go see what I can find on the arrival of the Tornado."

An hour and a half later, two Air Force majors and a tech sergeant sat in the briefing room, in front of them, a copy of the Russian facilities map. There were three locations circled, all marked ABANDONED on the map.

"Our best guess is that this Amur-3 is one of these three facilities," Gritt said. "The old photos all show that they were abandoned in 1954 or before. What you are looking for is any recent activity. We need photos from the closest road or railroad to each of the facilities. Once you locate them, take a few minutes over the target for a detailed camera run. Any questions?"

The mission planners took over the briefing, providing additional maps and overlays showing Russian radar and fighter bases. "You will need to stay well south of Khabarovsk. They are installing a new radar at the airbase. We don't know if it is operational; there is a lot of air activity in the area. We don't want one of their MIGs to stumble into you."

The Tornado flight crew studied the map in front of them. "So, routing half-way between Vladivostok and Khabarovsk and across China south of Yichon should keep us clear of any radar?" asked Major Kennedy. His six-foot, average build body, rigidly upright in the old oak chair. His focus was as intense as any man Gritt had ever known.

"Any we know about. "You will need to stay below three hundred feet to the coast and then climb. That will take you below the fixed radar."

"We didn't have time to change the camera package on the plane," replied Kennedy. Optimum altitude for this package will be nine thousand feet AGL. The targets all seem to be remote enough that there should be no low-level air traffic in the areas."

"What is the distance, round trip, using this route?" asked the second major. Gritt guessed that he was both the co-pilot and the mission's intelligence commander.

"To the farthest target, nine-hundred-sixty miles."

The two pilots looked at each other and shrugged. "Might as well have them fuel the axillary tanks. We could probably make it without, but if we have to outrun a MIG or dodge any weather, we can use the extra fuel."

"What is the best estimate of weather over the targets?" asked Kennedy.

"The whole region has been under a stable high pressure for the last three days."

Gritt dropped his pencil on the pad in front of him. "We flew that RB-47 out on the ramp the length of Kamchatka yesterday; there was occasional thin cloud cover and almost no wind. If you have to get down in the bushes, to get below any fog, can you still film the targets?"

The sergeant looked at his aircraft commander for permission to speak. Kennedy smiled and nodded. "Sir, I can reconfigure one of the cameras for a thousand feet above ground level. We won't have any redundancy, but at a thousand feet we could see whether there was cream in your coffee."

"That might make sense," offered Gritt, "but this is your mission."

"Sergeant, how long will it take to make the change?"

"Give me a half-hour, Sir. I'm the guy sitting in back with the guns. I don't want to have to fly this again."

"Go get started, Sergeant," Kennedy said. "The men the general is looking for are our men. If we have to go back to find them, we will, but we are pushing our luck on this mission."

"What time do you want to be airborne?" asked Gritt.

"If we are off the ground by noon, we should be back just in time for happy hour," replied Kennedy.

His co-pilot shuffled the materials in front of him into a folder. "That would put the sun at our backs for the photo runs. We should get really good contrast."

"You gentlemen want some lunch before you go?" asked the general's aide.

"Nope, hungry keeps us on our toes," answered Kennedy.

CHAPTER 28

AMUR RIVER BASIN, CHINA AND RUSSIA

GRITT WATCHED THE RB-45 begin its takeoff roll. Paint covered the Air Force markings on the plane, mottled greens and browns on the fuselage and upper surfaces, powder blue underneath. The noise, already ear splitting, exploded as Major Kennedy triggered the JATO rockets attached to the fuselage, giving the heavy plane a boost in power as it rumbled down the runway. The external rockets would be jettisoned as soon as the plane cleared the boat traffic offshore.

The RB-45 scooted across the Sea of Japan at three hundred feet, reaching the Russian mainland in less than an hour. The pilot picked a low spot in the coastal mountain range, climbing only a thousand feet after he was confident that he was inland of any coastal defense radar.

Crossing the border, the crew could pick out the sparkle of sun reflecting from Russian MIGs to their north and Chinese MIGs to their south, both circling high in the clear sky, each watching the other. Cracks in the communist wall were already beginning to show. Once clear of the border, Kennedy allowed the plane to climb until he was two thousand feet above the Chinese plain.

An hour later, his co-pilot picked out the smoke and steam rising from the Chinese city of Yinchuan to their north. Giving the city a wide cushion before turning northwest, they continued their climb. At nine thousand feet, the Amur River was unmistakable as was the gap in the forest where the Trans-Siberian Railroad made its way from the Pacific to Moscow. It was almost exactly three hours from takeoff when the crew picked out the Zeya River's confluence with the Amur and turned back east, their first target only forty miles to the south.

An unplowed rail siding, where a smaller river crossed under the tracks, marked what the crew hoped was access to the first gulag. Through his binoculars the co-pilot picked out a narrow road through the trees and in the distance a large opening. The pilot swung the plane around and lined up on the road. As they crossed the railroad, they activated the cameras, switching them off after less than a minute, as they passed over a large field of collapsed wooden buildings. From almost two miles in the air, it was clear; there was no trace of activity.

They passed over a small settlement along the tracks. Photographing it took only thirty seconds of film. Below them stretched endless forest.

The second rail siding also appeared to be abandoned. From the cockpit, the two-story concrete buildings only a quarter mile from the rail line appeared empty. There was no hint of steam or smoke, heavy snows having crushed the roofs of outlying wooden buildings.

Second growth trees stood where once a rail spur ran to a massive scar in the hillside behind the buildings. Millions of tons of gravel for the rail bed had been extracted from the hill, and all of the large timber cut from the surrounding hills for railroad ties leaving only small trees and brush even a half century after the railroad was built. They made a single photo pass over the unoccupied facility.

"Nice day for flying," offered the sergeant from the tail gunner's compartment. "I looked this one over really good. There hasn't been any activity down there in years."

Kennedy looked down at the map strapped to a tiny folding table. "I hope this trip wasn't a waste of time. I know General Gritt by reputation. If we don't find Amur-3 here, he will just send us out again."

"Seems to me, Sir, that's what they pay us for. Besides, if it was the three of us down there somewhere, we would be praying that the folks back home were looking for us."

The co-pilot was studying his map. "We need to divert to the north for about ten minutes to bypass what appears to be a town just down the tracks."

"What the hell?" Kennedy said. "Let's get it on film. The men in the photo lab can look for some sign of an old gulag."

"OK, camera's on in about six minutes," replied the co-pilot. "I just worry when we fly over some place that may have a telephone."

A lumber town came into view. Small roads stretched out from the rail yard onto hills denuded of trees. The camera pass took a minute.

From the tail, the sergeant called, "There has to be a dozen small roads stretching out into the hills. Suppose we should follow a couple of the larger ones to see if one of them leads to this Amur-3 place?"

"I don't think so," replied Kennedy.

"I agree," offered the man in the co-pilot's seat. There are probably a thousand people in a town that large. It just doesn't look like a place the Russians would stash American prisoners, too many eyes. Someone could see something and accidentally spill the beans." The co-pilot dropped the dividers he'd been using to measure map distances into a pocket. "The next two hundred miles are all forest. The last target is about halfway to the next town."

Fifteen minutes later, a large lake began to emerge from what looked like surface haze in the distance. The co-pilot studied the hills below. "We have some surface wind out of the east down there. It is kicking up some snow."

"Keep an eye on the tracks. We're still looking for a rail siding."

"Hot damn," exclaimed the co-pilot. "There is a siding coming up and there appear to be a couple of rail cars sitting there."

Kennedy began a wide turn to the right, giving him a better

view of what his co-pilot was watching. "We will set up for a pass over the rail siding. We can shoot the whole thing in ten seconds."

From the tail came a call. "There is a road from the siding going inland toward that frozen lake. The road begins just east of the siding and runs northeast toward the end of that lake."

"All right let's shoot the whole thing. Did anyone see any smoke in the distance?"

"You probably wouldn't see any with the wind," offered his co-pilot.

"I can see the road," replied Kennedy. "I will slow us and then hold us over the road; film everything until I say stop. On my mark, three two one, camera's on."

Kennedy found that he was fighting a strong wind from the east as he tried to stay on the northeast track. "It's blowing at least thirty up here. You couldn't feel it when we were nose into the wind."

"The wind is smoking on the ground," offered the sergeant. "The trees along that lake are whipping. The lake is completely blown clear of snow. It's so clear you can see huge rocks and fallen trees under the ice."

Two minutes later, Kennedy started tiny turns left and right. "Camera's off. Dammit, I lost the road."

"It just ended," came a call from the tail. "But you hit the jack-pot. There is a small clearing in the trees with two-story buildings and some smaller structures. The road leads right into the clearing and there are vehicles parked beside the buildings. I can see smoke or steam coming from at least two."

Kennedy turned to the man at his right. "You're the mission commander, Monty, what's next?"

"I think we should make a wide circle and come in over that frozen lake. Let's drop down to a thousand feet and buzz whoever is down there. Might as well fire up the other camera and get some close-ups while we are at it. With the trees and the wind, they won't hear us coming."

"OK, if we are going to do this, let's make it pay. I will slow us to one hundred fifty knots. That clearing can't be more than a mile in diameter. Fire the camera on my call. We should get everything from the lake to the end of the clearing in two minutes."

Kennedy swung the plane to the right, studying the hills between the clearing and the railroad. "We are going to have to climb like hell to get over those hills."

The mission commander laughed. "Aren't you the one who always describes this type of problem as the difference between flying and driving a bus?"

They took their time setting up the camera run. Kennedy descended into the narrow valley where a river flowed from the frozen lake. Wind bounced the 60,000-pound aircraft. He dropped the flaps ten degrees to increase lift as the plane started over the lake. He checked his watch. It took almost two minutes to reach the spot where the road skirted the lake. "Camera's on," he ordered.

From a thousand feet above the ground, no detail escaped the men in the plane or the camera. The road skirted the lake for less than a mile and then twisted through the forest for four more. Just before three concrete buildings came into view, a guard tower stood at treetop level, no one visible in the howling wind. There were old wooden buildings that all showed signs of recent repair. As the Tornado raced over, a man standing behind one of the buildings looked up.

"Camera's off," called Kennedy, "hold on."

He pushed the throttles to full take off power; his heart pounding in his chest as the jet engines slowly spooled up. At 70 percent power, he turned toward the lowest hill in front of the plane and began to climb. The plane accelerated slowly, the flaps improving lift, but holding down airspeed. Kennedy watched the ground rising to meet them, even as the plane clawed for the sky.

Kennedy lowered the nose, increasing airspeed while the plane closed on the rising hills in front of them. He bumped the flap handle to full up just as he jerked back on the yoke. The Tornado's nose turned skyward. Below the left wing, the tops of the trees crept from two hundred feet below the aircraft to a hundred feet. Out of the windscreen the blowing tops of the trees on the ridgeline were still above the cockpit. Instinctively he slammed the throttles forward, realizing they weren't going to move any further.

From the co-pilots seat, he heard praying. "Lord, please, I don't want to join the men being held down there."

The treetops were now only ten feet below the wings. The plane was still climbing but the airspeed indicator was falling like a brick dropped from the top of a building, the weak buffet of a stall starting to shake the plane. In five seconds or less they were going to fall out of the sky just like that brick. Kennedy began counting, "One-one thousand, two-one thousand, three-one thousand."

At five, Kennedy pushed the nose down. The Tornado rolled into controlled flight, just over the tree covered hills.

"When you get a chance, Sir, pull over at the first filling station so that I can clear the pine needles out of the gun barrels?"

"Sorry about that, Sergeant. I was counting on the wind on the nose to slow us, but that meant flying into rising terrain. Maybe we should have started the photo run from the other direction, but I wanted to make sure we got the entire camp."

"You think I am shitting you, Sir? We drug the tail right through the trees at the top of that hill."

"Write me up, Sergeant. Send your report to the mission commander's office. You might have to wait a bit for any action, though, I think Monty just had a heart attack."

The sergeant laughed. "Did you see the sign painted on top of the front building?"

"No, I was a little busy."

"I don't read Russian, Sir, but there was a word in Russian followed by a three. Can we go home now?"

"On our way. We will follow the exact same routing." Kennedy climbed to 7000 feet and headed southeast.

The plane was south of Yinchuan, turning east when the sergeant reported company. Two tiny specs were falling out of the sky behind the plane. "Gentlemen, we have some Chinese company coming." The sergeant raised his well-used binoculars to study the approaching planes. "Two MIG-15's painted green, not silver."

Monty looked over at the pilot. "How do you feel about the fuel if we make a run for it?"

"We might make it, but it will be really close. We didn't plan on head-winds."

"All right, I am going to try to talk our way out of this."

Monty switched the radio to the Chinese air-to-air frequency and began a deliberate transmission in Mandarin. An exchange began, that lasted for five minutes, the gap between the Chinese fighters and the Tornado disappearing.

The two fighters moved to less than three miles behind the Tornado, and then took up stations to the left and right.

"I don't know what you told those boys, but it isn't raining bullets back here yet. They are sitting to either side, herding us." The officers could hear the stress in the sergeant's voice.

"I told them that we are a test flight of a reverse engineered American Tornado bomber out of Fushon. I told them we were having engine problems and asked them for an escort. One of the Chinese pilots recommended staying away from any major towns or cities in case we need to bail out."

Kennedy looked in awe at Monty Chin, next to him. "Thank you, Sir."

"This only bought us fifteen minutes, if I guess right. Those guys out there are probably on the radio right now, checking out our story."

Kennedy glanced down at the map strapped to his leg. "The Russian border is still a half hour out."

"When they come at us, we will have to make a run for it. In the interim, we are conserving fuel," replied Chin. He paused. "It will make for a bigger fire when we hit the ground."

What do you think they will do when we don't turn south?"

"When we get close to the border, I'll call the Russians and tell them that we are an experimental bomber that strayed over the border into China by mistake. I will tell them we are being chased by Chinese fighters and ask them to put some MIGs in the air to scare them off. Be ready to pedal as fast as you can when I call."

The follow up call from the Chinese fighters came before it was expected. Monty asked for fifteen minutes to try to arrange a radio relay with mechanics at their base and then switched to a Russian ground control frequency and made his call. "Turn on all of the navigation lights," he ordered, then start a slow turn toward Vladivostok and pour the coal to it."

Black smoke billowed from the four engines, as they struggled toward full power. Behind them, the two MIGs rolled to the south as they had expected the larger plane to do. Monty switched back to the Chinese frequency, explaining that their base recommended more fuel to keep the engines cooler.

The Tornado stretched its lead over the Chinese fighters to more than five miles before the Chinese pilots figured out what was going on. As the Tornado flashed over the invisible line that separated The Soviet Union and China, six silver streaks rolled over from well above them and dove toward the border. As the Tornado streaked under the Russian fighters, Kennedy turned the plane straight east toward the Sea of Japan only a hundred miles away. He pulled the power back to reduce the smoke, diving toward the cover of the forest below.

"Major Chin," came a call from the tail, "I still feel better when Major Kennedy is flying but turning a language scholar into a pilot was one of the smartest things that I have ever seen the Air Force do."

"Thanks Sergeant. It makes you wonder what might have happened if we had put Japanese American pilots in the air in World War II."

CHAPTER 29

GENERAL MOLOVIC SNUFFED out his cigarette. Inside, his stomach churned, both from the message he'd received that morning, and from what he'd just seen. In almost seven decades of life, he had never struggled with what was right and wrong. Duty always directed his actions, but duty was becoming a confusing concept.

On the day of his marriage, he and his beloved wife sung that old peasant song, "Holly Mother Russia." His fellow cadets formed an honor guard to escort them to the train for a honeymoon at her parents' dacha in the Crimea. Now, she was gone. The same goons that turned his life inside out arrested Sofi. She'd died of a heart attack in the car.

Decades in uniform demanded that he march into the camp commander's office and report the over-flight. Those bastard Americans were rubbing salt into his wounds, flying right over the prison. He and Sofi had given. Both of their sons died fighting as Russian armies smashed Berlin, and now Sofi was gone in one more insane internal fight among Russians.

The door in the administrative building banged open. Rasputin flanked by two guards stormed into the courtyard. For the fifth time in two weeks, Rasputin waved his pistol.

"Do you have the courage to use that? Offered Molovic.

"Escort the general to the interrogation room. Make sure his hands and feet are secured," ordered the colonel, his face scarlet. "I will be along in a minute or two."

❄

Rasputin lashed out with his belt, knocking Molovic's hat from his head, opening a gash in his scalp. The second swing slashed open the general's cheek.

"That plane was one of yours, wasn't it?" screamed Rasputin. "Your influence over your men has made you some kind of God; they are more loyal to you than Russia. What are they going to do, bomb this place and kill us all?"

Molovic licked the blood dripping down his face and onto his lips.

"I am going to report that pilot to Moscow. By tomorrow, he will be in a cell next to yours."

Molovic's hands were chained above his head, his feet to the floor, Rasputin ordering his restraint. If his feet had been free, he would have kicked the little prick in the balls. He could feel his hands wrapping around Rasputin's neck, choking the life out of him. Molovic looked up to make sure his hands were still restrained, the thought so real.

"I wouldn't do that Colonel Rasputin," he replied. "You have no idea who was flying that plane. I have three sons of senior ministers to Premier Khrushchev in my squadrons. Any one of them might be saying goodbye. You started this. You better make very sure that you don't elevate it too far. There are men in the Kremlin that would be happy to step on any pissant colonel that fucks with their families."

"You and your American compatriots will all admit your guilt before I leave. When I get to Moscow, I am never coming back to this wilderness hell hole, unless it is to shit on your grave, Molovic."

"It is still *General* Molovic, Colonel Rasputin. I don't understand your hatred of the Far East. It is all part of Russia."

Rasputin lashed out with his belt again, opening a cut on

Molovic's chin. "Then I will explain." Rasputin pushed his face close to the general's.

Molovic closed his eyes and shook his head. "Listening to your babble will be a waste of my precious time."

Rasputin pulled away, his face scarlet. "We could bury you tonight."

"We will see who is buried and when, Colonel."

"I am through coddling you, General. When you leave this room, it will not be in that grand uniform you work so hard to maintain. It will be in pajamas, like the rest of the prisoners. You will work with your hands just like the other enemies of Russia. You will be interrogated every day until you sign your confession."

"You are going to torture a general of the Air Force, Colonel, without permission of your masters in Moscow?"

"I am going to do whatever I have to."

❀

The door to the cafeteria creaked open, and Molovic was shoved into the room. He wore the same striped pajamas as the American prisoners eating their lunch. His feet were bare. He found a seat at a small table in the corner, alone, the other prisoners watching.

McGrady and Davis also watched, their rice half-eaten. "A plant," offered Davis. "They put him in here to check up on us."

"I don't understand," replied McGrady.

"In the old camps, they put people in with us that were obviously Russian. They were there to check on escape plans and to talk up how much better our lives would be if we cooperated. I haven't seen one in years."

"Two things, Colonel. First, I don't think anyone here is going to really trust a Russian general. Secondly, I am new here, but didn't you say that there was nowhere to go if we did get out of here?"

"Then why is he here?"

"I met the general the first day we landed in Khabarovsk. If you can help me over to his table, let's find out. It might help if we treated the general to some rice."

Davis helped McGrady into a chair next to Molovic, who used a rag to wipe away the blood dripping from his fresh wounds. McGrady introduced the two men, as Lt. Carter placed a bowl of rice with fish broth in front of the newcomer. Carter found a chair and seated himself, as the general explained his new status in three sentences. He closed with, "The Politico is pissed off that one of my pilots buzzed the prison this evening, you know, to say goodbye."

The general began eating the tasteless goo, as did McGrady. After a couple of minutes, Davis went back to his table followed by Carter. Without looking up, Molovic whispered, "If Rasputin knew that it wasn't one of mine, he would piss his pants."

McGrady, whose mouth was full of rice, managed to mumble, "Oh."

"The jet that tried to blow the roof off this afternoon was one of your B-45's, I think you call it a Tornado. There were glass camera windows in the fuselage. I think your folks are coming to get you." The general went back to eating.

CHAPTER 30

FAIRBANKS, ALASKA

GRITT FOUND PLENTY of time to study the photographs. It was a 3000-mile flight back to Fairbanks, more than seven hours locked away with the Blackbirds in their cramped cage.

Before he left, he'd dictated a comprehensive report and handed it to Major Chin. It was to be encoded at the American embassy in Tokyo and sent to his boss, the Director of the CIA.

The two ELINT operators with him couldn't really understand how a pilot could get claustrophobia, since pilots spend so much time in an enclosed space. His explanation of being able to see outside and having control of the plane were foreign concepts to the men.

All three men kept up a steady banter. The electronic techs discussed the details and nuances of their intercepts as the general pulled one photo after another from an envelope, making notes on the back. Three hours later the exhausted general finally fell asleep in his seat.

The techs covered the sleeping man with a blanket then tugged a worn file from between two radios. They spent the rest of the trip working on their plan to use surveillance technology to get rich in Las Vegas.

The RB-47 touched down at seven in the evening. To Gritt, the four days he was gone seemed like a month. He didn't bother to go by his office. He needed a drink, one away from the people he served with. He parked his old jeep on the street and headed into his favorite bar. He ordered a Jack and water from the bartender, and then sloughed off his coat. "You can't carry that pistol in here," laughed the bartender. "The rule applies to everyone."

Gritt unbuckled the holster around his waist and handed the Model 11 automatic to the bartender who hung it on a peg behind the bar. Picking up his drink, he headed for his table, stopping short. Carmen sat in the corner booth, working on a margarita.

"What are you doing here?" he asked.

"I figured when you didn't get back yesterday, and your office nervously told me not to worry, that you would need a drink when you got in. I just wanted to protect your reputation."

Chad's strange smile and questioning eyes coaxed her to finish.

"Don't you know that drinking alone is a sure sign of being an alcoholic?"

Chad leaned over and kissed his wife, noticing that she'd taken the time to find something tight and low cut before leaving the house.

"Isn't there a basketball game tonight?" asked Chad.

"That was last night. The replacement coach kept your son on the bench, and we still won. It was a good experience for him. And, in case you are wondering, when I heard you might fall out of the sky today, I put the kids on a flight down to visit their grandparents in Anchorage. It's spring break. I figure you are going to be buried every day, but the nights are mine for three whole days."

Chad slipped into the booth next to his wife, slipping his hand under the table and onto her thigh. She put hers on top of his and squeezed.

"Welcome back, soldier," said Carmen. "We are going out for dinner, but we don't want to be home too late." She pushed her face against his shoulder and then slid it up to where she could sneak a quick kiss on his cheek. Chad was not the kind of man who felt comfortable with public displays of affection.

Gritt burst through his office door a little before seven the next morning. While most of the building was just coming alive, his office was humming. Gritt poured a cup of coffee from the fresh pot on the bookcase and stuck his head into Dan Greiwe's office on the way to his own. "Dan, give me the thumbnail version," he said.

"The director's office wants to know if there is a C-123 transport in Alaska. It will be easier to requisition for whatever you are contemplating. His staff indicated that there are six stationed in Anchorage.

I have a phone number for you from the Director himself pertaining to whatever team you are trying to pull together. I have a name of someone who can get you any special weapons that the team needs. Oh, and your friend Mrs. Wilson called twice on the radio. She wants you to give her a call tonight around six. How was your trip?"

"Grab a cup. I'll fill you in."

The day ended at seven, not because there wasn't more to do, but because they ran out of time to coordinate with the people east of the Mississippi. Chad turned into his driveway, the auxiliary gas heater under the passenger's seat, combined with the heater that came with the old jeep, barely able to keep the windows clear. A cold air mass rolled in from the arctic all day, dropping the temperatures to twenty-two below zero. It brought a smile to Chad's face; he just hoped that it was just as cold in the Amur basin.

He hung his heavy overcoat in the hall closet and flipped the heavy fur hat he substituted for his regulation Air Force cover onto the shelf above the hangers. In the living room, Carmen sat on the coach, her feet folded under her, a crocheted blanket covering her body and legs. Across from her, Susan McGrady rocked slowly in the old maple rocking chair. "Can you tell me anything?" she asked.

Chad sighed, an obvious sign to Susan that there was either no news, or what news he was about to offer was not good. "Susan, you need to remain positive. In the last three days, more than fifty men have been working on finding Pat and his crew."

"Did you find them? Are they alive? If I at least knew that, it would be easier."

"Susan, you will be the first to know when I have something solid. I spent the day talking with people from DC to San Diego working on the problem."

Carmen came to his rescue. "Chad didn't mean that Pat and his crew are a problem. What he means is that this is no different than any other day in our lives. With the men we love doing the work they do; we have to accept that we will be treated like mushrooms. Learning to live in the dark is part of the deal."

"I suppose I could make some wiseass comment about bullshit, but I really realize that you can't tell me anything," offered Susan. "I just wanted to see your eyes when you delivered the company line. Your eyes didn't tear up. I will take that as a good thing."

Susan rose, picking up her fur coat from the chair next to her.

"Why don't you stay for dinner?" asked Carmen. "We were going to grill some steaks, but with the weather I decided to fry them Mexican style with onions and peppers."

"Thanks, but I promised Rick's girlfriend that I would pick her up for dinner. We will be meeting that village girl that Bob Walsh has been seeing."

Chad helped the woman into her coat and walked her to the door. He hadn't noticed her car parked across the road as he drove in. Susan turned and kissed Chad on the cheek. "You are in for a treat. That saucy wife of yours is going to cook dinner in a negligée. I ruined your surprise homecoming when she threw on that robe when I arrived."

Susan couldn't hide the tears in her eyes. Chad took her arm, then walked the woman to her car and waited until she started it before jogging back through the bitter air and into the house. Telling Susan that he knew that Pat was still alive but that she might never see him again was worse than letting her worry. There was nothing that he could say that was right.

"I didn't know that Bob Walsh was seeing a village girl," he blurted, as he dug his old wool sweater from the closet and walked back into the living room.

"Susan is talking about Dr. Imanov. Don't you remember introducing Christine and Bob at the Chamber of Commerce dinner?"

Chad remembered, but it didn't matter. Carmen threw the robe over the back of the couch and slipped her black apron over her new red silk negligée. "Here, tie this in back for me," she requested.

Chad could tell that there was little in front, under the apron, by studying the back which did little more than turn his wife's curves a pale shade of red. "Aren't you going to be cold, dressed like that?"

"Not while I am cooking. You are going to get a fire started, and then come in and open the wine." Carmen turned to face her husband and wrapped her arms around his neck. "When are you going after them? You know you should leave missions like that to men who can at least run. But I know better than to try to talk you out of going. When are you leaving?" She reached up and kissed him and turned for the stove before he could see her tears.

Chad laid a fire in minutes. He struck a match and touched the edge of a page of advertising from the *Fairbanks News Miner* crumpled under the kindling. He waited a moment to make sure that the fire caught and headed for the kitchen.

Chad forced himself toward the table where a bottle of cabernet waited. He avoided staring at his wife who was busy with a frying pan at the stove. He fumbled with the corkscrew, jerking the cork from the bottle with a *pop*. "Christine would get a hoot out of being described as a village girl. After years of college in southern California and Med School, Fairbanks is about as close to the village as she wants to live."

Chad filled a glass and placed it on the counter next to Carmen, then stepped back.

"I would love to see your face right now, Chad Gritt," laughed his wife. "You got really quiet when you stopped behind me just now."

"Guilty as charged. You haven't lost a thing since we visited that beach house in Mexico back in 1941."

"Just keep your hands to yourself until after dinner, Romeo."

The next morning, Chad dropped his toothbrush into the porcelain holder above the sink. He slipped on a pressed shirt and began buttoning. "I talked to Ellen Wilson on the radio yesterday. She needs some help, so I thought I would fly up there tomorrow. I will be back by dark. I can't wait to see what you have planned for dinner."

"I was thinking of a bowl of oatmeal, but you will like the presentation," laughed Carmen.

"You know, I love you," uttered her husband as he tightened his tie. "It has been a long time since we had time alone. Still, I'm happy the kids will be home the day after tomorrow."

❀

Gritt dropped onto the wooden swivel chair behind his desk. He picked up the family picture from the corner and stared into the faces of a teenage boy, younger daughter, and dark-haired wife. He sipped his strong black coffee from an ancient mug stenciled with the sketch of a World War II P-38 fighter. He twisted his body to the right, relieving a small fraction of the permanent pain in his left hip.

"You ready for me, boss?" asked Dan Greiwe from the doorway.

Gritt put the picture back in its normal place above his phone. "Yup, where are we this morning?"

Dan dropped into the seat across the desk, handing a small stack of sheets to his boss. "The folks in DC finally got it on the C-123. We can't fly non-stop from here to Japan, and even with refueling in the Aleutians it is just too tight. They have asked for the loan of one belonging to the South Korean Air Force. They promised that any South Korean insignia would be removed, and that if we lost the bird to give them a new one."

"Did the South Koreans agree?"

"Not yet, we only asked a few hours ago, but we made it clear that the plane needed to be at Chitose by the end of the week."

"What about the team?"

"That retired officer, Lt. Colonel Pulver, we talked to yesterday sent us a telex this morning. He is definitely in and has selected a second-in-command, some master sergeant he served with in Korea. They were both Rangers. They are putting together four more shooters and one medic. The boss has given them his checkbook to make this happen. They will be here on Thursday. Somewhere, they requisitioned a DC-6 and a pilot who is checked out in both the six and C-123. The pilot has a lot of off-runway experience."

Gritt drew a line through three of the items on the yellow pad in front of him. "What about the Bombardier snowcat?"

"The U.S. Army in Korea has a dozen of the B-12 models. If we get the C-123 from the Koreans, then we will borrow one of theirs."

"You know, there is a damned good chance that we will leave it behind after the mission," replied Gritt.

Greiwe smiled. "I didn't think anyone needed to know that before we got back."

Gritt crossed off another item. "And weapons, where are we on them?"

"The boss is sending a dozen High Standard .22 silenced pistols with Pulver. He also found two Winchester model 70's with scopes silencers and ten silenced M-1 carbines. He gave Pulver access to the armory at Fort Ord, for anything else he needs."

"With you and me, that's a total of ten. Have you done a weight and balance yet on the C-123?"

Greiwe slid a graph across the table. "We are good. We even have room for four barrels of fuel and two pumps. We could position them under the wings before we head for the gulag. The pilot could spend his waiting time pumping fuel. We will only need extra avgas; there will be plenty of jet fuel for two takeoffs.

"Dan, I am going to fly out to visit Ellen Wilson tomorrow. Just stay on this. Keep up the appearances of business as usual so we don't invite any eyes that we don't need but stay on this."

Gritt stood and headed for the coat rack.

"If I need you, where do I find you, Sir?"

"I am going home to change and then take Carmen out for an early lunch. You know where to look. After that I am going flying. I am going to try to find some glare ice and practice landing on it."

"The folks at Fairchild Aircraft sent out a flyer some months ago about a program to put some kind of skis on their C-123 airplane. Do you want me to follow up with them?"

Gritt paused at the door. "Nope, we don't have time. If that lake is covered in snow, we are shit out of luck."

CHAPTER 31

WOLF PACK LAKE, ALASKA

GRITT CRAWLED INTO the back seat, lifting four jerry jugs of avgas into the luggage compartment. He figured he couldn't go wrong with an extra twenty gallons of gas. He was airborne ten minutes later.

Gritt looked down at the Bettles airport an hour and a half into his flight. He glanced at the map in his lap and turned more west. Ellen's lake should only be another twenty minutes.

Right on time, a frozen lake appeared over the cowling. He circled, picking out the cabin on the south shore. There was little obvious wind in the trees, but the bouncing airplane told him that it was blowing. He circled a second time, looking for smoke coming from the cabin.

Below on the lake, a man stood, a rifle over his shoulder. *What the hell,* thought Gritt. He circled to take one more look. Near the shore, about a hundred yards from where the man stood, Ellen was walking and waiving at the plane. Behind her, two rifle targets were pinned against the steep bank.

For practice, he touched down on a spot blown clear of snow, the skis making a scraping sound. Moments later, his skis slid up onto a layer of wind-packed snow. He taxied over to where the two people stood waiting, and pulled the fuel mixture to off, shutting down the engine.

"Looks like a beautiful day to fly," greeted Ellen, giving Gritt a huge hug.

"It is. I've flown in some lousy weather, and I have been through some really rotten landings, but almost any day is a good day to fly," replied Gritt.

Ellen turned to the tall dark-haired man next to her. "Anton, this is Chad Gritt."

Anton extended his hand, his brown eyes studying the man in front of him. "In Russia, a general would demand that he be introduced as a general."

"And you have to be Anton Bidkov, a recent immigrant to the United States," replied Gritt.

"I was teaching Anton how to shoot a rifle with a telescopic sight, but it will only take a few minutes to get some coffee heated." Ellen turned toward the cabin.

Bidkov slipped the rifle sling over his shoulder and motioned Gritt in front of him. "Let's talk while we walk," answered Chad, choosing instead to walk next to the Russian. "I only have a couple of hours before I have to get back."

"I am listening."

"Ellen tells me that somewhere out in this lake is the remains of a TU-16 bomber. She also tells me that there is almost nothing left of it. I believe you were the pilot."

Anton nodded. "The rest of my crew died in the wreck. We have found almost no trace of the men."

"I won't try to interrogate you, Anton. I would do a lousy job if I tried, but how many men did you lose in the crash?'

"Five."

"Ellen tells me that you aren't going back."

"There is only one thing that would take me back. I would like to confirm where my wife, Natalya, is. Ellen thinks she is dead. It would confirm my government's latest betrayal."

"But you want to stay in the States?"

"I would like to try to make a new life with Ellen." Anton stopped, a frown on his face. "Until I know what happened to Natalya…"

He hesitated only a few seconds. "Maybe I can buy one of those amazing de Haviland Beavers that brought the generator and make a living flying people around Alaska."

"Have you ever flown a small plane?"

"Only when I first started flight training."

"Ellen," Chad yelled, "get the coffee started, were going to get Anton back on the bronc that threw him."

"Come on Anton, let's go commit an act of aviation."

Anton looked at Gritt like he was out of his mind. "I don't understand any of your last two sentences."

Gritt turned toward the Cessna. "Do you want to go flying or not?"

Gritt put Anton in the pilot's seat and then slipped into the co-pilot's seat next to him. It took only ten minutes to talk Anton through the controls. With his hands and feet following Anton's movements, Chad smiled as the fellow pilot taxied back, to take off into the wind.

The takeoff was amazingly smooth for a pilot with no time in the aircraft type and no experience on skis. They climbed the plane to two thousand feet to allow Anton room to practice some rolls and turns. The man was a natural.

"Let's fly on up the valley a ways, so we can talk," suggested Gritt.

Anton rolled the aircraft smoothly into a 180-degree turn, his toothy smile reflecting the afternoon sun.

"Here's the deal, Anton. My country is constantly responding to Russia's pronouncements that is has hundreds of new jet bombers and thousands of nuclear bombs ready to drop on us. We fly over the Soviet Union to try to figure out just what the threat is. If we could better understand the Soviet capabilities, we would like to stop those missions. Just about the time you crashed on Ellen's lake, I sent a plane out to try to find the TU-16 you were flying. It was shot down, and now all three men in the crew are being held."

"I am sorry about your crew. Our mission was to drop papers over your base in Fairbanks warning you to stop flying over Russia. My men are dead, yours are in prison. The men who send us sit in their warm offices, or in ornate taverns drinking Scotch or vodka."

"Our intelligence says the engines on the TU-16 are giving your pilots some trouble. Did an engine failure cause your crash?"

"Yes, but it was caused by a bird strike into the engine. The engine exploded, causing a fire inside the plane." Anton looked over at Gritt, pain in his face. "My men burned. I tried to crash through the ice to lose the airplane, but even more to shorten our death."

"Every pilot in the world fears a fire in the air."

"It is even worse than you can imagine."

"My government will want to question you about Soviet air capabilities. You will not be tortured, so I guess you will tell us whatever you feel comfortable telling us. In return, I have assurances that you will be able to stay, but since we don't know how your government will react, we should probably give you a new last name."

"I don't understand."

"Most Russians who come to the States are ignored. But once in a while, your government will send men over here to make sure people they are afraid of don't talk."

Anton nodded. "Will you be there when they question me?"

"No. I probably shouldn't tell you this, but I am going to try to rescue my crew."

"Ellen thinks that Russia holds a number of Americans."

"Not any Americans that they admit to holding. Anyway, I am only going after the three men I lost looking for your plane." Gritt looked around at the snow-covered hills. He hoped it wouldn't be the last time he saw them. "I have a bad leg from the last war. I have a wife and two children. I don't want to go. This mission scares me."

Anton looked at Gritt. "Sometimes you have no choice."

Gritt smiled. "We should probably get back. We don't want to worry Ellen."

Anton rolled the Cessna into a smooth turn and headed back to the lake.

"Does it feel good to be flying again?" asked Gritt.

"You have no idea, General. Thank you."

"Are you willing to meet with the people they will send to Fairbanks to talk to you? If you would like, I can have one of my staff meet with you before they arrive. I will try to arrange for them to sit in on the discussions."

"I will talk to them. But I don't want to end up in some American gulag."

"I will discuss your case with an attorney friend in Fairbanks. This is a national security matter, so he probably can't get any guarantees, but he knows how our system works. I don't think you face any prison time."

Anton greased the Cessna onto the ice, landing smoother than Chad did. They taxied right up to where Ellen waited at the wooden table by the shore.

As they climbed out of the plane, Anton shot the woman a huge smile. "Do you need help turning the plane around?" he asked Gritt.

Ellen managed to carry three scalding cups of coffee toward the Cessna, leaving a brown trail in the snow.

"Yup, thanks for the help. I also have four cans of fuel behind the back seat. I would appreciate you handing them up to me. I will need the extra fuel to get home."

Anton climbed back into the plane, handing the cans out to Gritt. Chad climbed onto the strut as Anton opened the cans, and screwed the spouts in. He handed the first one up to Chad, who spilled a little fuel as he lowered the spout into the opening of the fuel tank.

"Do you know where your men are being held?" asked Anton.

"We have some intelligence on their location. One of our planes flew over the place a few days ago. It was abandoned for some time, but there are definitely people there now."

"Where is this camp?" asked Anton, curious about the Americans ability to mount a rescue in Russia.

"It's northwest of Khabarovsk. Some place called Amur-3." Gritt emptied the first can and lowered it for Anton to grab. Nothing happened. Gritt looked down. Both Anton and Ellen stood frozen, looking at each other."

Finally, Anton looked up, retrieving the empty can and handing a full one up to Gritt. "You have to take me with you," uttered Anton, his voice shaking.

"Let's pour the other two cans in the other wing," suggested Chad, "and then you can tell me why a guy who doesn't want to go back, suddenly wants to go to Siberia."

Chad finished pouring the third, and then the last can of fuel into the pilot's side wing, then climbed down, thankful that it was thirty degrees warmer on Ellen's lake than in Fairbanks. He and Anton resealed the metal cans. Then all three carried cups of coffee to the table.

"What's this about?" asked Gritt.

"Let me go get a map while you two talk," replied Ellen.

"I told you that there is only one reason I would go back," started Anton. "My wife was a scientist who was exiled because she wrote a report that was different than Comrade Stalin wanted to see. She was sent to a gulag in the Far East. She wrote for a while, and then the letters stopped."

Chad sipped the coffee that was barely cooling despite the cold. He waited for more of the story.

Ellen trotted back down the trail, Jack romping at her side. She spread out a map of Russia. "Have you told him?" she asked Anton.

He shook his head, no. "General Gritt, Natalya was sent to the Amur basin. Her letters were from a gulag called Amur-3."

Ellen pointed to four circles Northwest of Khabarovsk. "It has to be one of these gulags."

Chad pointed to the one closest to Khabarovsk, the most isolated camp. "We have determined that this is what they are calling Amur-3."

"Chad, I believe that everyone who was originally imprisoned at Amur-3 was released the year after Stalin died. Those who didn't go home are probably still there," said Ellen.

"Based on the photo we took, there aren't more than a couple of dozen people including the guards. I saw photos from three years ago. The place was abandoned then. Now there is a small group there. There were obvious signs of repair."

"I didn't mean that there were any Russian prisoners," replied Ellen. "All of the gulags have graveyards."

"General Gritt, I need to know if Natalya is really dead," finished Anton.

"We have a full team going in. I don't have room for anyone else on the plane. We will be landing on a frozen lake and then we have to take the prisoners with us when we leave."

Gritt watched the anguish in both Anton's and Ellen's faces. "I will try to find any records of those who died there."

"Do you speak Russian?" asked Anton.

Chad looked at the sky. He'd totally missed that. There was no one on the team who spoke Russian. "No, none of us speak or read Russian."

"If you can't talk to the guards, even if you surprise them, you will have to kill them all or they will fight. You don't know what it is like to be assigned to a place like Amur-3," continued Ellen. "Those who do not fight will be shot after you go."

"What could I tell them that can help?" asked Gritt.

"You won't know until you get there. It will depend on the leaders who survive the assault."

"General, Chad," started Anton, "I need to find out. I owe the Soviet government nothing. Let me be your mouthpiece. There will be hell to pay if you succeed. Still, most of those assigned to this camp are exiles, not politicos. They don't deserve to die because you ordered your planes to fly over Russia."

Chad thought through the plan. Both Anton and Ellen were right, he needed a Russian speaker. That meant someone would have to stay. He would have a couple of hours flying home to figure that out. "Ok, Anton, I will send a plane for you on Friday morning. We will be leaving Fairbanks a day or two later."

Chad turned to Ellen. "Will you be alright out here alone?"

She forced a smile. "I was alone until the plane crashed on the lake. Besides, until Anton knows for sure what happened to Natalya, he will always wonder. It will always be in the background between us."

Chad circled over the lake one more time, rocking his wings. Both Anton and Ellen were out on the lake throwing a stick for that bear that Ellen called a dog.

CHAPTER 32

THE GUARDS CAME for Walsh only an hour after he curled up on his thin mattress. Their courtesy was something new. They waited while he carefully folded his thin blanket at the foot of the bed. He was marched to the interrogation room. He headed for the chair; bracing for what he knew was coming. *It could be worse; they could torture me like the others,* he thought.

The guards grabbed his arms and pushed him toward the concrete wall at the back of the room. There, his hands were manacled to two rings over his head and his feet, to shackles embedded in the floor in front of him. Then both guards left.

Walsh stood against the cold wall for an hour before the door opened. Aunt Star rushed into the room, placing a chair right in front of him.

"I not see darkie man before," she started. Star tugged Walsh's pajama bottoms down where they folded over his feet. Star began to giggle hysterically. "You not so big." Star began unbuttoning her blouse, pulling it from the gray wool skirt she always wore. She threw off her blouse and unclasped her bra, dropping both over the chair back. "You like Russian girl?" Star sat in the chair. She began to fondle him.

"I am engaged to a doctor at home," blurted Walsh.

"This word means you have a wife?"

"Not yet, we will be married next summer." Walsh looked down at Star's face. The woman wasn't as old as he originally thought. *She is attractive,* flashed through his mind. Walsh managed to fight off a sick stimulation and numbing fear. He closed his eyes.

Star giggled, as she saw the first indication that he noticed her. "You want this Russian girl?"

"No," blurted Walsh, "I am waiting for my fiancé." The vision Davis had planted helped him regain control.

"American mens killed my husband. American mens shoot his plane. Now Americans mens should take his place. Russian girls need a man. Beside, you never going home, darkie."

Walsh was over his momentary weakness. The more he ignored Star, the more her hands and lips flew over his body. Every time she touched him, he twisted away, as much as his shackles allowed. Star continued the game, giggling as she became more forceful.

Finally, she stopped, a laugh rumbling from deep within her, ending in a screech. "I now show you what happen when you say no." Star opened the door of a small metal cabinet next to where he was chained. She pulled two coiled cables with brass clamps from the cabinet, clamping one on his left thigh and the other on his genitals, her screech turning into a scream.

She slid her chair next to the box. "Next time you will not say no," she screeched, as she pushed a button in the box, sending electric current racing from clamp to clamp.

The first jolt lasted only seconds; the pain so startling that Walsh made no sound. Star's laugh became hysterical. The next jolt lasted a minute or more, longer than Walsh's brain could contain the pain. His scream drowned out hers. Two-dozen black and white Russian ravens, exploded from their roosting tree a hundred yards from the gulag.

Star quit trying to talk to him. The pain went on until her screeching ended in a fit of gagging and uncontrollable coughing. Star pulled the cables, allowing the clamps to rip flesh as they tore away. She recoiled the cables neatly in the cabinet and stood. She pulled up the front of Walsh's shirt and rubbed her breasts over his chest and then stepped back to admire the pain and terror in his eyes.

The woman turned away, suddenly modest. "I will see you again," she mumbled, as she dressed. Without looking back, she walked from the room.

Walsh didn't have any idea how long he hung in his shackles before the two guards dragged him from the chamber back to his cell. They folded his blanket over him so that the double layers helped shut out the bitter cold of his cell, then they left.

As usual, the cells were unlocked at six. Most of the captives headed to the cafeteria for their breakfast of black bread and tea. Davis and McGrady made their way to Walsh's cell instead. The man lay in a fetal position, drenched in sweat. "It will hurt like hell for a couple of days, before you will want to live again," voiced Davis. "You have to keep eating. Don't let them win by dying."

"I'll bring you some bread and a bottle of water," added McGrady, shocked by the appearance of the tough as nails man in front of him.

The two men walked toward the cafeteria. "He kept his family jewels," observed Davis. "The blanket wasn't soaked in blood."

"I thought that anyone cut that way would die," whispered McGrady.

"Nope, Star ties off the veins and sews them up, just like what they do to a man in some normal medical procedure." Davis looked over at McGrady, studying his face. "Don't try to figure it out. You will just go insane trying to make sense out of any of this. The only way we win is to live and take care of each other. He will want to sign the confession to get out of here, we can't let him do that."

"Is this what happened to the two men who died?"

"One of them was tortured by Star. The other was a former survival trainer. The two men were captives for years, and both spoke Russian fluently." Davis stopped walking.

"Both slipped away one night when they knew that a train was going east, planning on making their way to the coast and stealing a boat. They were going to try for Japan to tell the world what was happening here. The men wore clothes stolen from the laundry so that they could pass for Russian.

"Were they discovered on the train?"

"No, somehow a couple of the guards just happened to be at the rail siding when they tried to slip into an empty boxcar. They were both shot on the spot."

"Is the rail siding always guarded?

"No," replied Davis, "after you have been here a bit longer and we get to know you better, I will have Carter share our intelligence files with you. We have the train schedule nailed. We know every guard by name, and the only time they ever go to the siding is after a train stops."

CHAPTER 33

FAIRBANKS, ALASKA

LT. COLONEL PULVER came with the pedigree of a super soldier, but in person he was the opposite of what everyone expected.
The man was at most, five feet-seven, and soaking wet he couldn't
have weighed one-fifty. His buzz cut hair was gray, as was the slim
mustache above his narrow lips. It was hard to see the pupils of his
strange gray eyes.

The DC-6 pilot was day to Pulver's night. The man had to be in
his fifties, with bulk like a pastry chef who liked his own creations.
He'd been a pilot for TWA before he lost his medical, and before
that a multi-engine pilot in the U.S. Army Air Corps. Gritt had
heard his name before, in clandestine services circles. Jose Martinez
was more Cuban than Cuban American, and with 30,000 hours
in the air, more experienced than everyone in Gritt's command
combined. His bald head glistened with sweat from the exertion of
his own laughter.

The two men sat with the general in the back corner booth of
the Cottage Bar. While Gritt nursed his drink, the other two, were
working on their third; several previous missions together welding
them into brothers in arms.

"The first place we crossed paths was in Indonesia, fighting the
locals who had declared independence," replied Jose Martinez. "We

were kinda' on loan to the Dutch, who were trying to hold onto the colony."

"Jose moved us around, using anything that would fly, and my unit would help local Dutch troops chase down rebels," Pulver said. "By the end, people were dying by the hundreds. Our last mission was to take thirty commandos behind Indonesian lines. We raided a prison camp where a hundred Dutch and British mercenaries were being held. Everyone knew the war was lost, and our side was worried that they would be slaughtered the day after an armistice was signed.

"We got a reputation for that kind of mission. We have worked together in five or six other fights, some you probably know about and a couple, we didn't want to discuss with the U.S. Government. There are always details that are better kept between the shooters."

Gritt smiled, documenting that the not-so-subtle message got through.

"My sergeant and I spent some time in a Chinese Communist prison," Pulver said. "Jose here plopped some beat-to-shit DC-3 onto an abandoned airstrip with a dozen of my old troops and got us out. We know what your guys are going through. When Allen called, it was a no-brainer. We both spent some early years on the wrong side, brutes fighting people trying to live their own lives, their own way. Since then, we have made sure we were on the right side, and on this, we are. The commies killed as many civilians in the Second World War as Hitler."

Gritt finished his drink and reluctantly ordered another. Both kids were singing in a concert that night, and he needed to be there. If everything went to shit in Russia, he wanted them to remember that he was there. Still, this was the time and place to discuss some off the record details.

"Tomorrow morning, a man is going arrive," Gritt said. "He is going with us. I am not telling Allen that he is going. But you need to know, that technically, he is probably still on the rolls as a Russian Air Force Major. He has a personal mission to this Amur-3 place and a personal beef with the people who commanded him. This is one of those details you referred to earlier. Besides, we need a Russian speaker. The boss would like to do this with as little loss of life on the other side as possible. We don't want the Russians holding a press conference with a pile of dead guards behind them."

"General Gritt," replied Pulver, "even if we have complete surprise, there will be sentries that we need to dispose of."

"Eric is right," added Martinez. "If this camp is anything like some of the others we have taken, the men we are rescuing aren't going to give those who have been tormenting them goodbye cards."

Gritt sat back in his chair, realizing that there were probably a lot of things were missed in the original plan to rescue his men. "I don't want to leave that pile of bodies that the boss is worried about."

"General Gritt," started Jose.

"On this operation, Chad, would probably be more appropriate, since none of us will be in uniform and no one will carry any ID."

"We understand the politics, Chad. But if you think Eric here is going to shoot any of our own guys to stop them, then you better call this whole thing off."

"General, we know your reputation as well. On the ground as a shooter in the Aleutians, stealing an airplane right off a Japanese Air Base, strategizing the surrender of Japanese on Okinawa, pinpointing enemy command and control positions in Korea, you are a legend. You fired your rifle. You shot down enemy planes. Sometimes you hate to pull the trigger, but you still do it to complete the mission."

Chad thought about the crazy mission that he led into mainland Japan during the war and how a half dozen Japanese radio operators and guards, really just young boys, died so that no one was left alive to disrupt the mission. "We do what we have to do," he agreed.

"Now it is going to be damned cold where we are going. How many of your men have cold weather gear?"

Jose smiled at Gritt. "Until Allen called, we were all in the canal zone, trying to figure out how to keep the rebels supported by the communists from ousting Batista from Cuba."

"First thing in the morning, get your troops together and I will have my aide, Major Dan Greiwe, escort all of you to a great surplus store downtown. Buy what he suggests, not what they want to sell you. And if you wouldn't mind, I need to outfit the Russian who is coming with us. He is almost exactly my size, six-two, one-ninety-five, and lean. Please pick up one of whatever you buy for yourself for him."

Eric Pulver polished off his third drink and held up a finger for another. "Any chance that this Russian officer is still playing for the other side?"

"Based on what I know, I don't think so, but he will be unarmed."

"He's your guy, General. If someone needs to shoot him, it's up to you."

Gritt rose; he barely had time for dinner before the concert. He couldn't imagine having to tell Ellen that he killed Bidkov, but she was probably the only woman in the world who might understand. "I concur. The Russian is my problem. I will keep him close and keep an eye on him, but I am counting on your team for help. Let me give you two some ideas for dinner."

Jose held up his hand. "Chad, remember where we came from, the time change is deadly. We ate our second lunch a couple of hours ago. We're having dinner right now."

✻

The same ski equipped plane used to deliver the generator buzzed the cabin an hour after first light. Ellen picked up the two cups and placed them into the pail she used for dishes.

"I know you have to go," she said. "Are you ready for what you might find?"

Anton picked up the coat that Ellen gave him. "No. I don't think you can ever be ready for something you pray never happened. But I need to go."

"You know that there is a good chance that some men are going to die on this mission?" asked Ellen.

"I have been thinking about that. If your friend Gritt's people are really good and they achieve surprise, it will be Russians who die. Russians seem to attract death."

Ellen walked to the waiting plane with Anton, the throb of the huge rotary engine echoing through the trees. "You just make sure that you aren't one of those Russians who die," she ordered.

As the Canadian built bush plane lifted from the lake, Ellen watched, her tears soaking the scarf pulled up to protect her face from the bitter cold prop wash as the plane taxied away.

❁

Gritt was at the Fairbanks airport, as the ski-equipped Beaver slipped and slid to the shack that served as the offices of INTERIOR AIR. The pilot was the first one out of the plane, running behind an old military boom truck to take care of a nature call. Anton climbed out of the plane; the same puffy down coat wrapped around him that he had worn on Chad's visit. He tugged, trying to close the zipper.

Chad waited for the pilot to return. Anton shook hands with the pilot before Chad handed the man a crisp hundred-dollar bill. "That should cover the flight."

"I'm available to fly your pilot friend back out when you two are done with whatever you are doing," offered the Beaver pilot. "Things are a little slow now, so I can go almost any time."

"Thanks Jim," said Gritt, leading Anton toward his old jeep.

"Nice flight?" asked Gritt.

"I told your friend, Jim, that I flew your Cessna, so he let me fly most of the trip. That Beaver is built like a Russian airplane; you know, stout. We Russians put huge engines on our planes and push the air out of the way." Anton laughed at the old Russian pilots' joke. Chad joined him, figuring that someday Anton would explain it to him.

"Anton, I am going to take you to my house. Carmen will get you some lunch. I will be back to pick you up at three for a briefing with the team that is going to Amur-3." Gritt stopped for a second before stepping on the starter switch. "You do have a watch?"

Anton pulled up the sleeve of the jacket. "Russia makes the best aviator watches in the world. But I haven't wound it since the crash. What time is it?"

Chad introduced Anton to Carmen who reluctantly agreed to the strange man in the house. All Chad told her was that Anton was a friend of Ellen's. Before leaving for his office, Chad checked to make sure that the jumpers that connected his home telephone to the network were still disconnected. In an emergency, Carmen could use the ring-down circuit from the phone in their bedroom. It connected right into his office on base.

"The C-123 will be in Chitose tomorrow. The track vehicle is already loaded on the plane. When it gets into the hanger in Chitose, a crew will go through the plane with a fine-tooth comb and paint out all of the Korean Air Force markings," said Greiwe. "Lt. Colonel Pulver and his guys rented a couple of trucks. They are out at the gravel pit, test-firing the weapons the boss sent from Seattle."

"How did the shopping go?" asked Gritt, looking through a small stack of telex messages.

"Everyone is set. They bought a lot of wool, and everyone will be wearing matching green down parkas and those ridiculous leather caps with ears. You know, the ones with rabbit fur inside. They have winter boots and gloves with liners."

"Wouldn't white parkas make more sense?" asked Gritt, looking up from the messages.

"Pulver and Sgt. Mosby figured that it wouldn't make much difference at night. I didn't know that you agreed to change the assault to a night operation," said Greiwe.

"Dan, this type of mission is what these guys do. Jose has never landed on ice before, so he figures that day or night won't make much difference." Gritt raised his hand, as Greiwe started to object. "I know, I know, it doesn't make much sense to me either, but both those guys figure that assaulting the gulag in daylight is a lot more dangerous than landing on ice at night."

The meeting that afternoon fleshed in a few more details, including a recommendation by Pulver that they take some stretchers in case some of the prisoners couldn't walk. Gritt hadn't thought about that either.

Gritt briefed Anton who was introduced as a recent immigrant from Russia. The shooters seemed concerned, but Martinez welcomed the fellow pilot with open arms. Originally, Gritt planned to be the co-pilot for the C-123 mission, but with Anton available, they could now share the duties.

Anton and Gritt pulled into the driveway at six. It might have been nice to show Anton one of the Fairbanks restaurants, but Chad insisted on a family meal. Friday was steak night in the Gritt household.

Anton marveled at the double bed and how comfortable the spring mattress was, as Carmen ushered him to his room at nine. On the bed was a duffle bag. Anton began transferring items from three large paper bags of clothes from the shopping trip.

"He is a very nice man," commented Carmen as she climbed into bed.

"I hope so, he certainly has Ellen Wilson's attention. Did he try to use the phone while I was gone?"

"No, the phone was out of service anyway. I'll have to run by the phone company in the morning to report it."

"I'll take a quick look in the morning," committed Chad. "Probably just some frost in the outside connection." He climbed into bed with his wife and switched off the table lamp.

Carmen slid across the bed onto Chad's shoulder. He wrapped his arm around her. "I know you can't talk about this trip, but you better come back."

He kissed her forehead and then tilted her chin to reach her lips. He ran his free hand across her shoulder and down her side. "I'll be back. My office will have updates on when, but they won't have anything for three days. If everything goes as planned, I will be home in four."

He let his hand slip down toward the front of her gown. Carmen caught it and pushed it back onto her side. She said nothing, but he could feel moisture on the shoulder where she pushed her face up onto his neck.

CHAPTER 34

THE FLIGHT TO Chitose took just over sixteen hours, including a stop at the Navy base at Adak in the Aleutian Islands. Everyone aboard was too wound up to sleep except for Jose, who, after briefing Gritt and Anton on the DC-6, proved he could sleep anywhere. An aide to the base commander, curious to find out why they were there, escorted them to a small Japanese inn just off base. The commander had been ordered to "Provide all support necessary," in a directive from the Secretary of the Air Force but knew nothing of the mission. An hour later, Gritt and Greiwe pulled up with two borrowed vans, to take everyone to dinner.

Pulver's shooters ran through the photos and maps provided by Gritt all the way across the Pacific. They felt ready, the mission still two days out. They were disappointed when the Saki stopped flowing at midnight.

While the non-pilots inventoried their gear and arranged for four barrels of fuel and two battery-powered pumps the next morning, the pilots spent hours flying the C-123. After refueling, they parked the plane next to the DC-6.

Anton and the rest of the team moved their small mountain of equipment from the hanger where they were staging the mission. The boxy cargo area of the C-123, already carrying the snowcat, held it all with room to spare. Gritt and Martinez visited the weather office.

"Skies should be clear. We're one day past the full moon, so you should have maximum illumination for the next couple of nights. There is a good chance that, as the high pressure moves east, there will be increasing winds starting tomorrow," offered the briefer. "There is also a chance of some nighttime fog here in the Chitose area, but it shouldn't be heavy."

"When you say wind, what are you talking about?" asked Jose.

"Winds over the target today in the ten to fifteen knot range, from the east. But those could build to twenty-five to thirty late tomorrow."

Gritt looked over at Jose. "We go tonight instead of tomorrow night?" he asked.

Jose nodded his head. "Thanks."

Gritt shook the captain's hand. "Thank you for flying up from Honshu to brief us. There was no one here at Chitose with the clearance for this type of mission."

"Just bring 'em home, General. Monty Chin said to tell you that he and his crew put their butts on the line for this, so he expects the mission to be a success."

The two men made their way back to the hanger. Gritt took Pulver aside and explained the weather.

"Everyone into the cars," called Pulver. "We will need some rest for the mission tomorrow. Since we have nothing else to do, its naptime. I will get you all up at about seven for dinner."

Pulver and Gritt stood as the other eight men on the mission headed for the vans. "For all but Mosby, Martinez and myself," explained Pulver, "this is new for them. If I tell them we are going tonight, none of them will sleep."

"Where did these men come from? On the plane, there was more Spanish than English," observed Gritt.

"All served in the Rangers, and most put that training to work as professional soldiers," replied Pulver. "I looked for colleagues who spoke Russian. There weren't any, so we drew from the men we were training for the Cuban conflict. Our friend Allen is paying well to get your men back, General."

CHAPTER 35

AMUR-3 GULAG

TWO MEN IN the hall were practicing sit-ups. At the other end of the hall, other men spotted each other doing chin-ups. The makeshift gymnasium in the hallway outside their cells was a lifesaver. Even though their bodies were wasted from poor food and brutal treatment, the gym allowed the prisoners to maintain some muscle tone. Those exercising were also sentries.

In the center cell, Lt. Calvin Carter opened a worn newspaper, an old English language edition of Pravda, the official Soviet newspaper. Davis watched his intelligence officer carefully unfolding each page to avoid tearing the soiled and tattered sheets. Carter pointed to tiny dots and dashes, curved and straight above and below certain words and photos.

"The paper's a file of notes on the gulag, our guards and the prisoners," said Carter. "It is also a listing of their ranks and skill sets." McGrady watched as Carter pointed out the names of all of the guards.

"So, this is how you keep track of the men who have been reduced to making us less than human," offered McGrady, scratching at dozens of scabs from rubbed skin.

The night before, Carter and Davis used one of the knives in the kitchen to cut the cast from his body. No one knew if the ribs healed, but McGrady's body was withering from inactivity. "You have been here long enough to be read into the security files," offered Davis, as he sawed away at the plaster cast. "You are the second ranking officer. If something happened to me, you would take command."

McGrady ran his finger down one page. "Who dreamed this up?"

"One of the men who died. He spent a month training Carter here on the system before he made his run for it," answered Davis.

"How does the system keep track of our own men?"

Carter pointed at one of the symbols and then turned to the first page of the paper. From the top, he traced his finger over every line of every story, looking for that same symbol. By the time he reached the bottom, he'd pointed to letters that phonetically spelled out Colonel Robert Davis, Air Force, pilot.

With McGrady watching, he quickly ran through the names of the other prisoners in order of rank, including Walsh and Flores. On McGrady's page, the page number at the top had two dots above the numerals indicating that he was now the second ranking officer in the camp.

"Very impressive. The marks in places where they have no meaning make the coding tough to see," observed McGrady. He continued to scratch at a scab until it bled. God, how he wished the signal allowing the men to go down to the river would sound, so that he could bathe. "Is there some reason you aren't listed, Lieutenant Carter?"

"I hadn't noticed. I just assumed my predecessor listed me when I came into the camp. I'll take care of the entry tonight."

"There are only three of you Navy types here then?" asked McGrady.

"True, Sir, two from the Korean conflict, and I was the only survivor when the Russians shot down our surveillance plane just north of the Korean border. MIGs with Chinese markings attacked us had Chinese markings, but I think they were Russian."

"Were you over land?"

"No, we were in international waters. They probably set a trap for us like they did your crew."

"What were you flying?"

"A P-4M."

"A Mercator, huh. And you were the only survivor. They must have fished you out of the drink damned fast."

"We hadn't noticed, but there were a lot more fishing boats than normal and even a couple of destroyers under us when we bailed out. I was picked up by a fishing boat and nearly beaten to death before they handed me over to a destroyer."

"What was your job, if you don't mind me asking?

"I was on a ride along. I can fly, but while I am a brown shoe sailor, I was in photo intelligence. Funny, that has helped me here. Since I don't know much about our strategies or aircraft capabilities, I am not much use to the Russians. But I can keep an eye on them."

Davis watched the exchange, a puzzled look on his face. "I can vouch for Carter's skills. He can put together the tiniest pieces into a picture that none of the rest of us see. It's almost telepathy the way he anticipates our jailers. He has saved at least one life by figuring out that the guards were going to do a cell search. Deerwater was hiding food in his cell for an escape. Carter figured out they were coming, in time for him to dump his stash when we went to the river."

"I wasn't questioning Lieutenant Carter," replied McGrady. "It's just that he doesn't have the normal arrogance of a gold wing pilot." McGrady tried to laugh. He nodded to Carter.

"Colonel Davis, when we wrap up here, I would like to spend a few minutes with you to discuss your command structure," added McGrady. "I would like to do it before we go to the river. It has to be about zero out there today, so I suspect that after I plunge into the current and rub myself a minute, I will be about finished for the rest of the day."

"We're done, aren't we Carter?" asked Davis.

"Yes, Sir."

Davis took McGrady's arm and helped him to his cell at the end of the hall. The two men sat down on the only seat, the bunk.

"I think I can trust you, Sir," started McGrady.

Davis nodded. "You keep that suspicious mindset, and you may be the only one here who makes it home."

"There may be more going on than you think. I am going to tell you something that should stay between us two."

Davis looked at the man across from him with a puzzled smile. "Okay."

"That General Molovic who is now one of us, told me something that has to remain a secret. It may be bullshit, but it is something we need to think through just in case."

"You sound like a prosecuting attorney lecturing a detective."

McGrady took a deep breath. "The plane that buzzed us, the one that everyone assumed was one of Molovic's people…"

"Yes."

"Molovic says it was one of ours. He told me it was a Tornado with camera windows. He thinks they are coming for us."

"Why would he tell you that?" asked Davis, anger written all over his face.

"I think he wants us gone. But gone in a way that he ends up back in Moscow where he can defend himself. Someone in Moscow has accused him of treason. They questioned his wife until she died of a heart attack. I know how he handled us when we were first captured. He tried to buffer us from that politico. Everything he did, you would have done for the USA. I think he believes that if we are rescued, he will get a chance to clear his name. Even if he dies in the process, it would be better than spending his life here."

"That sounds like a load of crap, Colonel."

"I thought so too," replied McGrady, "but I can't figure out how telling us this helps the general. They have beaten that seventy-year-old man more than my own crew. What would he gain by lying about the Tornado over flight?"

"We should be discussing this with Carter, he's our intel officer."

"Not now, please. The thing we need is to figure out how to get the men together and out of here quickly if the cavalry shows up. If this leak, then someone will die. If we are the only two who know, then it will be you or me."

"There is something more, isn't there?" asked Davis.

McGrady nodded his head. "I was told the Air Force sent fighters out of Japan to help the Navy Mercator that was under attack a year ago. They saw the plane going down in flames. They didn't see any chutes. The report didn't mention any unusual Russian ship activity."

One of the men seen earlier doing sit-ups stopped at the open cell door, two buckets in his hands. "It's almost time," he said.

❈

General Molovic sat in the office of the camp commander. His face was bruised, his lower lip split. It was all he could do to walk into the commander's office, the pain in the bottoms of his feet from the beating the night before, excruciating.

"Colonel Rasputin tells me that the visit from the low flying jet was one of your men. He has asked me to report the incident," said Nasidna.

"That is because the Colonel is too big a coward to report it himself."

"And why would that be, General?"

"Because Colonel Rasputin knows that there are several sons of ministers, men close to Comrade Khrushchev, in squadrons that report to me. The fathers would react forcefully to protect their sons. He knows my men consider this trumped-up charge against me as nonsense. Why would he put his career on the line if he can talk you into reporting instead?"

Nasidna opened a file on his desk, sliding it across the table at Molovic. "The MVD is going ahead with formal charges against you, General Molovic. It appears that Colonel Rasputin's reports have condemned you."

Molovic smiled, the effort opening the split on his lip. He dabbed at the blood with the sleeve of his pajamas. "Since I have told him nothing, I have no idea what his reports might say."

"You are here under lawful orders," snapped Nasidna. "You still hold the rank of general, but you don't appear to have any authority left and you certainly have no friends in Moscow. You are just one more prisoner to me."

"We shall see," replied Molovic.

"Don't use that insolent tone with me, Prisoner 032. Your life means nothing to me, but if you have information about some type of attack to rescue you, it would be better for you to tell me so that I can head it off."

Molovic asked for a cigarette. He was surprised when Nasidna tossed him a pack. He tapped out a cigarette and slipped it between his torn lips. Nasidna handed him a lighter. He lit the cigarette, relishing the harsh smoke, but he said nothing.

"I have heard no reports of any attempt to rescue you, General," offered Nasidna. "Since you were arrested, a dozen KGB agents have been assigned to keep an eye on your former forces. They have reported nothing. You will find me very observant; I know every-thing going on, in and around this camp."

"Then you know that Colonel Rasputin is just a little boy mas-querading as a colonel. He's a selfish little shit who stirred up more of a storm than he ever expected. Now, he wants to pull you into the shithole with him. He is afraid of his own shadow."

"I will be there when they stand you up against a wall and shoot you, Molovic," wheezed Rasputin, standing behind Nasidna's chair.

"General," interrupted Nasidna, retreating from his prisoner number insult, "If you assure me that there will be no attempt to attack this camp to rescue you, I will believe you. Not only that, but I will return you to your own room and get you out of those silly pajamas."

"What, and leave me naked?"

"No General, your uniform will be cleaned and returned to you.

I will also insist that Colonel Rasputin here gives you time to heal before his next session."

"Will you stop this bastard from torturing me?"

"I don't have the authority to do that. Honestly, I think you are probably guilty, but I don't really care. The offer is, your uniform, room, some decent food and a few days respite. Take it or leave it."

Molovic finished his cigarette, crushing it out in the ashtray on Nasidna's desk. He tugged another from the pack and lit it without asking. "Pavel, I can assure you that I know of no plan to rescue me from this camp. If you want to put that in writing, I will sign it."

As Molovic showered for the first time in days, and put on real clothes, he hummed "Holy Mother Russia" to himself. He was too good a chess player to fall for the faints tried by Rasputin and Nasidna. *That bastard really believes that he knows what is going on in the camp,* he thought.

CHAPTER 36

THE AIR FORCE'S C-123 with a maximum load has a range of just over a thousand miles. When empty, it can cover nearly twice that distance. For an aircraft that can carry fifty soldiers, it can take off and land on amazingly short runways. When Martinez started his takeoff roll, their airplane's fuel tanks carried enough fuel to cover 1700 miles. The problem was, the target was just over 800 miles from Chitose, leaving no reserves. Even with the extra 200 gallons of fuel in barrels, it would be tight.

Martinez pushed the throttles of the huge Wasp radial engines to full takeoff settings and followed with the throttles of the two jet assist engines on the wings. The plane, some called a flying whale, rumbled down the runway, clawing its way into the air quickly. Martinez shut down the jets and rolled the radial engines back to climb power. They would follow almost the same routing as the photo recon plane before them.

"God, I am happy that lake is at least three miles long," offered Jose. He leveled the plane at 300 feet for its run to the Russian mainland.

"Me too," replied Gritt sitting next to him. "But just so you know, there might be some snow buildup along the lake. We don't dare hit snow berms at any speed. That would collapse the landing gear. We may not have three miles of clear ice."

Jose laughed. "Just once, I am going to fly a mission with no bad news just after takeoff."

The plane climbed over the coastal mountains north of Vladivostok and then dropped low again as it crossed the Chinese border. Once the plane was inside the Russian and Chinese radar shield, they climbed to ten thousand feet heading directly toward the Amur-3 camp.

Gritt gave up his co-pilot's seat to Anton, then made his way to where Pulver, Mosby and their team hunched in canvas seats in front of the snowcat. "Let's run through the plan once we land. When we get close to the camp, Anton will approach the guard tower. He will tell them that he was dropped by a passing train, but got his Jeep stuck in the snow and was forced to walk. He will try to get them to come down to help him."

"And just why would the Russians drop one man and a vehicle from a train?" asked Pulver.

"As we discussed, to interrogate the prisoners," replied Gritt.

Pulver and Mosby looked at each other.

"You are damned lucky we came along," replied Pulver. "Generally, when we hit a prison, we find one of two things. Sometimes the people we are looking for are long gone. Or, we find our targets and a bunch more that no one even knew to look for. The one thing we always find is plenty of bad guys – interrogators – already at the facility."

"Do you have a better idea?" Gritt scowled.

Mosby replied with a toothy smile. "Just get him close enough to call out for help in Russian. When the sentries stand up to see what is going on, we will take them out with the silenced Winchesters. It may be hard for him to see two of his countrymen killed, but the guards have to go before they can sound any alarm."

"That's not what Anton agreed to."

"Neither of us really trust your pet Russian," replied Pulver. "If he can't handle it, he needs to stay with the airplane."

"Or he can wait with me," offered Gritt. "He has some unfinished business at the camp. He thinks his wife died there."

"General, just let us do our job. None of us need to die there. We are going to be outnumbered by at least four to one, but we're ready and unless this is a trap, they aren't. If your friend Anton can get most of those in the camp to surrender this could go really easy. But if there is resistance, we don't have time to negotiate. Once we take out the guards, this all has to happen in about five minutes so that they don't have time to radio for help. This lumbering plane wreck is really vulnerable crossing hundreds of miles of Russian and Chinese territory. If they get MIGs out looking for us, we are all dead."

Gritt dropped onto the bumper of the snowcat. He started to argue against the change in the plan, and then stopped. "I'm happy to have your expertise."

"When we get there, we will knock down the radio tower next to the building by the parking lot. If there are any overhead telephone wires, we will cut them.

Both Sergeant Mosby and I are sure that the prisoners are in the back building, the one closest to the river. That means that the center building is for administration, and the one next to it is the barracks. We hit the barracks and administration buildings first. Sergeant Mosby and you will go into the admin building. You need to clear both floors, but I doubt that there will be more than two or three people there. The critical one will be in the communications center. Don't give him time to call."

Mosby looked at a three by five card in his hand. "Lt. Colonel Pulver will lead three men into the barracks. Your Russian guy could really help there if we can trust him. If he can announce that our entrance is just a drill and ask everyone to assemble in the lobby, maybe we won't have to kill as many of them."

Pulver pointed at a tall gangly kid at the end of the row. "Max there will go directly to the prisoner's building. He is the best shot we have and our medic. His job is to neutralize any guards before they can kill the prisoners. He will release the captives, evaluate them for evacuation and hold them in that building until we arrive."

Gritt looked at the two men. "This is a lot different than the plan we discussed the other afternoon."

"It's simpler and faster," replied Pulver, "and safer. We didn't want to debate this mission with you or your Russian friend. If this all goes well, only six of the Russians at this camp will die. If it doesn't, we will have to kill all of them. Now, unless you want to abandon the mission right now, this is how it is going to go."

Gritt's last conversation with the director had been explicit. "No big pile of bodies for the Russians to publicize but get your men out." Gritt puzzled over two conflicting orders. *Every mission is full of conflicting orders,* he thought. *The German strategist, Von Moltke pointed out that no battle plan survives contact with the enemy. This plan couldn't avoid contact.*

"Are we turning around?" asked Pulver.

"Nope, but we may have to arrange a big funeral pyre. The boss said, no pile of bodies, he didn't say no bodies."

Mosby punched his boss in the arm. "Allen told you that Gritt was one of us."

Gritt climbed back into the cockpit just as Jose turned the plane toward a distant frozen lake that reflected the moon like a mirror. "Tailwind most of the way. We are fifteen minutes early. I'll roll the plane up on the right wing to give you two a look at the camp."

Through his binoculars, Gritt picked out four bright lights below. They lit up the front of each building and the parking area. There were no other lights. "It looks totally deserted," mumbled Gritt.

"General, Russia is not like your United States," responded Anton. "From what I saw of Fairbanks, you light up your schools and your buildings, even your parking lots. Electricity in Russia is scarce. In a place like this, it comes from a small generator that uses precious fuel. They use only the lighting they need to."

Gritt noted that Anton used they not we. "Anton, are you sure you are ready for this? Pulver wants you to simply call for help so that he can get a clean shot at the sentries. There will be a number of Russian casualties."

"I knew that when we discussed your plan. I will try to save as many of them as I can." Anton looked over his shoulder at Gritt, the pale red light of the nighttime cockpit giving the general a dev-ilish look. "You promise that I will have a half-hour to search for Natalya's records."

"That was our agreement. If we can capture some of the staff alive, maybe one of them will know where to look."

Jose flew ten miles past the lake before he reduced the power on the radial engines. "We should be well past where they can hear us. By the way, thanks for giving me Major Greiwe to help fuel. I am not as spry as I used to be. I worry about falling off one of the wings. Hell, I don't have a medical or a pilot's license anymore." He laughed.

"Neither do I," replied Gritt. "I lost mine right after the war."

Both Anton and Jose couldn't hide their surprise. Before they could respond, Gritt turned from the cockpit. "I'll make sure every-one is buckled up."

"Good thinking," replied Jose. "On the ground, one way or another, in five minutes."

"Let me go," offered Anton, "you have a lot more experience landing on ice."

'Stay put," replied Gritt. "You are the better pilot. You probably even have a license."

As Gritt checked the straps securing the snowcat, Anton watched Jose drop the C-123 into the river valley used earlier by the Tornado to hide its approach.

Anton keyed the intercom, while following Jose's actions. "I have never known a general who admits that anyone knows more than him," he said. "The general told me that he really didn't want to be on this mission."

"No one hates war more than a warrior. He is a different kind of cat, but I would follow him into any battle," replied Jose. He dropped close to the river below. "I know you looked the lake over, how does the ice look?"

"The entire south side of the lake appears to be clear. You will probably have some crosswind from the right."

"I just hope the ice holds our weight," worried Jose. "This is all new to me."

"We Russians build rail tracks across frozen lakes like this. Just stay offshore from any valleys running down to the lake. There will be open water around stream mouths. Oh, and no brakes, use the props and flaps until we slow."

Jose dropped the landing gear and added more flaps to the wings.

Inside the fuselage, the only indication that the plane touched down was the sound of the wheels spinning. Gritt's experience on ice allowed him to feel the tiny slips and skids, as Jose fought wind over glare ice. Everyone felt the plane twist sideways, the snowcat thrown against its lashings. The plane skidded the other direction as Jose fought the wind, overcorrecting. The back of the plane erupted with Spanish profanity as the plane spun twice before coming to a stop.

"A bit more wind than forecast. My technique needs a little work," mumbled Jose. Anton sat staring straight ahead.

"One nice thing about ice," continued Jose, "the plane slides instead of digging in and tipping up onto a wing. I don't think we damaged anything, but maybe you should do the takeoff." Jose began to whistle like nothing happened. "Better check in with our passengers."

"Anton says we're still at least a mile from where the road comes down to the lake." Greiwe sat next to Mosby, an intercom headset clamped over his ears.

"Get ready, but we still have a long taxi before engine shut down," Greiwe announced.

In moments, the team was out of their seats. Some were unstrapping the snowcat and pallets of fuel while others stacked the men's packs and weapons along the ramp.

The plane slid to a stop. Greiwe tugged the headset from his head and wiggled past the snowcat to the rear of the plane. He lowered the ramp. Cold flooded in, hitting the team like a train. "Let's go," called Pulver.

The men rolled the two pallets of fuel down the ramp, and then positioned them under the leading edge of each wing. Each pallet carried two barrels of fuel, a battery in a metal box and a small electric pump with a long hose coiled on top of the barrels.

A twenty-mile an hour wind blew the cold through any gaps in their clothing.

Gritt climbed into the cab of the snowcat and pushed the starter. Nothing happened. He tried again, still nothing. A quick scan confirmed the ignition switch was on. It dawned on him that it was on before he took a seat. Leaning out the window, he called, "dead battery, get me one from the pumps."

The cramped quarters inside the plane made it difficult to install the new battery. Pulver's men spread out, rifles pointing into the dark forest. If this was a trap, one man with a machine gun could kill them all in seconds. Finally, the snowcat engine turned over and caught. Gritt ran the machine onto the lake.

Jose and Dan stood looking at the empty battery box under the left wing. "Sorry you guys," called Gritt. "You are going to have to pump each side, one at a time. We're going to need it all, so how long do you need?"

Dan smiled at his boss, frozen breath shooting from his mouth. "I'd say fifteen minutes per barrel. Probably an hour, maybe a little more in this wind."

The original timeline called for the entire mission to spend only an hour on the ground. They'd already used a quarter of that time. "Then quit standing around." Gritt looked over at Pulver, "mount up."

Pulver leaned two silenced M-1 carbines against the plane's ramp. "Just in case," Mr. Greiwe. He disappeared into the idling tracked vehicle.

CHAPTER 37

ELLEN STARED AT a pile of lined sheets, the latest chapters in her book. She tore them into tiny pieces and tossed them into the fire. She'd written the new ending only two days before. The final chapters moving from a "woe is me, what do I do now," to dreams of a Cinderella ending.

Her check-in call to the young lieutenant in Gritt's office the previous afternoon stirred fears she hoped were forever buried. Nothing in her dream ending had changed, but the news that two FBI men rousted Gritt's office that afternoon, looking for information about a Russian officer who was flying around the North Pacific on government airplanes brought back bad memories. Perhaps it would be more honest to wait for the real ending anyway. She just hoped it would be as much fun.

Ellen knew that if she did nothing the FBI would be at her lake in days. She would tell them nothing of Anton or of the two of them. Anton, the character disappeared from her writing, his few belongings packed into a trunk hoisted into a tree along her trap line. The lesson became brutally clear when goons in Washington shined a spotlight on Walt's life. Some in the government took what they called evidence and twisted it to say what they already believed.

The other lesson she learned was that the best defense was a good offense. She picked up the radio for her morning check in. "If they ask, Lieutenant, tell the FBI that I am on my way to Fairbanks. If you wouldn't mind, would you call Carmen Gritt for me and ask if I can leave my dog at her house for a few days. Oh, and can you check on flights from Bettles for me. I'll stand by the radio for your answers."

She began packing. The first item in her bag was her personal diary with the names and direct phone numbers of old friends still in the government. Inside the front cover, written in bold lettering, was the number of the phone next to President Eisenhower's bed.

CHAPTER 38

GRITT DROVE WITH his head out of the side window, the cold engine not generating enough heat to overcome the bitter temperature and steaming breathe of eight men. He started down the lake, toward a spot along the shoreline where the bank rose gradually to the road. In the mirror, he could see Greiwe on the left wing ready to begin fueling.

The track around the lake and into the trees hadn't been used in days. Windblown snow filled the rough dirt road six inches deep, except where wind pushed it into drifts in the turns. The bombardier crushed the crystalized snow, riding over the edges of the drifts.

In the seat next to Gritt, Pulver scraped crazily at the frosted windscreen.

"What is our speed?" he asked.

"Ten miles an hour," replied Gritt, finally able to see through the tiny opening in the frost.

"We will stop in fifteen minutes," said Pulver. "We leave the snowcat and walk the last half mile. I will put a couple of men out in front to make sure we see the camp before they see us."

"That isn't going to be a problem. When we flew over, there were four floodlights lighting up the compound.

"That's good," replied Pulver. He turned to Mosby behind him.

"Did you here that, their security is all focused on keeping an eye on the people inside the camp." Pulver put his hand on the dashboard and pulled up his sleeve so that he could study his watch as they drove.

The windscreen was just clearing when Pulver ordered, "stop."

Pulver and Max, the sharpshooter, waited until Anton was in front of them before shouldering the two silenced Winchester rifles and starting toward the camp. Pulver turned to Gritt. "Let us get out in front about two hundred yards and then follow Sergeant Mosby," he ordered.

Around Gritt, the shooters were mumbling quietly as they waited. "What are the men saying?" he asked.

"Yesli uy dvigayetes', ya up'yu tebla," replied Mosby. "While you were changing the battery, your friend Anton taught us. It means 'If you move, I will kill you,' in Russian. Grit shouldered his scoped Winchester 30-06 hunting rifle and tried the phrase himself. "I think you just said 'Hey mister, I think you have a cute butt. That could be, ah, misinterpreted in a prison," laughed Mosby.

A tiny flash from a shielded flashlight where Max, Anton and Pulver had disappeared into the shadows got the men moving. The sound of five men walking in the old snow sounded like someone crushing bags of potato chips. Steam shot from their nostrils. They looked like monsters from a Romanian graveyard, thought Gritt, struggling with his bad leg to keep up.

In front of the men, Pulver stopped to study the lighted compound from a couple of hundred yards away. He sent Max through the trees to the left.

"How well this all goes is really up to your acting skills," he whispered to Anton. "Try to get them to come help you, but if all they do is stand up in the guard booth, that will do."

"How do you know that there will be more than one?"

"There are always two, in case someone gets sleepy. I will be on your right with a round in the chamber."

"What is a round?"

"I will have bullets in the gun. Give Max and me five minutes to get in place before you walk up."

Anton watched Pulver disappear into the shadows. He checked his watch and waited. Then he began a stumbling walk toward the guard tower. The tower rose on four logs planted into the ground. A ladder extended twenty feet to an opening in the floor. Above the floor, four short walls of rough-cut lumber extended up about three feet. Posts at the corners supported a flat roof covered by snow.

Anton saw no one as he walked. That made sense. Anyone sitting in the cold windswept box would try to stay out of the biting gusts. He walked until he was thirty yards from the guard booth, then he dropped to all fours and called in Russian. "Please help me, help me, I got lost. I fell in the river and I am freezing."

Above he saw two heads pop up, but one disappeared instantly. He watched as a pair of legs appeared on the ladder heading down. The man reached the ground and ran to where Anton waited on his knees.

Anton lunged at the man, knocking him from his feet. He jumped on the flailing man, holding him down, his hand over the man's mouth. To his left he heard a muffled puff, and then a second from his right. "You are a very lucky man," whispered Anton. The other guard just died."

The guard mumbled under the hand pressed over his mouth. "Do not scream or call out," ordered Anton or I will kill you." He slipped his hand from the man's mouth just as Pulver pressed the silenced muzzle of a High Standard pistol against the man's forehead.

"Are you here to rescue General Molovic?" asked the terrified guard.

Anton pushed Pulver's pistol from the man's head. He held up his palm, silently asking for time.

One of the shooters slipped up next to Anton, tugging two feet of electrical wire from a pocket. He pulled the guards hands behind his back and wrapped them tightly with the wire.

"Tell me about Molovic," said Anton.

"His cell is in the administration building on the second floor, next to the interrogation room."

Anton struggled to digest what he was hearing. The man who planned his mission to America was here. The man who let him believe that Natalya was alive was here. "Tell me why the general is here."

"They say he is a traitor. They say he lured the Americans here to trade them for the crew of a Russian plane, which he stole. They say he is working with the Americans."

The rest of the team arrived, crowding around Anton and the Guard. "How many men are in the administration building tonight?" asked Anton.

"Only the clerk at the front desk and the man in the communications room. And General Molovic," he added. "Only the political officer and the two KGB men believe the general is guilty," stammered the guard. "The rest of us can see that the general is a patriot."

Anton dug a cloth bandana from a pocket and stuffed it in the man's mouth. Then he turned, motioning for Gritt and Mosby to follow. "There is a very important general being held here. He is the man who sent me to America. I will tell this guard to talk to the man at the front desk and to the man in the communications room and tell them to surrender. He thinks we are Russians here to rescue General Molovic. The general is in a cell on the second floor of the administration building. Please take him too. Tell him Anton Bidkov has come to even the score." Anton walked back to the guard. "Point to where the staff is sleeping."

The guard pointed at the building Pulver had identified.

"Now point at where the Americans are being held."

Again, Pulver and Mosby's analysis was on the money.

Anton pointed at Gritt and Mosby. "You will take those two men to the administration building and tell the clerk and the radio operator to go with them. If you don't, they will kill all three of you. Then show the tall man where the general is being held. Do you understand?"

The guard nodded.

Anton turned to Pulver and whispered, "You were correct. The building on the right is where the staff sleeps. The one on the left is where the Americans are held." Anton tugged his bandana from the guard's mouth and motioned for Gritt and Mosby to take him. Gritt rebalanced the sling from his rifle on his shoulder and drew the silenced .22 from a holster.

After they started, Anton motioned for the rest of the team to gather around. "There is a Russian General being held here. There are also some KGB interrogators here. They are very dangerous. They will not surrender."

Pulver slipped the High Standard pistol from its holster and handed it to Anton. "Thanks. Stay out of the light until we can survey the building. You lead the way."

Behind them, the snowcat with the last shooter driving crept up, its lights off.

CHAPTER 39

THE CLERK AT the front desk of the administration building never looked up as three men entered, careful not to slam the door in the wind. Gritt put his pistol into the captured guard's ear and pushed him toward the counter. The trembling man began mumbling in Russian. The clerk dog-eared his book, and stood, facing the barrel of a silenced pistol. It was only then that he noticed the guard in front of him, his hands bound. Moments later, Mosby pulled the clerk from behind the counter and wired his hands behind his back. He bound the man's feet, stuffing a glove liner into the clerk's mouth.

"I never thought to bring something to secure prisoners," whispered Gritt, his English startling the guard from the tower who'd finally quit shaking, his eyes turning angry. He glared at Gritt.

Mosby pushed the guard from the tower down the dimly lit hall. A single door showed light seeping under it. Mosby silently turned the handle, pushing the guard in front of him. As the door opened, the guard began yelling in Russian.

Mosby pushed the guard out of the way as the radio operator reached for a pistol. The silenced .22 fired, *pft, pft, pft.* The radio operator slid from his chair, two bullets in his neck and one just above his ear.

Gritt turned angrily toward the guard next to the door. He

pulled the glove liner from his right hand and shoved it into the man's mouth; then dragged the man out of the room, leaving him next to the clerk, behind the counter "Watch these two while I go find the general," he said to Mosby. He slid his rifle from his shoulder and leaned it against the counter, cocking his silenced pistol.

Without his cane, which Gritt chose to leave in the airplane, he struggled up the stairs. There were two rooms showing light. He stopped at the first one, a room with a metal door to his right that could be bolted from the outside. The door was closed but the bolt open. Gritt checked to make sure that the safety on his pistol was off. He pushed the door open, the hinges creaking. From the hall, he could see little. The room was mostly to his right, hidden by the door. To his left, a bucket used as a toilet and a roll of toilet paper sat in a tiny nook. There was no one using the makeshift toilet. He slipped through the door, the pistol in front of him, scanning. There was a narrow cot with a single worn blanket, and a few clothes on some shelves. Two pictures rested on a table against the far wall, but there was no general.

Gritt started to back out of the room. "Behind you," boomed down the hall in accented English. Gritt spun just in time to see the profile of a man in the hall. He ducked back into the room as two bullets slapped the wall next to the door.

Gritt looked around. A string hung from the single light fixture in the room. He tugged the cord, plunging the room into darkness. Then he slipped into the nook next to the stinking bucket and waited.

He could hear someone moving down the hall, breathing heavily. He realized that his own heavy breathing might give him away. He held his breath. Moments later, a pistol in a hand slid through the doorway. Gritt waited, until arms, then a shoulder and a head followed the pistol. He pushed the High Standard pistol against an ear and squeezed the trigger twice. The man holding the pistol dropped, folding like the wet towel you drop on a hotel bathroom floor. Gritt pushed the pistol against the back of the man's head and squeezed the trigger again to make sure.

Gritt slipped into the dark hall, empty as far as he could see. He moved toward where light flooded the passage. Inside the lighted room, a man sat, his hands chained to the seat, his legs chained to a ring in the floor. His face was swollen, and his hands bled onto his neatly pressed green wool trousers from where someone had tugged out a fingernail on each hand.

The man looked up, a serious look on his face. "As a general officer, I can't believe that I didn't tell them you were coming, but they didn't deserve it. I assume you are American, here for your flyers."

"And you must be General Molovic. I am to give you a message. Anton Bidkov says that he is here to even the score."

"You must be General Gritt. One of your men mumbled your name when he was asleep in my hospital. He kept saying, General Gritt will come. And now you have. Would you mind unchaining me so that I can get dressed? I was the one who warned you about that KGB scum. I assume you shot him."

Gritt looked down at the hand and leg cuffs constraining Molovic. "Do you know where the keys are?"

"On the desk in the corner. Spaciba."

Gritt pulled the chains from Molovic's legs, and then opened the cuffs on his hands. The general stood, walking to where his shirt, tie and coat hung on a rack. He pulled a handkerchief from his coat pocket and began to wipe the blood from his face and hands. "Is Major Bidkov with you?"

"He is. He is trying to get the rest of the guards to surrender so that we don't have to kill them."

"I am pleased that he is alive, although I know now that I am guilty of the treason that they say I committed. I gave your country one of our most advanced aircraft and a crew to tell you what it is capable of doing."

Gritt liked the man in front of him. It was easy to like someone that probably just saved your life. "Anton was the only survivor of a crash in the Alaskan wilderness. Your TU-16 was completely burned. If I knew earlier that it was there, I wouldn't have sent Colonel McGrady and his crew over Russia to find it."

"And if you had not been sending reconnaissance aircraft over Russia, I wouldn't have set a trap to shoot them down. I wanted to trade for Bidkov and his crew." Molovic finished buttoning his shirt, his torn fingers leaving bloodstains on each button. "How did you find this camp?"

"One of our radio listening teams intercepted a communiqué from a Colonel Rasputin, advising that just captured Americans were being moved to a camp called Amur-3."

"So, you flew one of your Tornado recon planes over the camps until you were sure which one it was," added Molovic.

Gritt nodded his head, trying to come to grips with how much the general seemed to know." He held his pistol next to his leg, unsure whether Molovic was a threat or not.

"You are much younger than I expected," Molovic continued, slipping on his coat.

"You, General, should be retired to your dacha somewhere, not rotting in one of your own gulags."

"Not my gulag. Our new premier is closing gulags all over the country. But there is a group of still powerful men who survived Comrade Stalin's purges by learning to be like him. I doubt that more than a handful of men in Moscow even know that this camp exists." Molovic looked at Gritt, sadness in his eyes. "How many Russians have died here tonight?"

"The men I came with are just now going into the prisoner's quarters and your barracks. So far only three that I know of, including the man I just shot."

"I asked about men, not dogs," replied Molovic.

"I am sorry any have to die," replied Gritt. "All I want is my three men."

"General Gritt, you have stumbled into more than you bargained for. This camp holds American flyers going back to the Great Patriotic War." Molovic headed into the hall. "I will need to stop in my room for my hat and cold weather coat. There is something I need to show Major Bidkov before he shoots me. Now, let's go find Colonel McGrady and his new friends."

Gritt stood and mentally digested what Molovic said, then turned to follow. He lifted the pistol and slipped the safety on, then holstered the weapon.

At the base of the stairs, Gritt picked up his rifle and pushed open the door, the cold no longer an issue to his adrenaline filled body.

Mosby joined them as they headed toward the prisoner's quarters. He slid the straps of a pack from his back. "Give me just a moment to plant charges on the radio tower. I'll set them for three minutes."

CHAPTER 40

PULVER AND TWO shooters followed Anton Bidkov into the Russian barracks. One shooter remained outside to insure they weren't surprised from behind. There was only one person in the huge lobby. Anton pointed his pistol in the small man's face and ordered him to tell where the camp commander's room was and where the KGB men were. The man began pointing and jabbering.

Moments later, the man was face down in a closet, his hands and feet bound, a gag in his mouth. Anton pointed at a diagram of the building on the wall. "We should put the guards and interrogators in the gymnasium. There are no windows and only one door."

Pulver nodded. "We clear the ground floor and then go find the officers."

Pulver's silenced carbine was at his shoulder, as he led Anton to the gym. Pushing open the heavy steel door, he found the light switch. He picked up a steel bar and cut a length of rope from a weight machine. "This will work to secure the door, at least long enough for us to finish our work here."

Anton turned to one of Pulver's shooters. "Repeat what I taught you."

The man managed a rough version of "If you move, I will kill you," in Russian.

"Good enough. Stand inside the door. Just point your rifle at everyone who comes in. Only use the phrase if you see someone less worried than you." The shooter looked to his commander, who nodded agreement.

Starting on the ground floor, Anton went from room to room. He opened each door, and without turning on the light, told the occupants that there was an emergency meeting. It took less than five minutes to empty the ground floor, as sleepy men in their underwear trudged into the gym. Bidkov slipped through the door, ordering the men inside to remain silent. He didn't want to warn those on the second floor. He had no idea what Mosby's man's orders were, but it didn't matter. "The man with the rifle will shoot anyone who tries to warn that KGB scum upstairs," he warned in Russian then turned to Pulver. "The top floor will be tougher, but we already have eleven of the sixteen people in the building. The only people on the second floor are the camp commander, the medic, some Politico here from outside, and two KGB men."

"They won't be as easy to fool," commented Pulver. "We start with the KGB men in the room directly above the lobby."

As the two men started up the stairs, a commotion broke out in the gym. They could hear the shooter mumble his warning. The commotion grew louder. The shooter yelled his warning, followed by the sound of two muffled shots from a silenced carbine. "Someone just died," said Pulver. They raced to the gym and helped the shooter secure the door, lashing the steel bar to the door latch and resting it on the seats of two chairs.

They reached the top of the stairs and the KGB men's room just as someone locked the door from the inside. "Watch down the hall," Pulver told the last shooter. "We'll deal with this."

Anton called to those in the room telling them that he was a KGB colonel there to find out what was going on with General Molovic. Bullets smashing through the wooden door answered his call. Pulver pushed Anton to one side while leaping to the other side of the door himself. Behind them, the shooter dove for the floor.

"Grenade," barked Pulver.

The shooter rolled behind Anton, then jumped to his feet. He pushed Anton behind him. Tugging a grenade from his coat, he pulled the pin.

Pulver pointed his carbine at the door latch and lock and fired three rounds, and then he leaned back and lashed out at the door with his foot. As the door sprung open, more bullets ripped into the hallway. Pulver's shooter flipped the grenade through the door. First Pulver, and then the shooter followed the explosion into the room.

The exploding grenade detonated about four feet above the KGB man hiding behind his overturned bunk, driving what was left of him into a wall. There was a second bunk, but no second man."

Anton's ringing ears kept him from hearing the warning from Pulver, now kneeling next to the body. He stood in the doorway as Pulver and the shooter wildly gestured. Finally, Pulver pointed past him.

Anton spun just in time to see people disappearing into the far stairwell. He raised his silenced pistol and fired, shots peppering the door, but missing the runners.

When he turned, Pulver was right next to him. "We are missing one KGB man, one medic, one politico and the camp commander," he yelled into Anton's ear.

In the background, quick blasts signaled the end of the radio tower.

CHAPTER 41

"WE DON'T WANT any of those who went down the back stairwell to release the prisoners, yelled the shooter. The men raced down the stairs to the gym door. Whoever raced down the rear stairs hadn't made any attempt to free the prisoners. Pulver's man stood next to the door and checked the steel bar. "That should hold them for an hour or two."

The shooter outside the building was on a knee, pointing his weapon toward the back of the administration building. "Two people just ran into the administration building," he shouted, pointing. "Another one came out of this building and ran into the woods. It's really dark, but he may have a rifle."

"We will deal with them later," said Pulver, pointing at the shooter. "You go back and find a place where you can watch over the snowcat. Make sure nobody sabotages it." He positioned his other shooter to cover the areas between the buildings.

Anton and Pulver arrived at the prisoner's building just as the men from the admin building did. They pushed into the entry, stepping over the bodies of two guards. Pulver whistled twice, which brought Max from behind an overturned desk down the hall. Behind him, a line of men sat, their backs against the wall.

"I don't know what in the hell is going on," started Max, "but when I opened the first cell, the graying man sitting closest to us came out. He walked down the hall opening door after door. There are twenty American prisoners."

"As I said," voiced Molovic, "you have stumbled onto much more than you planned."

Behind Molovic, Anton raised his pistol, pointing at the back of Molovic's head. "You really are here," he spat in Russian. "My lucky day."

"Not yet," ordered Gritt, "you two need to talk, and then I need a few minutes with General Molovic. Then if you still want to shoot him, I won't stop you."

"Who's in charge here?" asked Gritt.

The first man sitting along the wall struggled to his feet and shuffled toward Gritt. "I am," said the man, extending his hand, "Colonel Robert Davis, U.S. Army Air Corps and a prisoner since 1945."

Gritt extended his hand. "Not a prisoner any longer, Colonel, my name's Chad Gritt."

"You are young for a peacetime, General." Davis turned and called down the hall. "Colonel McGrady, your ride's here."

McGrady walked right past Gritt. He extended his hand to Molovic. "When you told me about the Tornado recon plane, I wasn't sure that I believed you. Thank you for your silence with our jailers."

Molovic stepped to one side. "Colonel McGrady, this is Major Anton Bidkov, the pilot of the missing TU-16 that we discussed."

"So, you got what you wanted. Is the rest of the crew with the Major?"

"No, your General Gritt says they were all killed when the plane crashed, all but the Major."

"I am sorry about the loss of your men. But at least you got the Major back."

"I doubt that," replied Molovic. He turned to Anton. "Am I right, you are not staying in Russia?"

Anton nodded. "I only came on this mission because Amur-3 was the camp where they held my wife."

"Major, you were chosen for your mission because of top marks on the TU-16 flight tests. Colonel Rasputin recommended you. He was the one who presented information about your wife. I only learned that she was dead after you went missing."

Anton didn't hear a word. "You lied to me. You used me, and you would have had me shot if I became a risk to your crazy plan.

"All of that is true, Major. It seems our whole country is full of people who lie to protect themselves, or to further their plans."

Gritt pointed at Davis' empty cell. "I will give you and the general five minutes to talk before we have to get moving." The two men nodded then walked into the tiny room and closed the door.

Gritt turned to Davis. "Colonel, do you really have twenty men here?"

"With your three men, that is the total."

"I have no idea how to get all of you to the plane, but get your men dressed. We have to go." Gritt smiled at the older officer. "I don't suppose you ever flew overweight back in the big war?"

Davis smiled at the ridiculous question. "General, we are dressed. These are all the clothes we have."

"How about shoes?"

"Nope, when we are outside, we go barefoot. It isn't too bad in the summer, but we have to limit our exposure in the winter."

"How about coats, or hats?"

"No Sir, just a single blanket."

"Shit, you will freeze to death just getting to the airplane. And the inside of a C-123 is cold."

"At least we will freeze to death on the way home, General."

Pulver was listening. "The guards must have clothes in their rooms."

He turned to Mosby. "Sergeant, we will escort these men to the barracks to find all the warm clothes we can find." He checked his watch. "General Gritt, we are already behind schedule. I will meet you at the snowcat in fifteen minutes."

"We can't get everyone in one snowcat," replied Gritt.

Davis turned to the men in pajamas, crowding around them. "We will have to take the open truck. Grab your blankets and follow these two men. You heard all of this. We need warm clothes. Nothing is going to fit, all that matters is staying warm."

Twenty-two men headed toward the barracks building as Gritt knocked on the door where Anton and Molovic talked. "We have to go,"

The door opened, and Anton followed Molovic out. "The general has something he wants me to see," offered Anton. "It will only take five minutes."

"Are you still going to shoot him?" asked Gritt.

"Probably not."

"Good, the man saved my life."

"Do you still have your flashlight?" asked Anton.

"I do," answered Gritt. He pulled it from a pocket and switched it on.

"We are going to the graveyard. It will be really dark." Anton retrieved his flashlight and handed it to Molovic. "We will follow you."

The three men walked around the side of the building toward the sound of running water. Molovic counted the rows of crosses as the trail wound through dozens of graves. He turned down the fifth row and stopped in front of the sixth grave marker. "Here is your Natalya," he said. He handed the flashlight to Anton.

"He will want a minute alone with his wife," suggested Molovic. He and Gritt moved toward the river, leaving Anton at the weathered wooden marker with the name Natalya Bidkov painted in chipping black paint. Anton knelt. He ran his fingers over the name. He switched off the light and stared up into the star-filled sky. The only sound was wind chattering the branches of the trees. His mother taught him to pray as a child, he tried to remember how.

Molovic and Gritt stood watching. "Only a couple of months ago, I told my aide that if we could get the politicos out of the picture, we warriors would talk, get drunk, and probably go fishing together. We would work out the problems between our countries," offered Molovic.

"I agree," commented Gritt. "If you would like to test your theory, I'm the guy. I own a plane on floats with access to the best fishing in the world." Gritt tapped the rifle over his shoulder. "We also have great hunting. You could go back with us. We will arrange for you to disappear just as we are doing for Anton. The woman who nursed him after the crash, an old friend, is quite taken by your pilot. I think Anton has already started his new life."

"It is a tempting offer…" started Molovic.

From a small hill next to the prisoner's quarters, a man rose from behind a wooden bench. Molovic started to shout a warning, as the man raised an AK-47 rifle and opened fire, the rifle set for full-automatic. The first rounds missed, but the man's sweeping motion caught the two men before they could duck. Gritt pitched against Molovic just as a bullet knocked the Russian general's leg out from under him. Both men tumbled, Gritt's flashlight flying into the river.

"I told you I would get you, you traitor," came a call in Russian. Grigori Rasputin waved his rifle in the air, screaming and dancing. "I told you, I told you, I told you, I told you."

Anton stuffed his flashlight into a pocket. In a crouched run, he slipped from grave marker to grave marker. It took only seconds to reach the two wounded men.

"The bullet only clipped my leg," whispered Molovic. "I think your friend General Gritt is badly wounded. You need to go get help."

Anton started to stand but ducked down again. "The man who shot you is walking toward us."

"It is that bastard Rasputin."

Anton rolled Gritt on his side and tugged the heavy hunting rifle from under his body. Working the bolt, he chambered a round and then slipped up onto a knee. The darkness made it impossible to see the crosshairs in the scope. Centering the middle of the man coming at him in the telescopic sight, he waited. Finally, Rasputin was silhouetted in the light of the building behind him. Anton pulled the trigger.

Rasputin's body stumbled backward three steps, the rifle in his hands tumbling to the ground. Then he collapsed.

"Is he dead?" asked Molovic.

"He is dead," replied Anton.

"Go get help," ordered Molovic. "I will stay with your new friend and see what I can do."

Anton laid the rifle against a grave marker and sprinted toward the light of the parking area. "Don't shoot me. I am part of the rescue team," he yelled. "General Gritt has been shot, he needs help."

In front of the snowcat, Pulver and his shooter were talking to Walsh, the first of the prisoners to find clothing. Anton stopped next to them, panting. "General Gritt has been shot. General Molovic is also wounded. They are near the river."

Pulver grabbed Anton and shook him. "Is the shooter still out there?"

"No, I used Chad's rifle to kill the bastard. They need help."

"How badly are they wounded?" asked Pulver in a practiced take-charge voice.

"Molovic was hit in the leg, but I think that General Gritt was hit in the chest."

Pulver turned to one of his shooters. "Find Max and the rest of our team and grab the stretchers from the top of the snowcat. I'll meet you down by the river."

He turned back to Anton, "show me where they are."

Colonel Davis and the rest of the prisoners were just leaving the barracks. "What happened?"

"Three people escaped our assault on the barracks. A man and a woman ran into the admin building, but the third ran into the woods. I think he just shot Gritt and that Russian general."

"Do you need help?" asked Davis.

"Get your men to the parking lot. My shooters and I will get the wounded men. We have to move. Get that truck in front started. Sergeant Mosby, go bring the snowcat as close as you can."

Max worked to stop the bleeding from a bullet in Gritt's chest and another that destroyed months of work by doctors who saved Gritt's left leg during the war. Pulver stuffed gauze into the hole in Molovic's leg and wrapped it in a tight bandage.

Pulver looked at his watch. They were a quarter hour behind schedule, and they still needed to get three times as many men to the plane as planned. Four of them lifted the two stretchers and headed toward the lights of the snowcat idling a hundred yards away.

"Are we all here?" he asked as they reached the parking lot."

"No," admitted Mosby. "Some of the prisoners borrowed guns. They went to pay off some old debts."

Four prisoners went from room to room looking for the camp commander and Aunt Star. Taking turns, one man would slam a door open and turn on the lights while two others rushed into the room ready to shoot anyone that moved. Davis covered them with a pistol. In the interrogation room, they found Star sitting naked on the desk; her clothes draped over the chair where her pistol belt hung. Davis left the three men who knew her best, continuing to look for Nasidna.

He found the man sitting behind his desk, a bottle of vodka in front of him, a glass in his hand.

"So now the shoe is on the other foot," said Nasidna. "Remember how many times you might have died, but I let you live?"

"Pavel, no prisoner will ever forget you. I am here for all of them," answered Davis.

"And you are alive."

"Only so that you could torment me more. I never faced you as an equal. Now, that has changed. You keep a Makarov pistol in your desk drawer. You have ten seconds to reach for it and kill me before I kill you." Davis began counting, "one, two, three."

Nasidna dropped his glass, the clear fluid flying everywhere. The arm of his chair was pressed against the drawer. He pushed his chair back and managed to get the bulky machine pistol from the drawer by the count of seven. With shaking hands, he fumbled with the safety. He started to point the weapon when Davis shot him twice with the .45 automatic. Pavel slumped forward. "You promised ten seconds," he mumbled.

"Now you see how painful broken promises are to desperate men," replied Davis.

A moment later, a woman's hysterical laugh, preceded three spaced shots. "That should account for all of them," said Mosby. "General Gritt killed the other KGB man earlier."

The two stretchers were moved to the back of the truck. The wounded men were covered with blankets. The rest of the rescue team and twenty former prisoners piled into the snowcat and truck and started toward the lake.

CHAPTER 42

MOLOVIC SAT ON his stretcher, his hand holding a compress against a hole in the Grit's chest. "Can you speak?"

"Yes," whispered Gritt.

"We can't let this ratchet up the tensions between our two countries," said Molovic. I will find out who is responsible for holding your countrymen."

Gritt nodded. "Maybe, too many bodies. I am sorry," he managed.

"One is too many," replied Molovic. "Tell me again, how you knew to come to the Amur-3 camp?"

"One of our radio intelligence operators intercepted a transmission from some colonel named Rasputin bragging about capturing my men." Gritt paused, fighting for another breath. "He named this camp as where they were being held."

"Rasputin was an idiot. He's the man who shot us. He was the one who lied about Anton's wife. Anton killed him."

The medic placed his hand on Molovic's shoulder. "He is bleeding inside his chest. He needs to rest; we are hours away from a hospital."

The snowcat led the way to the C-123. The truck's narrow tires slowly pushed through the snow berms that the cat crawled over.

It took the cat ten minutes to reach the track down onto the lake. The truck fell slowly behind.

Out on the open lake, bright moonlight illuminated the plane. Pulver could see the barrels and pallet under the right wing pushed clear of the plane, but on the left, the hose still extended up onto the wing. Jose and Greiwe sat on the barrels, waiting for the approaching snowcat.

"What's wrong?" asked Pulver, leaping from the cab of the Bombardier.

One of the shooters steered the snowcat to a position twenty yards behind the plane, leaving it running, its lights illuminating the open back of the aircraft. Two shooters and McGrady and his crew climbed out of the cab of the snowcat, along with Anton, helping two prisoners who could barely walk.

"We finished the right wing, but halfway through the first barrel on the left, the battery went dead. We will need the one from the snowcat," answered Jose. "It's going to take another twenty minutes to finish fueling."

As the men rose, Greiwe caught the movement of the truck coming through the trees. "We have company," he yelled. He raced to the ramp, and picked up a carbine, working a shell into the chamber.

"Relax, we have a lot of company," replied Pulver. "The truck is with us. We found seventeen more prisoners than planned. General Gritt is badly wounded in the back of that truck. We also have a wounded Russian general."

Greiwe laid the rifle back against the ramp and started toward the truck.

"Let my men take care of the general," suggested Pulver. "We need to get going."

The truck stayed on the road, coming to a stop fifty yards from the parked

plane. Two men lifted Gritt's stretcher from the truck bed carrying it across the ice into the plane. They placed Gritt on a bench above the cargo deck just below the cockpit.

Molovic tossed off his blankets and stood. Pulling a shovel from the bed of the truck, using it as a crutch, he began making his way to toward the plane. Mosby helped Davis get the rest of the prisoners on their feet and started them single file for the plane. Their feet wrapped in towels; the prisoners could barely walk across the wind polished ice.

It is always the same, thought Mosby, *they stay tough in the face of the enemy, but when rescue is near, their bodies begin to fail them.*

Jose scratched his head, doing some mental math. "We were going to leave the snowcat to reduce weight. Still, we are going to be damned heavy on takeoff with all these new men."

"We can leave the rest of the fuel," suggested Greiwe. "That cuts about five hundred pounds out of your takeoff weight."

"With a headwind, we are already down to no more than fifteen minutes reserve," replied Jose. "The loop down into China adds a half-hour to our flying time."

The Russian general, using a shovel to keep him upright, stumbled into the light. His pants leg was red with frozen blood. "You are heading to Chitose?" he asked.

Greiwe didn't know whether to answer the Russian.

"He's okay," called Pulver from the back of the snowcat. "He was a prisoner too."

"Yes, we are based out of Chitose," replied Greiwe.

"You can cut a half-hour out of your flying time if you fly a straight line," replied Molovic.

"That would take us directly over Khabarovsk with all of their fighters," answered Greiwe.

"You will be taking Anton with you. I will give him the radio frequencies for Khabarovsk intercept control. Anton can tell them you are on a flight to Yuzhno, Sakhalinsk. By the time they figure out your subtle course deviation, it will be too late to catch you."

Thinking through the chart he'd memorized, Jose punched

Greiwe in the shoulder. "It will be tight, but that should give us enough fuel."

"How badly is General Gritt wounded?" asked Greiwe, turning toward the plane.

Max leaped from the end of the ramp onto the ice. "It isn't good. His hip is broken, and the round he took in the chest clipped his breastbone. His heart is still pumping, and his lungs sound clear, but a bullet in the chest must have hit something important. He needs a hospital as fast as we can get him there."

"Let's get the hell out of here," shot Greiwe, as he pulled himself up onto the left wing. He dropped the fueling hose and clamped the cap onto the fuel tank. The men around the plane began to clear everything in its path. The line of prisoners continued to plod toward the plane.

Jose removed the pump and instinctively slapped a cap on the half empty barrel. Pushing it over, he started it rolling away from the plane. "Line up the men, we will want the heaviest near the front," he called.

"Let me help you with that barrel," called Anton. He passed the line of prisoners and helped Jose tip over the full barrel. Then he froze.

He turned toward the prisoners. "Calvin, Calvin Yerkovitch, what are you doing here?" he blurted.

His question was answered by silence. Anton pointed at the second man in line.

"You must be mistaken, Ruskie," replied the man. "My name is Calvin Carter, Lieutenant, United States Navy."

"Don't bullshit me, Calvin. I spent too damned much time trying to help you get through basic flight school," answered Bidkov, "and still you failed."

"You must mistake me for someone else."

Bidkov continued to point at the man. "That man is Calvin Yerkovitch. His parents moved to Russia right after the war, proud communists. His father taught English at Moscow University. His mother writes an English language column for Pravda."

"Mr. Carter, come here," ordered Davis.

Calvin took two steps, forward and then bolted for the ramp of the plane. He grabbed the M-1 carbine leaning against the ramp and swung it toward Jose and Anton. He started firing from the hip.

Anton dove behind the full barrel. He heard shells slamming into the metal and then the sound of bullets hitting something softer. Jose groaned and collapsed onto the ice.

"You will all move out onto the lake," screamed Calvin. He picked up the second carbine. "Drop your weapons and move far enough for me to reach the truck."

Six rifles were pointed at Carter. None of the shooters could get a shot at the man without hitting their only ride home. "You aren't going anywhere," called Pulver.

"I will shoot this plane full of holes if you don't start moving," repeated Calvin.

"What are you, a Russian plant?' asked Davis.

"All of the men in that Navy plane died in the crash. It was easy to take one of their names. You fools made me your security officer. Now, get moving."

The Russian spy backed up the ramp, raising his rifle, aiming at a cluster of hydraulic lines. "If I die here, you all die here too."

Calvin's face twisted into a shocked smile, he twitched and stumbled. He slowly turned and then the men outside heard the unmistakable, *pft, pft, pft, pft* of a silenced .22 pistol. Calvin's arms dropped, the rifle tumbling onto the ramp, and then he sagged onto his knees, rolling out onto the ice.

Half a dozen men rushed the plane. Calvin lay in the light, his eyes wide open, his chest pumping red bubbles of blood from his mouth, streaks of steam escaping holes in his coat. Then his chest stopped heaving. From his stretcher, Gritt allowed the empty High Standard pistol to clatter onto the deck.

"Let's get the hell out of here," barked Pulver. Move. Come on. Move. Get the prisoners loaded and that fuel barrel and the body out of the way."

Anton backed into the light of the snowcat headlights, dragging Jose by his coat collar. "Our pilot is dead."

"And General Gritt isn't in any shape to fly," called Max, kneeling over the unconscious man.

"You flew most of the way here," replied Pulver, pointing at Anton. "You fly us home. Get up in the cockpit while we finish clearing the area for you to turn around."

"I don't have a license, but I flew before my eyes went bad," called Greiwe. "I guess I'm the co-pilot."

"Shit doesn't anyone in America have a pilot's license?" snapped Anton as he turned to Molovic. "Engine start in three minutes."

Finally, only Pulver and Molovic remained on the ice. "After you, General," said Pulver.

"I'm staying. I'll give you an hour to get moving before I free the men you left in the gymnasium. With my tormentors gone, I will organize the survivors. We will cremate the dead, all except for the shithead that started all this. I want to hand the body to his father personally and tell him privately just what a prick he raised."

Molovic turned, using the shovel to hobble toward the truck. When he opened the door and climbed in, he finally took a breath. If it had been him watching an American officer walk away, he might have shot the only person who could stop the takeoff.

Molovic watched as the left engine belched smoke and flame and started, and then the right. Anton was a pro. He gave the engines, sitting a couple of hours in the cold, time to warm up before he pushed the throttle forward on the right engine and locked the left brake. The plane began to slide, but it also began to turn for the taxi down the lake. As it straightened out, Molovic heard the unmistakable whine of jet engines.

He hadn't noticed the small jets on the wings outside the huge radial propeller engines. The Russian general watched for a dozen minutes until the huge plane slipped through another turn. The thundering plane roared over his head, barely above the trees, it's engines straining to lift the heavy load, the jets shooting fire from the back of the wings.

"It was too bad that Major Anton Bidkov died in that crash in America," said Molovic. He watched the plane jog toward the railroad tracks where the pilot knew there would be no steep hills as he climbed. "If Bidkov lived, he would be honored for what he was trying to do to protect the Soviet Union," offered Molovic.

The only audience for his speech was the wind.

He started the truck and put it in gear. There was work to do, just not too quickly. He would leave the guards where the Americans put them for an hour. It would take another couple of hours before the technicians could rig emergency communications. In the interim, he would draft a report, one that would get him on the next train to Moscow. The five days that it would take to get there would give him plenty of time to develop a plan for the Air Force to take credit for freeing the Americans from renegade Stalinists. In return, the Americans provided firm information about a missing Russian bomber that crashed after getting lost in the Arctic.

CHAPTER 43

"WHERE IS THIS Yuzhno?" asked Greiwe.

Anton leveled the plane at 10,000 feet. "It is the largest city on an island just north of Japan. It's less than an hour flying time north of Chitose. During the War, the southern half of the island was Japanese and the northern half Russian."

"Is that what the Japanese used to call Karafuto?"

"Yes," answered Anton, walking the fuel mixture back, trying to find that magic place where he optimized fuel economy without burning up the engines. He quietly thanked Gritt for the time he'd spent flying the piston engine Cessna. "Keep a close eye on the engine temperatures."

"There is a legend about General Gritt and this Karafuto place. He led a raid that rescued some Japanese American prisoners from Karafuto. The story is that he stole a Japanese flying boat and flew it to Alaska. He walks with that limp because some young kid in the American Navy shot the plane down while he was landing."

"That story is told among Russian pilots. Only the way we tell it, a Russian pilot stole the plane late in the war and flew it to Khabarovsk."

"We are right at red line on the engine temperatures," said Greiwe as he tweaked the fuel mixture. "Thank God it is so cold.

In warm weather we would burn the engines to a crisp without adequate fuel flow to cool them."

"I never believed the story about a Russian pilot stealing the flying boat," continued Anton. "Why would he fly it to Khabarovsk when Russia had a military runway on the north end of the island?"

"We are coming up on the air base." Anton didn't really believe that they would fly over Russia's most powerful Far East airfield unchallenged. He wiped his hands on his pant legs trying to dry them.

"If the winds down there are anything like those on the lake, your former comrades may not have any planes on standby," offered Greiwe. He took a deep breath to calm his nerves. "If they do, at least there will be emergency services at the airport when we crash on their runway."

"You don't understand us," answered Anton. "I've seen standby aircraft sitting with their canopy propped open in driving snowstorms."

"Okay, that still leaves the chance of rescue if we turn this flying whale into a landmark on their runway." Greiwe's stomach felt like it did after eight cups of coffee.

"Maybe. But while they offer you first aid, they will offer me a bullet.

Anton's call to the sleepy Russian air controllers allowed the C-123 to fly right over the air base at Khabarovsk. Their routing would take them toward the northern end of Hokkaido, only fifty miles from the southern end of Sakhalin Island and the town of Yuzhno. As the plane left the Russian mainland, Anton pulled the throttles back, setting up a slow decent, stretching their fuel. They were a hundred miles from the closest Russian fighter base when they turned southeast toward Chitose. The Russian controllers, watching them on radar, warned them that they were flying into Japanese air space. Their calls became frantic when the plane didn't turn north.

"I didn't understand any of your conversation with the controllers," offered Greiwe.

"When they asked if we needed emergency assistance, I told them no; we just decided to go get some sushi," laughed Anton.

Greiwe picked up the clipboard that Jose left between their seats and flipped on the white light above his shoulder. He scanned the board to confirm their call sign and the radio frequency for Chitose approach control. He dialed in the frequency. "We need to be closer to reach to Chitose."

Anton nodded as he leaned forward and tapped the fuel gauges. The needles bounced on empty. At least they still moved. In front of him, the Japanese island began to materialize out of the dark. "We are going to be running on fumes by the time we get there."

Greiwe checked his watch. It was hard to believe that they'd lifted off the runway in Chitose only eight hours before.

Pulver tapped him on the shoulder. Greiwe tugged one side of his headset from his ear. "How much longer? Gritt's breathing is becoming really labored. We need to get him to a hospital."

Greiwe repeated the message to Anton, waiting for an answer.

"About twenty minutes, unless something goes wrong."

Greiwe gave Pulver his answer. He looked up into the tough mercenary's face. The man was worried.

The left engine coughed, then caught again. "I think we are already on fumes," said Greiwe. He looked down. The sea below was a mass of whitecaps. Not as violent as fifteen minutes earlier, but still boiling. "We would never survive a water landing."

"We need the radial engines to land," replied Anton. The vision of the moonlit lake and the TU-16 smashing through trees flashed through his brain. "One crash in a lifetime is enough," he added.

"What?"

"We aren't going to lose this plane."

"We are running out of options about as fast as fuel," answered Greiwe, staring at a map in his lap. "There is nowhere else to land."

"Restart the jets," ordered Anton. "We are descending anyway. Run them up to takeoff power."

The plane surged forward as the jet engines slowly spooled up. "Now pull the radial engines to idle and roll the fuel mixture to lean. The jets won't keep us in the air, but they will allow us to hold our rate of descent."

"We can't have more than a few minutes of jet fuel left," offered Greiwe. "Jose only wanted enough loaded for two takeoffs."

"As Ellen Wilson says, sometimes our lives are in someone else's hands, but only if we listen to what he is telling us," answered Anton. "We will run the jets until they die. There's no reason to crash with anything in the fuel tanks."

Pilot and co-pilot sat in silence until they felt they were close enough to use the radio. "Chitose approach, we are a C-123 Provider on special assignment, assigned designator S as in Sam and A as in Adam. You have our identifier on file. We are about ten minutes to your northwest, at five thousand feet descending," called Greiwe.

The jets both flamed out at the same time.

"Provider, on approach to Chitose be advised that the airport is currently closed due to fog. Recommend that you divert to your number two destination."

Anton pushed the radial engine throttles forward again, but only enough to keep the heavy plane from turning into a useless pile of aluminum falling out of the sky. "You talk, I'll fly," he said.

Anton pointed to the fuel gauges. The needles were pegged on empty.

"Negative Chitose, we are at bingo fuel. We will need an ambulance."

"I repeat Provider, the airport is closed. We have one quarter mile visibility, ceilings indefinite, and heavy fog."

The left engine sputtered again. Anton switched on the fuel booster pumps, hoping that the electric pumps could squeeze any remaining fuel from the tanks.

"And we don't have the fuel or the time to go anywhere else, Chitose. We will have to fly a NDB approach, what are your winds?"

"Winds calm. Altimeter is two-niner point nine five. Are you familiar with our NDB approaches?"

"Just give us an outer marker, any potential visuals, vectors and distance to the runway. Neither pilot, nor co-pilot is familiar with your approaches. Neither is current." He paused. "If we live through this, we will self-report our violation." Greiwe's attempt as humor fell flat.

There was silence for a full five minutes as Anton continued to allow the plane to descend toward the city of Sapporo, a bright smudge under the fog on the nose. Finally, Chitose called back. "Provider, this is Chitose. General McNamara is on his way to the tower. In the interim, what help do you need?"

"Just get us to that outer marker and vectors, then light up the runway. We are over the city now. Oh, and make sure the ambulance has a trauma team. You might also roll out the fire trucks."

"Provider, we have you on radar. Turn left fifteen degrees. Do you have time for a normal NDB entry and approach?"

"Probably not," replied Greiwe.

"Roger that, Provider. Here is my best cut on getting you down. If this works, we both self-report. If it doesn't, I'm keeping my mouth shut."

Anton rolled the plane onto a final heading as he passed over a stand of three radio towers with flashing lights. In front of him, there was only grey. "Switch to tower frequency and check in."

"Chitose tower, this is Provider on final."

"Roger, Provider. We can't see a thing, so let us know when you touchdown."

"God, I hope we didn't just rescue these guys to leave them spread all over the runway," commented Greiwe as he lowered the landing gear and increased the flaps.

"I think I see lights right in front of us. Call my decent in fifty-foot calls," ordered Anton. The left engine sputtered again. Anton rocked the airplane violently from side to side, trying to slosh any remaining fuel to where it might feed into the engines. He wiped his hands on his pants again, straining to grip the yoke with all his strength to keep it from slipping in his sweaty fingers.

Greiwe saw nothing out of the windscreen. "Four hundred feet. One hundred feet per minute decent."

"We put a fire truck with its lights flashing on the end of the runway," came a call from the tower. "We have a dozen vehicles with their lights on, paralleling the runway. Good luck, Provider."

"Were through three-fifty, coming up on three hundred, now."

"Keep the calls coming."

"Two fifty."

Okay," said Anton, "give me full flaps."

"Two hundred," called Greiwe, still seeing nothing in front of them.

"One-fifty. We should be almost over the runway."

"One hundred. Shit, there is the fire truck, left five degrees," snapped Greiwe.

The fire truck flashed below them so close that if anyone crazy enough to be sitting in it, they could have reached up and touched the plane.

"Lights left and right," called Greiwe.

The heavy plane slammed onto the runway, the headlights of vehicles on both sides blocking out the regular runway lights.

"Let's get this pig stopped," called Anton as he and Greiwe both pressed on the brakes, the tires skidding and smoking as Anton kept the plane between the lights with the rudder. They ran out of lights. The men could still feel the tires skidding.

There was no visual clue that they stopped, only that inner ear sense that the body was at rest.

"Are you on the runway?" asked the tower. "We can't see any lights."

"Fuck, we forgot to turn on the lights," sighed Greiwe.

"It was a secret mission," laughed Anton, as he fumbled though several lighting switches.

The left engine quit.

"Shut them both down," directed Anton. "We don't want anyone driving into a prop."

Two jeeps pulled up on each side of the plane.

"I'll go drop the ramp," offered Greiwe clambering from his seat. Moments later, the wail of a siren pulled up as the ramp began to drop.

Greiwe turned to where Pulver was already unstrapping Gritt's stretcher. "How is he?"

"Not good, unconscious. His breathing is irregular, and he is gasping." The two men carried the stretcher onto the ramp.

"Set it here," ordered a paper-thin young man with a stethoscope tossed over his shoulder. "We need some room." While the ambulance crew started an IV and got an oxygen mask over Gritt's face, the young man used scissors to cut Gritt's coat and shirt away and examined the wound. "Internal bleeding is compressing his lungs."

The ambulance crew helped roll Gritt on his side as the doctor reached for a scalpel and pressed it between two ribs. He held the cut open with a tongue depressor as blood poured onto the stretcher.

The doctor turned to the ambulance driver who was standing next to him. "Sandy, call the hospital and get surgery prepped. Have whoever is holding this groups ID's get them to the hospital while we drive."

He turned to Greiwe who was kneeling next to his boss. "Who is this man?"

"General Chad Gritt," replied Greiwe.

The attendants loaded the stretcher into the old International ambulance. "And Sandy," tell them to check on General Gritt's blood type, tell them we are going to need a lot of it."

The doctor leaped to his feet. As an afterthought, he called, "Anyone else hurt?"

"No," said Greiwe, as the ambulance door slammed shut and

the driver turned to retrace his way along the parked cars toward the road.

"Who are these men?' came a question from a graying man, still buttoning his shirt, the single star on his collar twisted at an odd angle."

"Sir," replied Greiwe, "you know about General Gritt's mission. I will fill you in, but I think that it would be better in private.

CHAPTER 44

GENERAL MOLOVIC CLIMBED the stairs, the pain from his wound no worse than a half dozen before. He made his way to Pavel Nasidna's office. He found the man's legs sticking from under the desk, the blood from two bullets in the chest pooled around the body.

Molovic stepped around the blood and rummaged through the desk drawers for a pad and pencils and the key to a small wall safe, which he knew would be hidden behind the picture of Premier Khrushchev. He pocketed the stack of bills from the safe.

Carrying the pad and pencils, he headed toward the conference room down the hall, stopping to spread Aunt Star's clothes over her lifeless body.

In the conference room, he began to write the kind of report that his old friend, General Blovinin, would appreciate. It spelled out how the leader of an American extraction team accidentally divulged how he knew to attack the Amur-3 camp. He also divulged that the American leader told him that found a crashed TU-16 on the arctic ice, burned, with no survivors. With no idea who Calvin really was, he credited an American prisoner with helping him escape from the plane before it took off.

Molovic, set his pencil aside and wandered back to Nasidna's office, retrieving the bottle of vodka and the glass from his desk. He picked up the unfired Makarov pistol and tugged a holster from the desk drawer. Resettled in his chair in the conference room, he continued his report, emphasizing how shocked he had been to find a prison run by the MVD, holding American prisoners, especially since the Soviet government denied holding any Americans for more than a decade.

He closed with several lines about knowing information that was too sensitive to send over the open radiophone system. He would hand deliver it.

Finishing a tumbler of vodka, Molovic strapped the pistol around his waist and headed down the stairs calling for any survivors to make themselves known. Twenty minutes later the survivors gathered in the gym. No one challenged the general that only hours before was a prisoner. He sent the men to dress in whatever clothes the prisoners left behind.

"We will probably abandon the camp," he told them. "It is of no further use since the enemy knows where it is." Molovic sent two communications men to begin patching together the radio tower. He put the rest of the men to work carrying the bodies into the old wooden supply warehouse. "Gather their identification and valuables."

"The Americans shot a man in the guard tower," added the survivor Anton had tackled.

"Put his remains in the warehouse with the others." Molovic paused. "There is also one body out by the graveyard. Leave it for now. I'll be in the conference room. Check in when you are done," finished Molovic.

It was almost dawn when the communications team managed to splice the cable to the radio antenna and pull the twisted frame of the tower upright using the truck and the van. A strange obese man stuck his head into the conference room. "The men have finished with the bodies, and we are ready to test the radio, General."

"Give me an hour to compose a message."

"But General, the Americans will get away."

"The Americans landed on the lake in a huge multi-engine plane. They have been gone for four hours. I suspect they are well outside our borders, don't you?"

Molovic stared at the half empty bottle of vodka in front of him. "Besides, I need some time to figure out how to explain how a small force of commandos can raid a Russian base and kill almost half of its staff, including two KGB officers. You guards let them escape without a single casualty. If we don't explain this correctly, a lot of you may end up in prison yourselves, maybe even worse."

The man at the door nodded, "thank you comrade General."

"Tell the men to get some sleep. We are all exhausted. We will meet at noon and figure out the next steps. "

The general watched the tired men traipse through the snow toward the barracks. Then he wandered down to the kitchen. He sat at a table, ripping pieces of bread and devouring them with chunks of sausage. He needed to soak up too much vodka. It wouldn't be appropriate for the men to find him drunk after his nap.

He checked his watch, waiting until the exhausted men would be asleep. Slipping on his coat, he crossed the parking lot to the warehouse. Inside he found nine bodies lain out on the wooden floor. Molovic rummaged through the shelves in the back of the warehouse, finally finding what he was looking for. He pried off the caps from two huge cans of paint thinner and wandered from body to body soaking them and the floor around them. He ran a stream of paint thinner to the door. Using his lighter he lit a piece of paper and dropped it onto the damp stain.

As he settled into Nasidna's private room, the warehouse began to burn. General Gritt was right, maybe there were too many bodies, but at least there would be no gruesome pictures. Not a single guard reported the fire.

In the afternoon, the men looked at the still smoking remains of the warehouse, but nobody wanted to see what might be left of their comrades.

Molovic sent two men to retrieve Rasputin's body. "Build him a simple coffin, I want to return the colonel's body to his father." The other men, he tasked with cleaning up the damage and gore from the attack; all but the chief communications clerk who he put to work, sending his report to General Blovinin in Moscow.

An old man knocked on the door of his makeshift office. "I found one of the American's rifles," he called, holding up Gritt's Winchester. "It was down by the river. It's probably the weapon that killed Colonel Rasputin."

"I am getting on a train to Moscow. I will take it with me as proof."

The man leaned the rifle behind the door.

"Are you the senior survivor?" asked Molovic.

"I am the oldest. I was sent to work the camps twenty years ago."

"Your name?"

"Oleg."

"Well, Oleg, you are now in charge here. You will make sure the men don't leave. Keep them busy until you hear from me. I will try to get all of you released from duty with a pension. I doubt that Moscow wants word of this fiasco leaking out to the public."

Molovic pointed to a note and a stack of rubles. Put this where it will be safe. If you don't hear from me within ten days, send that message and divide the money equally, then you and the others go home."

"What do we do? There are no prisoners to guard."

"Start with a small party to celebrate being alive. There is a case of vodka in Commandant Nasidna's room."

Just before dusk that night, the Moscow express stopped at the siding. Alexi Molovic, dressed in civilian clothes, boarded the train, tossing his small suitcase up to the conductor. "I need help getting this coffin into the unheated luggage car."

"What is the emergency, Sir?" asked the conductor. "We stopped because you set out the emergency signal."

Molovic handed the man his military ID. "I am traveling to

Moscow. There has been a terrible accident at this camp, and I need to get my report to Moscow before someone finds out and starts telling an unauthorized version of what happened." He handed the man Gritt's rifle, wrapped in canvas.

"Please tag this and put it into the luggage car, near the coffin.

CHAPTER 45

FAIRBANKS, ALASKA

TWO MEN WHO stood out like pro football players at a Girl Scout camp, met Ellen's small plane. They herded her toward a black Chevy station wagon. "I don't want to put you in handcuffs. You're an old pro, don't give me any trouble," ordered one of the men as he started to open the rear door. Next to her, Jack braced himself, his teeth bared as he glared at the closest agent. His partner picked up Ellen's luggage.

"Maybe you should help her put the dog in back first," said the other FBI agent, struggling with two huge bags.

The agent at the door began to push Ellen. "What in the hell do you think you are doing?" screamed Ellen.

"You have a record of un-American activities," he replied. "We're investigating reports of a Russian spy infiltrating an American military mission."

"Now be a good girl and get that monster on the leash into the back of the car," said the second agent.

"I'll go with you voluntarily, and I want you to note that in your report," replied Ellen, as she led Jack toward the back of the station wagon. "But if you use the "girl" line one more time, I'll rip your tongue out and feed it to my dog."

The man who stood at the rear of the station wagon took three steps back as Ellen coaxed the dog into the back.

Ellen moved to the side of the car, toward the agent that called her a girl. She stood next to him, glaring.

He pushed Ellen into the car, banging her head on the doorframe.

Before the driver could pull away, Carmen Gritt's Ford pulled up in front of the car.

A man in a suit slid from the passenger's seat, walking up to the curbside of the rented FBI vehicle. He motioned for the passenger to roll down the window.

Instead, the passenger pushed open the door, slamming it into the newcomer. The man in the suit slipped on a patch of ice and tumbled. The passenger leapt from the front seat, flashing a badge. "I would warn you not to interfere here," he said.

The man in the suit dusted off dirty snow as he rose. He reached into his shirt pocket and handed the FBI agent a business card. "I am Mrs. Wilson's attorney. Unless you have a warrant, I am taking her over to a friend's home for the evening. She will be available tomorrow morning at nine. My card has the address."

The man stepped past the agent and opening the back door, helped Ellen out. She walked to the back of the station wagon swinging the tail gate open, she snapped a leash on Jack, "Sit," she ordered. Her attorney picked up her suitcase and a large duffel bag.

The closest agent reached under his coat and drew a pistol. "Our instructions to interview Mrs. Wilson came directly from Director Hoover himself."

"Do you or do you not have a warrant?" asked the attorney.

The only sound was two ravens fighting over something across the runway. It was amazing how brutally cold air transmitted sound thought Ellen.

"No," he answered after a long pause. "But Mrs. Wilson is part of an espionage investigation. I again suggest that you not interfere."

"Not only am I not interfering, I am making my client available where you will have a warm conference room and hot coffee for your little chat. Now put that pistol away and go get a good night's sleep or get a warrant. I will see you tomorrow morning."

Ellen followed the attorney to Carmen's Ford and loaded all 150 pounds of Jack into the back as the attorney slid her belongings past the dog. She climbed into the back seat.

"It's good to see you again, Ellen," said Carmen. After I got your call from Bettles, I figured you needed some help. This is Chad's old hunting buddy, Bill Knox. In a previous life Bill was with the Justice Department."

Ellen reached over the seat to shake the hand of the man just slipping into the passenger seat. "Thanks."

"My pleasure, ma'am." Knox turned to Carmen. "Let's get the hell out of Dodge before the men in the car behind us start figuring out their options."

❊

The two FBI agents presented themselves at Knox's receptionist's desk well before nine. "We're here to interview a Mrs. Walter Wilson."

"Coffee?" asked the receptionist as she showed them into a small conference room.

"One black, one cream only," answered the older of the two men. "Thanks."

Ellen Wilson carried a tray with coffee, cream and four cups through the door held open by Knox. "Nice to see you again," she offered, her face blank. "I'm happy to cooperate, but I don't think I can tell you anything important."

"Let us determine what is, and what is not important," offered the man who'd drawn his gun the day before. Both agents filled their own cups, the one who had pushed Ellen stirring cream into his.

"Before we start," smiled Knox, "I have a telegram that you should read. He opened an envelope, unfolded a piece of paper, and handed it to the older agent.

The man to read the message in seconds. He handed it to his associate.

"Is this really from the CIA director himself?" asked the younger agent.

"It is," replied Ellen. "You will note that it directs me not to discuss any part of a possible ongoing agency operation."

"Other government officials cannot interfere in an ongoing Bureau investigation," snarled the youngest agent.

"Ask your questions, and I will answer what I can without violating the directions of Director Dulles."

The older agent finished his coffee while his partner fumbled through a half dozen mundane questions. Any that implicated Anton or anything about the mission to Amur-3 she refused to discuss.

The older man rose, a sly smile on his face. "I will give you credit, Mrs. Wilson, you seem to have friends in high places. You win for now, but I assure you that until Director Hoover himself is satisfied, we can make your life a living hell."

Knox pushed his chair back. "That was an illegal threat, made with no judicial backup. Get the hell out of my office."

CHAPTER 46

CHITOSE'S COMMANDER, GENERAL McNamara, sat quietly next to the conference phone, as the Director of the Central Intelligence Agency gave specific instructions to those in his office. All of the prisoners were to be issued new uniforms and all were to be confined in one wing of the base hospital. McNamara was to provide whatever medical assistance they needed, but the prisoners were not to associate with the public or even other military personnel. Even those who helped the men from the airplane were to be under house arrest. With modern air travel, it was still going to take the deputy CIA director two days to reach Japan. The director was calling from the office of the Secretary of the Air Force.

Dulles closed with, "I am very sorry one of the prisoners died of a heart attack this close to freedom. Finally, I want your doctors to do whatever they can to save General Gritt's life. If you have to send him to Tripler in Hawaii, you are authorized to use any resources you need. To all, thank you for a job well done."

The head surgeon canceled the VIP steak and egg breakfast that the base commander ordered. The surgeon feared that rich food after years on a meager diet might kill some of the prisoners. Instead, the men sat exhausted in the hospital conference room, dining on oatmeal with minimal milk and sugar, the first some of them tasted in a decade. As they finished, they were escorted to a table in the hall, where they were issued new uniforms and shaving gear. The plan to issue them new shoes was postponed after the doctors examined their feet. Instead, one of the enlisted men was sent to the base exchange for slippers.

At the next table, the men's ID and rank were confirmed, and each was issued a hundred dollars to be used in the base commissary where they would be escorted that night after it closed to regular customers.

On the next floor, the surgery was quiet, five people assisting a sixth as he patched a tear in Gritt's heart from Rasputin's bullet. The bullet had slowed as it pierced his breastbone, grazing the heart before slicing through his diaphragm and lodging in the muscles along his spine.

The damage to his hip would have to wait until he was stabilized. The actual surgery took less than an hour, leaving the patient with tubes draining both sides of his chest.

"He's in recovery, Major Greiwe," offered the surgeon. "I think the heart repair went as well as can be expected, and we sewed up the other damage from the bullet in the chest."

"What can I tell his wife?" asked Greiwe.

"Nothing. There is a tight lid on this entire matter until the deputy director arrives. And, anything you might tell her would be premature."

"What do you mean, premature?"

"The general still has a major surgery in front of him. If we don't start on the hip repair soon, we might have to amputate. The bullet appears to have been stopped by a steel plate and a cluster of pins from a previous wound. There is major damage to the surrounding tissue and the bone, but we can't attack that problem until he is stable from the heart surgery."

The doctor slipped a pack of Marlboros from his pocket, offering one to Greiwe, then lit his own. "I wondered how a man-made general at the age of thirty-six, but I can tell from working on your friend that he didn't do it through politics. The man's a warrior. He should make it through this, if that makes you feel any better."

"Thanks. I need to get a message to his wife. Ten years ago, she was an emergency room Army nurse. She deserves to know."

"I don't really know what you men were doing, Major, but looking at the nineteen men we are caring for, I can guess. I read a lot of history. Wars have started over less than this. Live prisoners usually mean dead guards."

"Yes Sir, but technically we are in peacetime, and the man is a general."

"All of us who have been working on your general are also confined to the hospital until someone says otherwise. This is one of those moments when we just have to accept that, contrary to popular belief, our superior officers got there through experience and intellect."

The doctor looked down at his clipboard, then passed it to a nurse.

"We're all going home to pack an overnight bag. When we get back, I suspect we will find that our wives hid several bottles of scotch in our bags while we weren't looking."

Greiwe wandered down the hall to a waiting room, reluctant to climb the stairs to his assigned room. Pulver and Mosby were sitting in the empty room.

"How is he?" asked Pulver.

"Not good, but alive."

Pulver scribbled a phone number on the back of a business card he was holding. "Here, keep us posted. Were headed home."

Pulver saw the anger in Greiwe's eyes. "Don't let it get to you, Major. It's always like this. The men upstairs will want to debrief everyone and make sure that the story that they want told, is the only one that gets out."

Mosby stuck out his hand. For the first time, Greiwe noticed that he was missing a couple of fingernails and there were scars all over his hands and wrists. "I would be happy to serve with all of you, anywhere, anytime," offered Mosby.

"Thank you and your team for everything you did over there. I am really sorry about Jose," replied Dan.

"Yeah, shit, this means we have to travel commercial," joked Mosby, but there was a tear in his eye.

"At least he caught the golden bullet before he had to quit doing what he loved most," Pulver said. "Someday you and the others may be able to tell the world what we did; maybe not right away, but someday. When you do this for a living, you can never tell."

The two men headed for the stairwell. Greiwe looked down at the card in his hand. These men deserved the phone call requested. He flipped the card over. In simple black ink it read, Pulver and Mosby, International importers, Jupiter, Florida.

A nurse walking by gave the haggard man laughing hysterically a strange look, but she didn't stop.

CHAPTER 47

TRANS SIBERIAN RAILROAD

MOLOVIC WAITED ANXIOUSLY. The train would only be in Irkutsk for fifteen minutes. He smiled as a willowy blonde woman made her way across the ramp, a four-year-old boy by her side, a huge suitcase dragging from the other hand.

"Your telegram surprised me, father. With what mother told me before they arrested her, I worried that I might never see you again."

"I am so sorry that I wasn't able to come to Sofi's funeral. We must hurry; there will be plenty of time to talk on the train. Molovic picked up little Sasha in one arm and grabbed the suitcase handle. He led Lena to the berths purchased for them.

"Your limping father," she said.

"We can discuss it on the train. Where is Ivan?'

"Drunk again. I left him enough money to stay drunk for a month and took the rest. He was happy to see us go. Mother was merciless about his drinking, and he knows that I hate it. Maybe, God, will show mercy and he will pass out on the train tracks, and it will finally end."

Molovic looked down at his daughter, watching the pain in her face, but he could think of nothing to say.

The family settled into seats in a mostly empty car. "Did you bring your mother's embroidered bag?" asked Molovic.

Lena sloughed off her coat, pushing the long strap of a brightly decorated fur purse from around her neck. "Do you want it?" she asked.

"No, my lovely daughter, you must keep it close to you. Your mother insisted on converting every extra ruble we ever saved to gold and jewelry. It is our savings. It is your insurance policy."

"Father, what is going on?"

Molovic rose, pulled a pillow from the shelf above the seat where he sat and motioned for his grandson to lie down. He covered the boy with his coat and then moved to the facing seat, next to his daughter where he could speak quietly. "I have become the target of the Ministry of Internal Affairs. I think it is behind us now, but I won't know until I reach Moscow."

"Mother tried to explain it, but it really didn't make any sense."

"I was one of a dozen officers who put together a secret mission, one that I couldn't even discuss with your mother. It did not go as planned, and now I am the one chosen to take the fall. At least I was. Now it has become an international issue and I may be the only one who can turn this pile of pig intestines into sausage."

"Then why are we rushing off to Moscow without telling anyone?"

"Because, to some in the MVD, sausage may not be enough. And you and little Sasha are not going to Moscow with me. I want you to take the train down to the Crimea, to that little dacha where we used to vacation with your mother's parents. You will wait for me there. If I don't get there within two weeks, borrow your grandfather's boat, put as much fuel as you can on board and go to Turkey."

"I don't know anybody in Turkey, father."

"I am going to give you the name of an American general that I know. Go to the American embassy and use his name, and mine, to go to America. Your mother's little brother lives in Chicago, America. Go to him."

"I don't want my son to grow up without grandparents," replied Lena, unable to stop the tears running down her face."

"Neither do I. I will do everything that I can to join you. If I do, that means that our lives in Mother Russia will continue. If I don't, that means that I am being buried in Russia. It also means that the irrational men, who have targeted us, may make you a target." He tapped his wounded leg. "They already took a shot at me. Sasha needs a mother."

Lena tilted her head against her father's shoulder. "None of this is fair. Families should not be torn apart just to satisfy some political grudge."

"Lena, my sweet Lena, you are not so naive. It has been going on in Russia for decades, maybe forever. Usually, it happens to people who are not party members, but not always. It is always justified by the threat of Russia's enemies. That is what I was trying to overcome. Anyway, we have two days together before you change trains."

❧

Molovic arrived in Moscow late at night. The temperature just above zero and it was snowing. It took only a small bribe to arranged to have Rasputin's casket stored along with Gritt's rifle.

Molovic checked into a hotel, awaking the next morning to a heavy snow. He gave the bellman a bag with his uniform, offering a large tip if he could have the uniform back that afternoon, cleaned and with the hole in the pant leg mended. Then he picked up three papers, including one in English and settled into the hotel restaurant for breakfast. Not one word on the Amur raid or freed American prisoners made the front pages of the papers. He spent the next two hours scouring every page. It was as if the Amur-3 raid never happened.

After a nap, he gave the hotel operator the direct phone number to General Blovinin's office and then settled in for the call to make it through the notoriously terrible Moscow phone system. An hour later, his phone rang, connecting him with one of the beautiful young women who worked in the Air Force Commander's office.

"Is Comrade Blovinin in this afternoon?" asked Molovic.

"No General, I am sorry he is not. He asked that you meet him this evening at his home. He has arranged for dinner at eight. Where shall I send his car?"

A late dinner meant that Blovinin was trying to keep the meeting off the radar. Molovic called the Bellman again. "I need a car right away to the Communist Party department store and back," he ordered. Only at the party store would he find a descent suit and shoes for dinner.

❄

Blovinin's house was on the bluff not far from Moscow University. Molovic stopped to appreciate the glow of the city below. Like all Russians, Moscow was where his heart was. Still, Molovic's years in the wilds of the Far East changed him. His soul needed more open space. He'd just arrived but needed to get out of Moscow as soon as he could. He knocked on the heavy wooden door.

"I will try to arrange for us to meet with the Minister of Internal Affairs and the Defense Minister. They want to keep the lid on this American raid on Russian soil. Evidently there has been no word about American prisoners from their State Department or in their papers," smiled Blovinin. The two men, dinner over, were seated in overstuffed chairs in the general's private office.

"It is also good news that our plane has been found and that it was burned completely," added Blovinin. "Do you believe the American who told you that there were no survivors?"

"I do. He offered the information as justification when I confronted him about American over flights," shaded Molovic.

"Tell me about this American prisoner who helped you," asked Blovinin, sliding a bottle of Jack Daniels across the table to his old friend.

"The Americans landed one of their Pathfinder transports on a frozen lake. I was the last prisoner loaded, still on the open ramp with one of their soldiers. The pilot had the engines running, and just started to taxi when one of the American prisoners leaped from

267

his seat and tackled me, knocking me back onto the ice. I heard them call him 'Carter.' We both stood to run, as the guard fired his rifle. I was hit in the leg, and this prisoner was wounded in the back, but he kept on pushing me in front of him until he dropped. I guess the Americans didn't want to stop their departure to search for me after I reached the nearby woods. This Carter should be recognized as the hero he was."

Blovinin shook his head. "Not if this never happened; now what is so sensitive that you couldn't put it into a report?" Smoke from his Cuban cigar rolled across the room.

"The way the Americans found the camp. They somehow intercepted a telephone message that Colonel Rasputin made from the camp. He bragged about capturing the American flight crew and told the other officers in the region where they were being held."

"So, somehow the Americans are listening in on our communications?"

"Not all of them I think, Johan. They intercepted the information while they were out looking for their missing spy plane. I surmise that they can listen to our radio-telephone conversations if they are close enough to a relay point."

"Where is Colonel Rasputin now?"

"In a box down at the train station. He tried to run away. One of the raiders shot him. I brought his body to Moscow so that I could give it to his father and tell the bastard that he raised a stupid prick for a son. With no way to dig graves for the others, we cremated them."

"And what about the survivors at the camp? What are they doing?"

"Waiting for orders. I think they should be briefed to keep their mouths shut about the raid and sent home with pensions. There is no reason to ever again use a camp that the Americans know about."

Blovinin rose, gesturing for his guest to follow him. "I will have my driver take you back to the hotel. I will use what you have told me to arrange the meeting. It will probably take a couple of days."

While the driver ran for the car, Blovinin leaned close to his friend. "There are a number of high officials who are very embarrassed by all of this. I think the loss of Major Bidkov's plane is behind us, but this is not over."

Molovic noticed that his friend was whispering. As he walked to the waiting car, he glanced back. Above Blovinin, in a room directly above the office, he saw the shadow of a man crossing the curtained window.

Molovic turned, grasping his old friends extended hand. "I understand. I'll stay as invisible as I can until you can get this under control."

CHAPTER 48

GRITT'S SECOND SURGERY began at almost the same time that the Deputy Director of the CIA began a meeting with the prisoners and Greiwe. "

"You will all be flown from Chitose to Hawaii where you will be housed in a hotel. Those of you who need continued medical attention have the choice of the hotel or staying at Tripler." Once you get back on your feet, we will fly your families over to be with you."

"Sir, have our families been notified that we have been rescued?" asked Davis.

"No, Colonel. We want you to send those messages yourself. But before you send them, I want you to each meet with one of my staff. Some of you have been declared dead, and all of you were reported missing in action. Only those of you who were captured after the armistice in the Korean War are undeclared."

"Just exactly what are you saying?" came a call from a man in the back.

"Some of you may find that your loved ones have moved on. All of you will find that the life you left is not the one you will be going back to." The deputy gave his words a moment to sink in, before continuing.

"You are all still in the military. Some of you may have earned several promotions, but for now, you are all being promoted one grade." The man turned to Colonel Davis in front of him. "Congratulations, General Davis."

What he hoped would be greeted with joy was instead greeted with silence as the men hadn't gotten past his last pronouncement. "I need your attention right here," he commanded.

The faces all turned back toward him.

"Two things are critical. First, we think there might be more prisoners in both China and Russia. Any chance we have of getting them out will depend on how quiet we keep your captivity and this mission." He waited for a response, getting none.

"Secondly, the president is going to propose to the Russians that we are willing to open our airspace to their recon aircraft, if they open theirs to ours. That means no more covert missions and no more shootdowns. If we open a major brouhaha with the Russians over your captivity, and make all this public, there isn't a prayer in the world that they will agree."

"Why do the politics matter to us?" asked Davis.

"This means that you were being held without the knowledge of the current Russian government. You were freed with the help of Russian officers who found you being held by rogue officials. Until you receive written permission to tell a different story that is all you are authorized to say. And I mean, say to anyone."

"Do you have any idea what these men have been through?" asked Davis.

The deputy director smiled at the men. "I am proud of your determination and your courage. I thank God that you are home. People will debrief you from your branches of the military and our staff. Over the next year, the director himself will interview all of you. We want to know what you experienced. We want to find ways to protect those still missing." The deputy, a man with two decades in the intelligence business, knew that there was little that the CIA could actually do, and he knew that the men in front of him knew that also.

"Those of you desiring to continue military service and who can still pass the medicals are encouraged to do so. Some of you are ready to retire, and you have earned it. Others may want to leave the service. Your country will make retraining and education money available. You all have back pay waiting. Oh, and one more thing. I flew in on a private DC-6. We will be flying to Hawaii on that aircraft, but if it is all right with all of you, I want to wait until General Gritt is strong enough to go with us. I am told that if his surgery goes well today, that will probably be a couple of days from now."

The deputy director didn't wait for a response. Instead, he rose and walked briskly over to where Anton sat.

"Mr. Bidkov, it's time for the two of us to have some lunch."

A military police escort led them to the officer's club and a private room. "Let me pass on the thanks of the American government for your assistance. General Gritt didn't tell us that you were going to be part of the rescue operation. Colonel Pulver says that your participation saved American lives."

"I did not go there to save Americans," replied Anton.

"I know, but in the end, that is what you did. You also saved Russian lives. I am sorry about your wife. I just want you to know that you will be granted permanent residency in the U.S."

"Are you still going to interrogate me?"

"Yes. But not until the dust from this mission settles."

CHAPTER 49

JUST BEFORE EIGHT the following evening a familiar face slid into the booth at the restaurant where Molovic was finishing a meal of smoked fish. Molovic hadn't seen Blovinin's aide, Lenov, since the meeting in the Crimea where the plan to drop leaflets on the American airbase was finalized. Lenov never said a word; he just pushed an envelope across the table and departed quietly.

Molovic ripped the end off of the sealed envelope. Inside, he found a simple note and five thousand rubles. The note read: *This is not going well. Given enough time I will get it all sorted out, but for now I am being blocked from a meeting with Zhukov. The MVD wants all this buried. It's probably best, if you find some place where you are hard to find for a month or two. Call me after that. Your friend Johan.*

Molovic prepaid for two more days in his hotel and asked that he not be disturbed. An hour later, he slipped out of the back entrance of the hotel with only his small suitcase and headed through the snow to the train station. His first stop was the freight storage office. Flashing his ID, he directed the clerk to pry open the top of Rasputin's wooden coffin. He slipped a note to Rasputin's father onto the still frozen body. It infuriated him that instead of looking the old bastard in the eye when he told him what an ass, he'd raised, that was forced to leave a note. But his own live daughter was more important than one dead scumbag.

Then he picked up the canvas roll with Gritt's rifle in it and bought a ticket for Khabarovsk, five thousand miles to the east, using his military ID to bump someone from a premium berth. He suspected they would try to find him, and the breadth of Russian gave them a lot of country to search.

The next evening, Molovic slipped off from the train at a rail crossroads and disappeared into the city. Early the next morning, he purchased another ticket, using Pavel Nasidna's name and ID for a train south to the Crimea. He was confident he wasn't being followed.

The small peach-colored house sat at the end of a road carved into the seaside cliffs. Below a winding path ended at a small boathouse where a twenty-year-old speedboat waited at the dock. White wispy clouds spotted a clear blue sky. Below, the Black Sea stretched all the way to Turkey, flat and peaceful.

"All I know is Russia," sighed Lena. "If I turn up in America, they will arrest Sasha's father."

"You can blame me for that," replied Molovic, "if you really care. I introduced you to him. He was one of my most promising young officers, not a pilot, but a man with a remarkable talent for logistics and transport. His father was the Minister of Transportation."

"It took me years to see that was the problem. Ivan felt that his success was only because of his father. He hated the man, but it was Ivan's weakness, not his father's strength that ruined our lives."

"Lena, we have to leave. Right now, there are probably men from the MVD looking for me. I laid a trail back toward Siberia, but they will figure it out. They are scared. What I found them doing could destroy them. They will not hesitate to kill all of us."

Molovic helped Lena load heavy cans of fuel onto the old cruiser that belonged to her maternal grandfather. The night before he'd bribed a cab driver to find a battery to replace the one that hadn't started the boat in years. He'd spent much of the night doing what he could to make the craft seaworthy. The old engine started and run better than he'd expected, but with years of growth on the bottom of the boat, it would be slow. Still, they would be in Turkish waters soon.

The two watched Sasha play on the dock as they loaded food and all the clothing she and Sasha owned. They stashed the jewelry and most of their cash in a box under the floorboards in the engine compartment. Gritt's 30-06 rifle went up behind the couch. Once they asked for asylum in Turkey, there would be little or no customs search.

"Untie the boat and get the engine started," said Molovic. "I'm going back to the house for my bag. My uniform will be helpful in convincing the Turks and Americans to take us in, although they will learn nothing from me that they don't already know." He handed his daughter a small pack, with his credentials and four files taken from the Amur-3 camp, along with a note to General Gritt with his best estimate of Russia's long-range bomber fleet. It was his last effort to stop American over flights.

He hobbled up the dock and into the small house just as a black Moskvitch 400 sedan pulled up in front. Molovic grabbed his bag, glancing out the window; two men were climbing out of the old car.

Molovic headed out the back door, and onto the path to the dock just as one of the men came around the side of the summerhouse. Molovic started to run, his wounded leg slowing him. He felt the bullet hit his back before he heard the shot. He dropped behind a planter and tugged Nasidna's Makarov pistol from a pocket. He could feel the air in his lungs escaping through the hole in his back. His vision narrowed as two men walked calmly down the path.

Molovic used the last of his strength to raise the pistol, resting it on the planter. He emptied the entire clip into the two startled men before he tumbled backward.

He managed to force his eyes open as two hands wrapped around his face. Lena leaned over him, crying hysterically. "Go, go now, you have to save yourself and Sasha," mumbled Molovic. "I love you."

❈

Thousands of miles away, a special train stopped at the Amur-3 rail siding. Twenty men piled out of a passenger car, while two others backed two large vans off from the flatcar behind it. They approached the unsuspecting camp. The guards, with no prisoners to watch, slept or played cards or gorged themselves on food from the kitchen as the twenty men took up positions around the buildings.

The MVD internal policemen started in the administration building, shooting everyone they found, before moving to the barracks and the prisoner's compound. The trained assassins took only minutes to eliminate the last eyewitnesses to what had gone on at Amur-3 – all but one. Oleg was ice fishing in a small bay on the lake, returning each day to a hole laboriously chipped through the ice. The cove where he fished was three miles from the camp and filled with fish. Hearing the sound of gunfire from the camp, he rushed across a peninsula that shortened the trip back by almost thirty minutes.

Oleg arrived just in time to see two vans pull onto the road to the railroad siding. Dashing into the barracks, he found the first of his comrades in the lobby, his body soaked in diesel fuel and burning. Four more of his friends were burning in their rooms. The stench of burning fuel and flesh forcing him from the building. In the administration building, more men lay under a pile of burning wooden furniture.

The attackers hadn't even taken the time to shut down the generator before they left. He checked the empty brass from the firing. Every one of the killers carried a Russian made weapon. He remembered what the general said about their lives being in danger.

Oleg made his way to the kitchen. He removed a drawer, reaching behind for the hidden money and note that Molovic left. In his hands, he held more money than he'd seen in his entire life. He filled a pack with what he would need to hike to the nearest town, almost two hundred miles away. There he could catch a train home without stirring up suspicion.

CHAPTER 50

GRITT LAY IN a makeshift bed in the back of the plane. A doctor and a nurse sat in seats across from the bed, wondering how they could finagle some leave in Honolulu. Next to Gritt, McGrady, Walsh and Flores were using the thirty minutes granted by the doctor to discuss their captivity.

Gritt listened, taking in what he could through the drug-induced cloud in his brain. The mattress patch on his heart was holding. There was twice as much steel in his hip as before the trip to Russia. The one thing he heard clearly was McGrady's promise that their wives would be on their way to Hawaii in the next week.

As Gritt's eyes closed, Walsh and Flores returned to the poker game in the front of the plane. McGrady knelt next to the doctor. "What's the real scoop on the general, Doc?"

"The bullet didn't penetrate the heart, just tore muscle. With the scarring, it won't be as strong as before, but he probably won't notice the difference unless he decides to become an Olympic sprinter. The hip, however, is really a toss-up. Any time you repair an old repair you have less good bone and muscle to work with. I think we saved the leg, but he will always need a cane from now on. He will never pass another flight physical."

McGrady smiled. He knew that if Chad could sit in a cockpit, he would fly.

❈

THEIR ROOMS WERE all on the ground floor of one of the Mattson Hotels that made Waikiki famous. The Army's Fort DeRussy, not far away, served as the debriefing center. Two psychologists and several nurses who specialized in physical therapy, also worked from makeshift offices there.

Of the thirteen longtime prisoners, five found that their wives had remarried. The men formed a small team of graying stallions who divided their recovery time between sessions with a psychologist and haunting the bars and nightclubs along the beach, looking for feminine trouble. The rest of the group, along with the Fairbanks Three, as they become known, swam and lounged on the beach with wives and girlfriends.

Carmen had arranged for a dog mushing couple she knew to fly out to Bettles and then go to Ellen's cabin to take care of her animals. The five women from Alaska took a commercial flight from Anchorage to Los Angeles. There they boarded a Pan Am flight for Honolulu.

An Air Force policeman at the hotel entrance directed them to registration. There a middle-aged woman in a bright floral dress suggested that they would probably find the men they were looking for on the beach.

Searching from the deck, Ellen found Anton sitting alone. He was under the shade of a huge umbrella, his gaze locked onto the ocean. She began walking, now nervous, stopping to watch him as he studied three surfers working waves kicked up by afternoon winds.

He was alone. The other prisoners were all sitting together, laughing and drinking beer some throwing a football. Near them, a group of women sat talking, Ellen assuming that they were trying to figure out how to make sense of the change in their lives that was coming with the freeing of the prisoners.

"Hey, it's me, BB," she said, walking up behind him. "If you don't have anything better to do, I thought you might buy a girl a Mai-Tai."

Anton never looked around. He just extended his left arm behind him and wrapped it around Ellen's legs, collapsing her into his arms. "You have too many clothes on," he said.

Ellen wrapped her arms around Anton's neck and kissed him, draping her body against his. "I'm happy you are safe."

"I am home," he answered. "Well, not exactly home. I am finished with Russia. I really like your Alaska."

"Me too," offered Ellen. "But it is a very lonely place without someone to share it with."

"While I stood at Natalya's grave, she spoke to me. She said, 'go now and be happy.'"

Ellen slowly unwound her arms from around Anton's neck. "You stay here. I'm going to the shop in the lobby to buy a swimsuit. I'll send the waiter out with champagne and a couple of glasses."

Anton kissed her hand as she stood. "See if you can find something green. Maybe the color of spring leaves; it will show off your red hair."

❄

The next day, the surgeons released Gritt to Carmen's care. Proud Air Force mechanics delivered a modified beach lounge, sporting eight large wheels that allowed it to flow over the soft sand. It quickly became a fixture on the beach, and the center of attention.

"You are as brown as that hussy I spent a week with in Mexico back in the early Forties," quipped Gritt to his wife.

"And you, General Gritt, just led your last combat mission," answered Carmen. "If they shoot up any more of you, we will have to replace your underwear with mesh bags."

"It was nice of my folks to take the kids," offered Chad.

"They are registering them for the end of the school year in Anchorage. The doc says you will be up in a couple more weeks, probably on crutches, and then I am to escort you back to DC to talk to your boss."

"Carmen's Escort Service, I kind of like the ring of that."

Added to all of the other spots on Gritt's black and blue body, he sported a bruised shoulder at dinner that night.

CHAPTER 51

THE OUTER OFFICE of the Director of the CIA was empty. In a world where plausible deniability was a way of life, the argument between J. Edger Hoover and Director Dulles was nothing that anyone would want to know about.

"You do not have the authority to block my investigation," screamed Hoover.

"You are such an ass," replied Dulles. "The operation that you tried to investigate saved American lives. It gave us greater insight into the Russians and their threat. Leave this alone."

"I have no intention of dropping this," replied Hoover. "You are hiding a Russian spy. You are protecting those who are helping him."

"If there really is a man like the one you refer to, he would more likely be classified as a defector; someone helping our side. But I really can't comment on whether he exists or not."

"I'll be the judge of the man you refuse to present. We know where the woman who is helping him lives." Hoover stopped while he looked through his notes. "It will be easy for my men to pick them up at that remote Alaska lake."

"Aren't you forgetting the president's directive? I was told he made it clear to you that you were not to interfere in our work."

"Neither he nor you control the FBI."

"Perhaps this will help you understand just what your authority is." Dulles slid two sheets of paper across the desk. He followed it with a sealed envelope.

"What's this?"

"The first sheet is a pardon for the woman you want to harass. It clears her of any possible crimes in the name of national security and her long-term service. The second is one for the mythical Russian you are hunting. It is made out to John Doe, and only the president and I have originals with his hypothetical real name."

Hoover turned scarlet, but he said nothing for a full five minutes while he looked over the documents. He picked up the sealed envelope. "What's this?"

"Frankly Director, I don't know. Your old pal Joe McCarthy is dead and almost completely discredited. It's not up to you to go after 'Tail Gunner Joe's critics.' Or is it that your feelings are hurt because you weren't read into this from the start?"

Hoover's face looked like a teakettle left over high heat after all the water evaporated.

Dulles paused just long enough to make sure that his next sentence stabbed Hoover like a sharp spear. "I would surmise that whatever is in the envelope reminds you that if you continue to bully people just because you are pissed off, that you work at the pleasure of the president."

CHAPTER 52

JUNE 8, 1960, never dawned; during summer in Alaska and you could sit on your back porch at midnight and read without a light in the land of the midnight sun. Chad and Carmen waited at the gate as the first passengers began to filter into the terminal at Anchorage International Airport.

After a full year recovering from his injuries, Chad had been transferred to a non-descript building at Elmendorf Air Force Base in Anchorage. He still worked for the CIA and maintained his status as an Air Force officer, but his job now focused on threat assessment, as the United States built Alaska into a wall of fighter planes to defend North America from Russian attack.

The first passengers off the plane from Seattle were a thirtyish woman and her seven-year-old son. She straightened little Sasha's collar and made straight for the tall man in the light canvas jacket and his wife. "General Gritt?" she asked.

"And you must be Lena Molovic, and this has to be little Sasha," replied Chad as he nodded an answer to her question.

"We planned on you spending a couple of days with us here in Anchorage before we headed out, but if you think you and your son are up to it, we would like to head straight out to Lake Clark and the family lodge," added Carmen.

"We have great flying weather today," nodded Gritt.

"I am the daughter of a pilot," replied Lena, "I grew up in a house where weather was always part of a day's discussion.

"Good, then let's run you downtown for a late lunch and some clothes appropriate for bush Alaska. We will call Ellen Wilson from a pay phone and have her get the Beaver and my Cessna all gassed up."

They waited a half-hour for the minimal luggage that Lena was traveling with to reach baggage claim. Gritt shifted his cane to his other hand to help Sasha with his suitcase. Lena responded to a call from the woman supervising the luggage arrival. She returned moments later with an aluminum gun case, one of three that were carried out to the floor by a ramper.

"I didn't realize you hunted," offered Chad. "I can't think of any seasons open right now."

"I don't hunt. I have carried this with me at every stop between Russia and here. My father wanted to return it to you, General. It is a rifle that you carried on your mission to Russia."

A shocked Gritt reached down and snapped off the pins holding the gun case closed. He lifted the 30-06, scoped rifle that he never expected to see again and opened the bolt, checking to make sure it was unloaded. Around him, other Alaskans, and the tourists arriving on the plane, ignored the man with a rifle in the airport.

"My father didn't have an opportunity to tell me the story of the rifle," smiled Lena.

"Tonight, around the campfire, I will fill you in," offered Chad. "It will be the first time I have spoken about that mission since I was debriefed. Even my wife doesn't know the story." Chad put his hand on Carmen's shoulder and squeezed.

After a two-hour lunch and shopping trip, the Gritt's Ford station wagon pulled up in front of Wilson Air Service on Lake Hood, only a quarter mile from the runway at Anchorage International Airport. Ellen Wilson met them at the front door.

"Lena, it's nice to finally meet you," offered Ellen. At her side, a two-year-old boy stared at the older boy and his mother. How is your Uncle Frederick?"

"He's great. He made full professor this year, and he still does some contract work for the State Department."

Ellen looked at Chad and Carmen. "Frederick was one of my contacts in Russia. He was one of those with the courage to speak out about the gulag system. His network helped me track the locations of the gulags and how many people were sent there. When the government started to close in on him, I helped him get across the border into Iran and then to the States."

The door banged, and Anton Wilson rushed across the room to his wife's side. "Jerry is all set. He can handle all the charters for the next four days, so we are off to Lake Clark with our friends."

He turned to Chad. "Your Cessna is fueled. Our ramp kid topped it off. I also threw twenty gallons of fuel into the back of your plane since you are traveling light. I think we should show Sasha here what fishing is like, Alaska style. If the weather holds, we can fish a different river every day."

"By the way, did you read the morning news?" asked Lena.

Chad shook his head.

Lena fished a copy of the Seattle paper out of her huge purse. "That weather plane that the U.S. said it lost out of Turkey – well, the Russians claim that they shot it down over Russia and are holding the pilot. Do you know this Francis Gary Powers?"

"One more thing to talk about tonight," replied Chad, shaking his head. His face turned from joy to sorrow and then back to joy.

Carmen helped her husband settle into the pilot's seat of the Cessna. He primed the engine, which came alive the moment he touched the starter. She watched as he used his cane to help push the left rudder pedal, steering the plane out onto the lake.

"Why don't you let me fly today?" she asked.

Chad realized that he hadn't used the radio to tell other pilots in the area that he was taxiing for takeoff. "Maybe a good idea," he replied. "Although, one of the things I love about flying is that I can concentrate so hard on being in the air, that I can drown out every other thought."

"You're thinking about that pilot that the Russians are holding, aren't you?"

"Actually, I was thinking that it will never stop," replied Chad.

He picked up the microphone and keyed the radio, announcing his intentions. "I'll fly. I need it."

ACKNOWLEDGEMENTS
THE OPPOSITE OF TRUST

THE OPPOSITE OF TRUST began with a discovery in a Russian archive. Spending many hours in libraries, museums, and archives gave me an excuse to stay out of the bars. This was during the time when the Soviet Union was disintegrating, and American businessmen were novelties. A hundred-dollar bill would hire a translator for a couple of days.

The efforts made by Soviet flyers to stop the surveillance of Russia by American planes was extensive and frustrating to them. The limited resources, both aircraft and especially fuel spread over vast distances made the task monumental. Their official records reflect no air losses to American airmen, but the four Russian veterans of that period with whom I enjoyed a cold Piva with each told a different story. Remember, this was at a time when everything they believed in was crumbling and perhaps also a period of real candor for Russians. The one thing that they repeated again and again was how dangerous and difficult military and political life was during the transition from Stalin to Khrushchev. But they were proud of their successes. The Russian Military Aviation Museum's most cherished display is Francis Gary Powers' U-2 spyplane, downed by previously secret anti-aircraft missiles.

Research on the American side was easier. There were books and declassified reports and news columns. But the aviation records all seemed sanitized. It was almost like the only espionage carried on by the west was centered on Moscow, St. Petersburg and in East Germany. Cloak and dagger spies were honored, airmen ignored. There are reports of aircraft lost along the West Pacific coastline. All were sketchy.

In Anchorage, Alaska there is a monument to military aviators lost on missions flown from the state. The names are there but finding details on their demise is a monumental task.

The period of the McCarthy anti-communist hearings and the aftermath on entertainment, business, and political leaders is well documented. The military, however, acknowledged little about how it impacted them.

From records on both sides of the Pacific, I pieced together historical bits and pieces of the COLD WAR in the air official history; then like my other stories, created a page turning novel that might just be a more accurate portrayal of the Cold War in the skies.

Passions, especially among men and women are intensified in times of conflict. Writing the story of an American diplomat and a Russian airman, both betrayed by their own government was a labor of love. Unlike most stories about people who were wronged, those I interviewed for this book all retained their patriotism. I thank them and the silent warriors in both nations who offered their experiences and help. To each, as agreed, your identities and lives will never be revealed by me.

For writing support, I would again like to thank Gabrielle Raffuse, PhD and best-selling authors Marc Cameron and Robert Dugoni. Rob Bignell, my editor helped make the book more concise. Thanks to my fans who volunteered as beta readers. You made *The Opposite Of Trust* a better story. The team at Damonza provided cover design and formatting to turn this manuscript into a book. DERRICK helped launch rodgercarlyle.com, and thanks to DACIA for social media help. Finally, my wife Carmen invests as many hours on each book as I do.

THE POLITICS: The Cold War between the Soviet Union and the west, especially the United States has been written about in both fiction and non-fiction since the 1940's. Most of the stories revolve around cloak and dagger spying; men and women, usually in

Europe, risking their lives to study the enemy. Little has been written about the espionage in the air, where real bullets were flying, and people were dying. I dedicate this book to the aviators on both sides.

That, to me is expressly important as the military tasked by each side was also battling political and bureaucratic struggles at home. Especially in Russia, the death of Joseph Stalin and conflict over his replacement created a situation where many military leaders spent as much time worrying about those behind them as they did about the enemy. The McCarthy hearings in the United States tainted American life for a decade. It remains one of our darkest chapters.

For those who are sticklers on military technology, historical battles, doctrine, and geography, please note that this is a work of fiction, a novel with all of the liberties afforded any author. I've taken liberties with the aircraft and especially with the early periods of electronic monitoring as part of air reconnaissance. Please forgive me as the goal was to emphasize the courage and skills of the people who actually flew the missions.

One other note, every nation has some deeply flawed, inhumane officers, some more than others. But each, also has highly principled men and women, people who could be your friend, whose only crime was national patriotism. Introducing them in my stories is an important part of defining the 'enemy.'

Thank you, reader, for giving me the privilege of the time you afforded THE OPPOSITE OF TRUST. I hope it was an enjoyable experience.

If you liked THE OPPOSITE OF TRUST, please consider posting a review on Amazon or Goodreads so other readers can find my stories. Thank you for reading my story!

www.rodgercarlyle.com
Goodreads Author Rodger Carlyle
Amazon Author Rodger Carlyle

ABOUT THE AUTHOR

RODGER CARLYLE is a storyteller who draws on an enormous personal library of experiences. An adventurer, political strategist, and ghostwriter whose love of flying began in the Navy, his experiences stretch from New York to Los Angeles, from Amsterdam to Khabarovsk in the Russian Far East, and from Canada into Latin America.

Through his passion for research, he treasures finding those events that are ignored or covered up by the powerful when some strategy or plan goes completely to hell. From there, he creates a fictional adventure narrative that tells a more complete story.

Rodger is comfortable in black tie urban settings, but he is never happier than in the wilderness. He has faced down muggers in San Francisco, intimidation by the Russian Mafia, and charging grizzly bears. Most of his stories take his readers to places they will never visit. He likes to think that he is there with them.

Visit Rodger Carlyle's website at www.rodgercarlyle.com